Escape From the Fringe

Central Worlds | Book One

Riley Collins

Copyright © 2022

All rights reserved.

ISBN: 1-7359029-9-3

ISBN-13: 978-1-7359029-9-9

Print Edition

Cover Art by: MiblArt

Editing by: Bodie Dykstra

To learn more about Riley Collins, see an updated list of titles, and join his mailing list go to his webpage at www.rileycollins.info.

Samsara Fleet Series

- Book One: For the Ones Who Remain

- Book Two: For the Ones Who Are Forgotten

- Book Three: For the Ones Who Rebel

- Book Four: For the Ones Who Liberate

- Book Five: For the Ones Who Prevail

- Book Six: For the Ones Who Endure

Central Worlds Series

- Book One: Escape From the Fringe

For Makaka Loka, who always encourages me to reach for my dreams.
Love, BAP

Chapter One

The Triple-Deuce

"It's not like it's the end of the galaxy." Tejal sighed dramatically as she gently nudged her daughter toward the door.

"It's *boring*."

"I'll try not to take offense at that, Daiyu." Tejal wrapped her fingers around her daughter's hand. "Everyone needs to work on the station. You know that. Maintenance can be interesting. You get to see how things work. Solve complex problems and make a real difference."

Dai scoffed. "Yeah, so we can mine more ore. What's the point? To make some rich jerk in the Central Worlds richer?"

"It's a job. A purpose. You're seventeen rotations old and you've graduated from crèche. You're an adult. Time to start contributing to the rest of the station."

"Maybe it's time to *leave* the station."

The empty threat hung in the air for a moment. Dai couldn't imagine following through on it. Station 222—or the Triple-Deuce, as the Orbiters who lived there called it—was all she'd known. The century-old mining station was cramped, creaky, and in the middle of nowhere, but it was her home. Every single person she knew lived there.

"You don't mean that." There was a sliver of worry in her mother's voice.

"No. I don't." Dai sighed. "I just want to find something that makes me happy, and I'm not sure if fixing broken mining pods is it."

"You always want the solution to be handed to you." Tejal's toned had moved from concern to lecturing. "Give it a dec. Thirty cycles should be enough time for you to get to know the job. You'll see it's a lot more rewarding than you think it is."

Dai's mother glanced at the wall and gave a small start. "It's already nine. You're gonna be late." She picked up the brand-new canvas tool bag Dai had received on her first day of training and placed the strap over her daughter's shoulder. "You'll need this." She touched the small pendant around Dai's neck and gently kissed her forehead. The necklace had been a gift from her father the last night she'd seen him. "Your father would be proud."

Dai wasn't sure that was true. But then again, she had only a faint memory of the man. Mostly, she remembered being fascinated with his bushy black beard and the wide grin nestled within. She remembered him as a cheerful giant, always laughing and joking. Sometimes, when he didn't see her watching, she'd see the smile drop and a look of melancholy sweep over the man. The purple crystal pendant was the only memory she had of him, a gift he gave her before he went out on what was supposed to be a routine delivery.

"Okay. Okay. I'm off." Dai returned her mother's embrace and rushed out of their small home.

The Triple-Deuce was a perfect sphere. At its core were the critical systems: life support, gravity, power, and the like. The living quarters were the next layer out from the center, and then came the public areas like the shops and the crèche, where she'd gone to school as a child. The outside layer of the station contained the landing ports, offices, repair shops, and storage facilities that were used for mining.

Dai waited at the front of the quarters she shared with her mother for one of the small automated skiffs that roamed the corridor to stop and pick her up. As soon as it came to a rest, she jumped on and plopped down on the center bench. "Observation dome, please." The skiff lifted off and glided down the passageway. Luckily, she was the only person aboard, so she wouldn't have to wait while others got on and off. She *was* late, after all.

The skiff got up to speed and soon Dai could feel small fingers of wind in her long hair as she coasted along a curved hallway that encircled the station. Each level had several main passageways that extended in concentric circles from the core. Ramps, sprinkled throughout, linked the levels together. After climbing countless levels and navigating several bends, the skiff came to a rest underneath the enormous glass dome at the top of the Triple-Deuce.

The floor underneath the dome was overflowing with plants. Large vines snaked up the walls, their leaves stretching out to capture the bright rays of light from the sun blazing like a malevolent iris in the dome's center. The room was one of her favorite places on the station. It was the closest she could get to being on a planet. She loved the smell, the warmth of the natural light, and the beauty of the plants that sprawled throughout the room.

Dai strode down one of the paths winding through the planters as branches and thorns tugged at her clothing. As she walked, she held her hands out, taking in the waxy feel of the leaves and stems around her.

"Think fast!"

Dai brought up her arms to protect herself but was too late. Something hit her neck with a sting.

"You're a jerk, Max." She bent down and grabbed the candy projectile from the ground, took a seat next to her friend on the bench at the edge of the sandy path, unwrapped the candy, and popped it into her mouth.

"Maybe. But at least I'm not late for training." Max pushed his blond locks away from his eyes.

"Are you tracking my schedule?"

"Your mom offered me a hundred credits to make sure you get there on time." He looked at her solemnly.

"Shut up!"

He broke into a smile. "Maybe not. But you'd better start taking this seriously. You're an adult. Technically, at least. What you do, like, matters."

"I already got this lecture from my mother today." Dai quickly looked around to make sure there was no one nearby. The bench was their regular spot to meet since it was in the center of the room, hidden from view by twisting bushes and flowers. But you never knew when someone would appear on a station. Space was tight. "Now, like you said, I gotta go to class. Were you able to get it?"

"Here you go," Max said. Dai felt a small chip press against her palm and quickly tucked it into a pocket in her work pants. "Be careful with it. I had to call in a few favors."

Max was a rotation older than Dai and had already started working as a porter in the commercial landing bays. He hadn't said it, but she suspected he'd taken the job so he could smuggle things onto the station. Things like the stimchip he'd just handed her. They were supposed to be amazing but were outlawed in the Central Worlds.

"Well, now we just need to get a stimpad," Dai said. That was going to be *much* more difficult. "Thanks. I owe you one."

"You owe me more than one." He chuckled. "But I know you're good for it." He gave her arm a small squeeze. There was an unspoken message in that gesture. They'd grown up together, and to Dai, Max was the brother she'd never had. She suspected he wanted their relationship to be more than that. He'd almost told her as much before. However, she'd made it clear that wasn't going to happen. But the man couldn't change how he felt, and neither could she.

"Now, seriously, you need to go." He playfully pushed her. "Even *I* think vocational training is important and I'm just about the least responsible person I know."

"Yes?" the secretary asked as Tak strode through the door.

"Howdy. Taksh Chan, here to see the mining chief." He bowed theatrically, raising his chempen in the air.

"So you're the consultant." The man behind the desk didn't look impressed. "Sit down. The boss's in another meeting." He motioned toward the row of chairs against the wall.

"You got kaf by any chance?" Tak asked as he forced a smile. "Seem to be feeling some travel sickness."

The secretary smiled and raised an eyebrow. "Travel sickness? Sure. Guessing that you never visited deck thirteen before, right?" He pulled out a small packet and tossed it to Tak. "Take this. There's no kaf. The machine's on the fritz, but these should help."

"You're a lifesaver."

Tak popped the tablets into his mouth, took a deep inhale from his pen, and slouched down on one of the cheap waiting chairs. He felt a dull stabbing in his temple and tried to piece together what had happened the night before. He'd arrived at Station 222 last cycle and decided to look around. He wasn't sure what he'd been looking for, but in the end, as the secretary had guessed, he'd ended up on level thirteen. After that, things got fuzzy. He remembered a few snippets. Laughing with a group of miners. Running through a corridor naked. An angry Grosk staring down at him as he poked him in the ribs with one of his front feet. A small light flashed on the combrace around his wrist, a message from someone. He'd check it later. It was probably from someone he'd met during his excursion and he was in no mood to read anything.

Tak rubbed his forehead as he slumped into his chair and waited for the drugs to take hold. The Triple-Deuce, as the locals called it, was as far from civilization as one could get. It was at the very edge of the galaxy, in the Fringe, the section of space that no government cared to claim. The station had been around for over a century, dutifully sending out mining pods to retrieve minerals from the surrounding asteroids, cleaning them, and then sending them away to be refined.

Tak had no idea why he'd accepted the assignment to come out here. There'd been some other options, but for some reason, he'd felt a desire to head to the very end of the galaxy. It was a decision he regretted as soon as he landed inside the rusty ball the Orbiters called a station. It was his job as a consulting geologist to travel to these dingy stations and advise their personnel on how to improve the mining yields. It wasn't the job he expected to have when he was a kid, but if life had taught him anything, it was that things didn't turn out as you expected.

"He ready yet?" The headache had subsided, but Tak was getting bored.

"*She* isn't."

Tak shifted in the chair, trying to decide if it had been designed for an alien species or to intentionally torture Humans. After having worked as a consultant for five rotations, he should be used to waiting. He was the last person the mining chiefs wanted to see, and they always made him wait. He figured he spent a quarter of his life just sitting in run-down offices like this one, sitting in an uncomfortable chair, waiting to meet someone as part of some sort of power struggle between corporate and the managers in the field. A wave of exhaustion from the previous night hit him, and he closed his eyes.

"She's ready."

Tak's eyes bolted open and he jerked up in his seat at the secretary's voice. Based on the tone, it wasn't the first time the man had called him either. He stood up and quickly pulled at the edges of his coat to smooth out the wrinkles, hating the feeling of the collarless garment against his neck and the press of the accompanying trousers squeezing his legs. The suit was awful, but it was the uniform of consultants like him. A sign that he was a professional instead of just a kid who knew some tricks to get a few more grams of precious material out of a rock—which was what he *really* was.

"Thanks."

He walked into the chief's office to find her sitting back in her chair, legs propped up and a predatory smile on her face.

She looked to be middle-aged, maybe forty rotations old, with close-cut white-blond hair.

"Siddown." She waved at the chair in front of the desk. "Seems like corporate decided I couldn't handle my own operation, huh?"

Tak had dealt with chiefs like her before. They saw him as a threat, a tattletale who had come there to report on what they were doing. It couldn't have been further from the truth. No one back at headquarters knew who he was or cared what he thought. It was a strange arrangement, with neither side really wanting him there, but he got paid nonetheless. However, he remained employed because he got results. Tak could always find a few ways to increase efficiency and improve an operation's yield.

"So, you're the big brain that's supposed to tell us what we're doing wrong?" She pointed at his forehead.

Tak took a hit from his chempen and gave the biggest grin he could muster. "Well, I wouldn't say that. But I do have a pretty good track record at finding ways to get the most out of the equipment."

She frowned, dimpling her cheeks and making her appear ten rotations older, and tapped at the panel in front of her. From Tak's viewpoint, the air above her desk appeared slightly darker than the surrounding space. From her angle, the darkness would appear as a screen. She was reading through his personnel file and the paperwork that corporate had sent ahead of him.

"Hmm. Near the top of your class at Ringolt." She continued scrolling through the file. "You've been able to make some decent improvements... fifteen percent on Station 765. Not bad." She turned off the screen and the air between them lightened almost imperceptibly. "Okay, Mr. Big Brain, I'll give you a chance."

"Glad to hear it." Tak cleared his throat and grinned. "I'm glad I told them not to send the real file."

"Mr. Brain, this little station and what we do here may seem like a joke to a spoiled kid from the Central Worlds. But it matters, and we matter. We supply the materials that make your simple, cushy little life possible. So you can either start helping or get the hell out." She pointed at the door.

Tak's face heated, and he shifted nervously in his chair. "Sorry. Just trying to lighten the mood."

"The mood's fine." She stood up from her chair and gestured to the door. "Let's see what you got."

Tak spent the next several standards with the chief, who went by the name Cookie, going through the entire mining operation. He was surprised to find that, despite the station's age, the equipment and processes were near cutting-edge. It forced him to reevaluate his opinion of Cookie. She kept her comments to a minimum, but he could tell by the way the workers greeted her that she had their respect.

"You get podsick?" Cookie asked, resting her hand on the hull of a mining pod. They stood in one of the landing bays, rows of pods on either side.

The answer was a resounding yes. Tak hated this part of his job. He hated getting into the tiny egg-shaped spacecraft, leaving the station, and touring the actual mining activities in deep space.

"A little." An understatement. "But I'll be fine." Maybe.

There was a small hiss as the chief opened the pod's hatch and climbed in. Tak crawled in after her, grimacing at the wave of stink that greeted him. For some reason he couldn't understand, the pods were either way too cold, and the miners spent their shift shivering, or way too hot, and they spent the time soaked in their own sweat. Based on the stink, this one fell into the latter bucket.

He sat down on the seat next to Cookie, the control yoke sticking up between his legs. She expertly went through the ship's warm-up sequence, then piloted them through the small bay door and into space. The entire front half of the pod was comprised of a transparent material which gave Tak an unfettered view of the stars in front of them. He took a sec to appreciate the natural beauty of space. It was something he never tired of and was the only part of this entire process he enjoyed.

"Right now my team's clearing a 'stroid not too far from here," Cookie said.

Despite what people saw in the holos, asteroid belts were relatively sparse, with hundreds of thousands or millions of kilometers separating each asteroid. To increase efficiency, mining stations stayed in one place while the asteroids orbited around the system's star. The mining crews would focus on whichever ones were closest to the base. Depending on the system, it normally gave them plenty of time to clear it of resources.

After a half standard, they arrived at the mining site. A swarm of pods glided around an asteroid, digging out chunks with their sonic drills and using their scoops to place the mineral-laced rock into steel nets attached to their rears. When they got back to the station, they'd empty the nets and then land. Mining operations always reminded Tak of holos he'd seen of bees on Earth.

"I have to say, this is one of the best operations I've seen," Tak said, trying to make conversation.

Cookie smiled slightly. "Well, at least you've got the sense to admit it, Mr. Brain."

"There still may be opportunities for improvement, though," he said. Cookie's smile vanished. "I think—"

"Yo, Cookie!" A static-laden voice shot out from the ship's radio, interrupting Tak. "We've got incoming."

"So?" She looked annoyed.

"It don't look friendly. Pretty sure it's them Jackals."

Cookie swore and slammed her hand against the glass in front of them. "Got it. Get everyone back to the station. We'll hold back until everyone's clear."

She turned to Tak. "Well, Mr. Brain, grab ahold of somethin'. We've got problems."

"Control to Miss Stromsky!"

Dai looked up at her instructor and jerked her arm underneath the table.

"Something on your combrace that's more important than my class?" Hiram tilted his head, his dark eyes aimed at her hidden wrist.

Her fingers fumbled around the device, trying to shut off the chat she'd been on. Small pings sounded from beneath the table as Max continued to message her, and the warmth of embarrassment crept up her face.

"Sorry, my mother was asking me to stop by the company store on the way home."

"Really, Tejal is messaging you during class?" The instructor regarded her coolly for a moment. "I know you're not thrilled about being placed on the maintenance track and you'll have a chance to reclass in a few decs." He sighed. "But I can't help you if you don't show some sort of dedication. You know all the things I'm teaching. Hell, you could probably teach half this class. But if you don't put in the work"—he gestured at the parts scattered across her work area—"then I can't provide you with a positive evaluation."

Like most people on the station, Hiram had known Dai since she was a child. He'd worked with her mom for rotations and most of the things he'd been teaching were things she'd already learned, long ago, from him or her mother. It was just so *boring*. She understood the concepts, but what she couldn't understand was why she should care.

Dai nodded sullenly and finally switched off the combrace. "Sorry, you're right." She did feel guilty. He was only doing his job, and she knew he cared about her. The only problem was she didn't know what track she wanted to follow. She knew it wasn't maintenance. But nothing else seemed any better.

He placed a reassuring hand on her shoulder and walked back to the front of the room. Thankfully, most of the students had paid no attention to their little conversation and remained engrossed in their own work.

"Class," Hiram announced. Everyone looked up from the piles of parts in front of them. A few had been so focused that they dropped their tools in surprise. "Take a break and return in fifteen tics."

With a collective sigh, most of the class stood up. Dai looked around at the familiar faces. These were people she'd grown up with. It was so strange to think of them as adults, learning a profession and going off to work. As the others broke into groups and walked out the door, she realized she didn't want to talk with any of them. The only thing they would want to talk about was class and maintenance, which were the last things she wanted to discuss.

Instead, she gathered her tools and placed them back in her bag as she waited for the others to file out of the room. After they'd left, she slung her tool bag over her shoulder—it was a gift from her mother; she wasn't going to leave it lying around—and stepped out into the hallway. She walked past doors leading to other classrooms and left the training facility, walking out onto the level's main passageway. It was quiet—everyone was working or sleeping—and she only passed a few other people and skiffs as she strode through the station.

What do I want to do?

It had been the only question on her mind for rotations now. Dai enjoyed repairing and maintaining machines, and she had a knack for it. What she didn't care for was the repetition that came from being a mechanic on a mining station. Growing up, she'd often had to sit with her mom at work when the crèche was closed for one reason or another and had a good idea of what life as a mechanic on the Triple-Deuce would be like. Every cycle she would sit in the same room, fix the same part with the same problem, and then return to the same cramped quarters.

"Ufffff." Dai ran into something and fell onto the patterned metal floor, instinctively flinging out her arm to cushion her fall. Her reaction spared her head but sent a small jolt of pain up to her shoulder.

"Dai, you okay?"

She turned over to see the eyestalks of Patroller Krishnal staring down at her. Despite his stern words, both of his mouths were crinkled in what she knew was a sign of amusement. The long, squat Grosk extended one of his chubby arms, which Dai used to pull herself up, wincing slightly as she rose.

"Sorry, Krish. I had my mind on other things." Dai rotated her arm gingerly, trying to see how badly she'd messed it up. Luckily, the pain was already subsiding.

"Training?" His actual voice was inaudible to Humans. A small translator hung around his neck, turning his high-pitched tones into Human speech.

"Yeah," she admitted.

Krish lifted the front half of his body from the ground, stood on his four back legs, and looked down at her. Most people couldn't read the facial expressions of a Grosk, but Dai'd been around Krish her entire life and could see the concern.

"Sometimes our only choice is the one we don't want to admit."

"What do you mean by that?" she asked. He was always like this: approaching his point in every way except directly.

"You're going—"

The station's emergency alarm blared, drowning him out. Dai looked up, annoyed. An evacuation drill. Now?

"Attention, all personnel. There are unidentified vessels approaching the station. Proceed immediately to the closest—" The voice cut off and the clang of a metal door slamming open sounded over the speakers. A moment later, another voice, female, could be heard. "You hear? There're Jackals attackin' the station. They sent out the security ships, but there're like ten of them."

A jolt of fear coursed through Dai's body and she instantly broke into a sweat. The Fringe had never been a safe part of the galaxy, but raids had been picking up over the past few rotations. Stories of stations being destroyed, ships being captured, and worse filled the news lately. Jackals were no joke.

"Did you fargin' look at the on-air status light?" The man's voice blared over the station's emergency broadcast system. "I'm on the mic."

"Oh, shrag. Sorry, Denny." A moment later, the faint metallic click of a door closing sounded over the speakers.

"As I was saying," the man continued, annoyance still evident in his voice, "all personnel should move to the closest evacuation area. This is not a drill. So do it right now."

The speakers clicked off, and the station's klaxon began ringing again.

Krish's eye stalks curved toward Dai. "I've got to clear this level and make sure everyone gets to safety. But you need to get going. Now." He dropped back onto all six legs and rapidly scurried past her. After a few tics, he stopped and swiveled his head back. "Stay safe, Dai."

Some of Dai's earliest memories were of riding on Krish's back as he ambled through the narrow corridors of the station, keeping the peace. As she watched her friend rush away, Dai wiped a small tear from her cheek. Would she ever see him again?

Things had suddenly become *very* real, *very* fast.

Chapter Two

The Triple-Deuce

"Jackals?" Tak asked for what felt like the hundredth time. He was struggling to keep the incredulity from his voice, especially since Cookie seemed to take the situation extremely seriously.

"Yeah, fargin' Jackals. Somethin' wrong with your hearin'?"

Jackals were something you saw in the holos. Tak knew they still existed, raiding ships and small stations on the Fringe. But it was still a little unreal to be speeding away from a fleet of them in a two-seat mining pod.

"What'll they do if they catch us?"

"They don't care about us. They'll sail right past." Cookie turned to look at Tak. "But if they get to the Triple-Deuce before we do, they'll decompress the entire station, lock all the bays, ransack the place, and leave us out here to die."

"Can this thing go any faster?" Tak looked at the nav screen with new respect. He could see the small dots of the Jackal fleet at the edges, barreling toward the Triple-Deuce.

As their small pod zoomed toward the station, Tak tried not to hyperventilate. He used his sleeve to wipe the sweat pouring from his face as he pictured other times he'd been this scared. Falling out of a tree as a child. Getting jumped when he'd been at university. The day he found out his parents had died. None of them, except the last, compared to this.

Cookie glanced over at him. "Kid, I'm gonna need you to keep it together. As soon as we touch down, we gotta get to the closest evac area."

"Isn't there, I don't know, security or something to protect the station?" Tak felt so helpless. So useless.

"Have you been listening to the net?" The chief shot him an incredulous look. "Yeah, we've got a few security ships, but there's at least ten of those scumbag vessels heading toward the station. Odds don't look good."

Tak felt a small glimmer of relief when he saw the light from the system's star reflecting off the outline of the Triple-Deuce in the distance.

"Listen up, Mr. Brain. As soon as we land, you get out of this pod and follow me. You understand?"

He nodded.

"Good. We'll only have a few tics before those Jackal ships are at the Triple-Deuce. Like I said, I don't think it looks good. When they make it past our security ships, then the first thing the bastards'll do is launch missiles and fire at the station. If we're not in an evac ship by the time they finish, we're screwed."

Tak nodded wordlessly.

"One other thing. I'm not paying your consulting fee. You didn't finish the job." She smirked.

"You get me out of here alive and I'll waive it." Tak was too focused on trying to breathe to come up with a witty retort.

"Deal. Now get ready."

One of the landing bay doors on the side of the station dilated open, and their pod darted through, crashing onto the deck with a heavy thud. As soon as the outer door closed and the atmosphere had been pumped back into the bay, the light above the pod's door turned green and Tak began fumbling at the opening lever.

"Not like that." Cookie leaned over him and shoved his hands away. A moment later, the door sprang open with a hiss.

Tak spent a few more precious secs trying to remove his restraints, then clambered out of the pod. A cool, crisp wave of station air hit him in the face. He felt something give and began to retch the contents of his stomach onto the metal floor.

"Let's go, Mr. Brain!" Cookie yanked at his sleeve, almost causing him to fall to the ground.

He followed the chief out of the bay and into a large utility corridor. An alarm, almost painfully loud, reverberated through the area, accompanied by bright red strobe lights on the ceiling.

"The evac areas are marked in yellow on the station map. Your combrace synced to the station?"

"Uh, no, not yet." Tak hadn't thought he'd be there long enough to need it synced. It was supposed to be a quick in-and-out assignment.

"Next time, maybe you do that, Mr. Brain." Small oval-shaped doors, each leading to a landing pad, flew past as Tak followed Cookie down the empty hallway. He had an uneasy feeling in his gut. Had everyone already left? Were they the last people on the station?

"It's up ahead to the left," Cookie huffed.

Faded yellow markers surrounded a large rectangular door with rounded edges. The mining chief slammed her open palm against the square button next to the door and it lifted open, revealing five rectangular evac ships and a small group of people walking up the ramps into them.

The ships were significantly larger than the mining pod they'd been in; Tak guessed at least twenty people could fit into each. He could see rows of chairs filling their windowless interiors through the rear doors.

"Cookie, you made it," a man cried, his relief clear.

"Yeah, barely."

"You're in luck," the man said. "We got room for two more."

"Have you seen Hu?" Cookie's lip trembled slightly.

"Sorry, no. But I'm sure he got on a ship. He was in crèche when the alarm went off. The teachers would make sure he's safe."

Cookie looked back toward the hallway with a pained expression. "I told 'im if anythin' were to happen, I'd come get him."

"You go to the crèche now and you're a dead woman."

The chief let out a shriek of frustration and ran a hand through her short hair. She froze for a moment with her head down and hands clasped on her head, then looked up. "Let's go." Tak wanted to cry. Her voice was a weak and broken rasp.

As she reluctantly turned and started walking up one of the ship's ramps, a small boy ran into the bay.

"Ma! I'm here! I'm here!"

Cookie spun around, sprinted to the boy, and picked him up, planting a firm kiss on his forehead. "Angel, what're you doin' here? Where's your teacher?"

"I ran away from her," Hu said. "I told 'er I wasn't leavin' without you. We promised we'd stay together, right?"

Cookie gently placed her head against her son's, her body shaking.

"We gotta go!" the miner said. He looked at Tak. "But there's not enough room for all of us."

"Why?" Tak could see there was still room in the ship. He could sit on the ground or on someone's lap if need be.

"These ships have nothin' beyond the bare necessities. You've gotta be strapped in for departure or else you'll be pancaked against the hull. Even if you survive, the life support systems can only support twenty people." He looked earnestly at Tak, his eyes wide. "Sorry, buddy, but someone has to stay behind."

"I'll stay," Cookie said. The words came out slowly, as if being ripped from her. "I can find another evacuation area. The Brain over here didn't sync up his combrace."

Tak could feel the weight of three pairs of eyes on him. He didn't want to, but he turned to look at Hu and the boy met his gaze. His wide blue eyes seemed to consume Tak. What was a boy without his parents?

"No, I'll stay." Tak hated the words as soon as they came out of his mouth. "Just go. I'll find something else."

"You sure?" Cookie asked.

"Yeah."

"Thank you, Taksh." Cookie gave him an awkward one-armed embrace, still holding on to her son. She checked her combrace. "There are still some evac ships by the observation dome. You remember how to get there?"

"Yeah," Tak lied. "But now I'm charging you double."

As soon as Krish disappeared around a corner, Dai turned and ran back to the training facility. As she ran, she thought about her mother. The maintenance bays were on the other side of the station, too far for her to reach now. When they'd heard more and more reports of the Jackal raids, they'd discussed what they would do if the Triple-Deuce had to evacuate and had agreed they would escape separately if need be. Still, she hated not knowing if her mom was safe.

The training facility was already completely empty. When Dai rushed into the classroom, all that remained were tools and parts scattered across the workstations. A tight band of fear constricted around her chest. *They wouldn't leave without me, would they?*

She followed the three-dimensional holo map above her com-brace to the nearest evac area. The door was open and the bay empty. The tightness around her chest grew to a dull throb. Why had she been kidding herself? She wasn't an adult. She was a kid. A kid who wanted a grownup to tell her what to do.

"Dai, there you are!"

She turned to see Hiram rushing toward her, his eyes wide and a small trail of sweat making its way down the side of his face. Dai felt a wave of relief wash over her. She was happy to follow and let someone else make all the decisions. Hiram was a *real* adult; he'd know what to do.

"I've been running all over, looking for you." He gave her a quick embrace, then grabbed her hand. "Follow me."

"I checked the emergency system," he said as he pulled her down a main corridor. "There are still some evac ships by the observation dome."

Dai felt a strange sense of detachment as they ran through the empty hallways, past shops she'd frequented all her life. Was this the last time she'd see the Triple-Deuce, her home? The only home she'd ever known. Would she see her fellow Orbiters again? Hiram? Krish? Her mom?

God, I hope she's okay.

"Hiram, do you know if my mom got away?"

The instructor looked back at her. "No, but she's a smart woman. I'm sure she did."

They rushed through the vacant main passageways of the station. It was as if everyone had suddenly disappeared into thin air. Bags, food, and equipment lay scattered on the floor. Steam still rose from the abandoned plates at the restaurants and cafes.

Dai followed Hiram up several ramps until they reached the station's dome. It's circadian protocols were active, causing the star above to be dimmer than it had been a few hours earlier.

"Through the garden," Hiram shouted, pulling at Dai's arm.

As they ran through the dense foliage in the center of the room, ignoring the sinuous, manicured paths that wound through the area, a loud explosion reverberated through the station. Dai could feel the vibrations of the blast shake the soil beneath her feet and had to grab the trunk of a small tree to steady herself.

A robotic voice joined the klaxons. "Hull breach detected."

"Keep going," Hiram shouted as another explosion rattled through the creaky structure of the station. The sound of creaking metal echoed from the decks below them.

They reached the edge of the chamber, and an enormous explosion knocked Dai off her feet. For a moment, she thought it was all over and the Jackals had breached the dome. But somehow, she was still alive. Above their heads, the glass of the observation dome held.

"They missed the dome," Hiram said, pulling her up. "Come on. They won't miss a second time."

Dai continued running, following her teacher, passing the empty cafes and bars where she'd gone to eat countless times, a pain stabbing her knee. Hiram hadn't noticed she was struggling and was now several meters ahead.

"Wait—"

Another blast knocked them to the ground again, and Dai heard glass falling to the ground behind her. The dome was failing. The Triple-Deuce, her home, was being destroyed.

She turned over and pushed herself up, her knee screaming in pain. As she stood, a steel barrier slammed down from the ceiling, splitting her off from Hiram with a loud thunk. *I'm not going to make it.* She heard another barrier slam behind her, isolating her from the observation dome. She was trapped.

Hiram's face appeared in one of the small portals in the door in front of her. He pressed his face against the glass, his eyes frantic, and mouthed something to her. Dai rushed to the door and pressed her ear against it. It was almost impossible to hear through the thick glass, but as she held her breath, she could make out a few words.

"—conduit on the outside skin... another two levels down—"

Dai pulled her head back and nodded. There was a small gap between the interior bulkhead of the station and the outer skin. Small maintenance shafts and utility conduits ran through the area between the different levels. She might be able to get to another evac area two floors beneath through the utility area.

She looked at Hiram for a moment. He was more than a friend. He was an uncle; he was family. Someone who had made her the person she was today.

"Love you."

"Love you, too," Hiram mouthed as he took several steps away from the barrier. His eyes were red and he held his clenched fists at his side. "Now go!"

Dai pressed her hand against the glass pane, letting it linger for a moment, and then looked around. The only option available to her was the Sicilian, a restaurant, on her left. Somewhere in the establishment, there must be a utility closet she could escape through.

The restaurant's dining room was a mess. The Jackal attack had knocked over the chic tables and chairs. The plates and glasses that had been on them lay in pieces on the floor. She rushed to the kitchen, and the glare of white work lights and sparkling chrome counters and appliances greeted her.

Where would the utility closet be? Dai had eaten there a few times but had never been in the kitchen. She frantically rushed through the cramped prep area, flinging open doors and cabinets, looking for something, anything. She could hear the steady beat of missiles striking the station with dull thuds, followed by shivers as the impact made its way through the structure.

"Raz," she cursed in frustration. There was nowhere to go. None of the doors led to anything but storage closets.

A small glint on the floor caught her eye and she bent down to get a closer look. A metal-lined square was embedded in the white-tiled floor. She tapped on it with her foot, and it gave slightly. It was a hatch that had been tiled to blend in with the rest of the floor. She grabbed a flat pry bar from her tool bag and wedged it into the small gap in the metal outline then levered up the cover and stuck her hands in the gap, pulling the plate off the floor.

Underneath was a small passageway that was barely big enough for her to fit in. Dai climbed, feet first, into the opening and crawled down the tight shaft toward the outside skin of the station. As she made her way through the passage, the tools in her bag clanged against the metal floor, creating a cacophony in the tight space. The light from the restaurant disappeared, and soon she couldn't see a thing. Rather than dwell on the terror gripping her chest, she focused on placing one hand in front of the other, pushing out the thoughts of her friends, her mother, and what was going on all around her. The sound of explosions had stopped, and she heard pings and tearing metal as the Jackals launched supersonic projectiles through the station's hull. The pea-sized titanium balls would overwhelm its ability to repair itself. They must be close to being finished.

She felt like she was in a nightmare. When Dai first heard the Jackals ravaged small stations, she had a hard time believing it. But she was living through it now.

She went to place her right hand down but felt nothing, and she pitched forward, falling for several secs before landing on her shoulder with a crunch. A blossom of pain radiated from her shoulder across her body.

Dai wanted nothing more than to just curl up and wait. To give in. But she thought of her mom. A woman who had given everything for her. Dai had to fight; she had to keep going. What would her mother do without her?

She felt around with her left arm, trying to keep her right as immobile as possible. She'd fallen into another conduit that led back toward the center of the station. With a small curse at her own stupidity, Dai realized she could use her combrace to light the passageway. She activated the device, and the small holo projection over her wrist cast a faint glow around her. In front of her were the dark metal walls of a conduit, with two more shafts that led down on either side of her. She peeked over the side but couldn't see anything beneath her except inky blackness. Thinking of her recent fall, she knew there was only one way she could go: toward the center of the station.

After trying to crawl and being rewarded with a sharp stab of pain in her injured shoulder, Dai turned onto her back and pushed herself along the narrow tunnel with her feet. The regular pings of the Jackals' shooting echoed around her, and she expected any sec to be her last.

Dai saw the outline of another portal above her head. A way out. She pulled herself into a crouch and pushed against the hatch above her with her left arm. It was heavy, heavier than the one she'd used to enter the network of utility tunnels. She wasn't able to do much more than lift it a few millimeters before being forced to drop it back down, causing dull thunks to sound through the passageway.

Dai screamed out in frustration as she realized she would die in the utility corridor. With a last cry of effort, she pushed against the hatch with everything she had and it suddenly—miraculously—lifted, revealing a beautiful shaft of clear white light and a strange man looking down at her with a frown.

Tak was lost. Completely and utterly lost.

After leaving the evac area, he'd run through the empty hallways of the station, trying to reach the observation dome at the top. As he ran, the steady booms of missiles shearing through the hull joined the constant shriek of the station's emergency system. As sections were breached, doors slammed down, isolating areas of the station that were under threat of decompression.

Tak had to constantly change direction while continuing to travel upward, gradually finding himself at dead end after dead end. With a jolt, he realized he'd been sealed in; there was no way to go any further. After everything he'd been through, the thought that he would die on a small mining station at the Fringe of the galaxy was almost comical.

He looked around for some sign of an evac area; they should be scattered throughout the station. Any signs and markings had been worn away over time and the residents hadn't seen fit to update them.

A dull thud came from nearby. At first, Tak thought it was the metal frame of the station trying to accommodate for several sections losing pressure due to the Jackals' attack. Then he heard it again. He looked around and began circling in the hallway, trying to locate the source of the noise. It was somewhere nearby. Another thunk, just ahead. Then there was a muffled shout of frustration and rage, barely audible over the station's alarm.

The outline of a square hatch stood out on the bare metal floor in front of him. It moved upward slightly, then dropped back down. Someone was trying to come up. Tak bent down and grabbed the recessed handhold on top of the hatch and pulled up with everything he had. He heard a yell from underneath as he lifted the door and dropped it onto the adjacent floor with a crash.

"Hello?" he called out.

A girl, several rotations younger than him, peeked her head out of the opening. Her expression was guarded, and her brown eyes darted around the hallway. She seemed familiar. Had he met her the night before?

"Who are you?" she asked, brushing the tangled mess of long brown hair from her face.

"I'm lost," he explained. "Do you know where the farg an evac area is?"

She studied him for a moment, then climbed out of the hole using her left arm. Her right was clearly injured by the way she held it close to her side. "How do you not know where the evacuation areas are? Isn't your combrace synced?" Tak shook his head and she groaned. "Just follow me."

The girl rushed down the hallway, and Tak followed closely. They descended to the deck below and came to a nondescript door. The girl pressed the square button next to it and the door slid open, revealing an evac area with an escape ship still resting on the landing bay floor. Tak couldn't help but shout in triumph.

"Farg!" the girl shouted.

"What?"

She pointed to a small placard on the rear door of the ship: *Do not use. Under repair.* Tak couldn't move for a moment, couldn't do anything. To come so far and then have this happen? It was like a twisted joke.

An explosion, larger than anything that had come before, shook the station and knocked them both to the floor. It even caused the ship to slide across the floor with a screech. Tak could hear air hissing somewhere nearby. The station was starting to decompress.

"I don't think we've got a choice," Tak said. The girl had what looked to be a tool bag across her shoulders. "Those tools?" She nodded. "Maybe we can fix it." Maybe *she* could fix it. Tak hadn't touched a tool in his life.

At least the pod still had power. Its ramp dropped smoothly when he pressed the button next to it. The bland, cream-colored interior had rows of seats but no cockpit, controls, or windows. The only thing in the cabin other than the seats was a small round-edged, rectangular box at the front, where he guessed the AI was housed, and a red button on the hull above it.

The girl rushed to the box and removed a panel. She pulled a small device from the bag and attached several leads from inside the box to the device.

"The flex drive and navigational system are on the fritz," she said after several secs. "We can probably leave the station, but I have no idea where we'll end up."

The barrage on the exterior of the station was becoming more intense. Old mining stations like the Triple-Deuce were hard to decompress, and Tak was guessing the Jackals were growing frustrated with how long it was taking them. The increased fire also increased the risk they'd hit something critical and destroy the entire station as well. The hiss of escaping atmosphere was growing louder from outside the ship as he hit a button to close the rear ramp.

"Well, I think that's settled," Tak said dryly. "Let's go."

"Agreed." The girl was already putting the device back in her bag.

As Tak sat down in a chair in front, the girl pressed the red button on the hull. "Provide voice confirmation to activate pod," a robotic voice instructed.

"Confirmed," they both shouted.

"Escape confirmed," the voice responded. "Departure in ten secs."

The ship's AI counted down from ten while Tak fumbled to get his restraints closed, and the girl slammed her tool bag into a small storage tub on the hull and jumped into the seat next to him. When the countdown reached zero, Tak felt the ship slide forward for a moment before catapulting out of the station so fast that it slammed him into his seat and knocked the breath from his body.

The cabin lights grew dim, and he passed out.

Chapter Three

Deep Space

D ai opened her eyes with a groan. It felt like someone had beaten her with a metal bar. Her knee was sore, pain stabbed through her shoulder, and every time she took a breath, her chest ached.

The man who'd saved her remained unconscious, his head lolled forward over his restraints. She studied him. He looked to be in his mid-twenties, with a mop of black hair and a chubby, childlike face.

When she'd seen him standing over her on the station, her first thought was that he was a Jackal. But it quickly became clear he was simply someone who'd been on the station at the wrong time. The Triple-Deuce didn't—hadn't—received many visitors, and she was curious why he'd been there.

As her mind turned back to her home, she started to cry. All her worries about becoming a mechanic like her mother now seemed so small and childish. Her home had been destroyed. She was in an escape ship to who-knew-where with a total stranger. And she had no idea if all the people she'd known and loved her entire life were still alive. Her cries turned to sobs as she thought of everything that had happened.

"Hey." The man was awake and looking at her. "I'm Tak," he said softly.

Dai tried to stop crying, but she just couldn't.

He waited patiently, the sympathetic expression never leaving his face. "I'm sorry for your loss. I'm guessing you're an Orbiter."

She nodded, still sniffling. "Yeah."

"I'm really sorry."

"I lived on the Triple-Deuce my entire life." If it surprised him, it didn't show. "Everyone, everything I knew, was on that station." She sniffed. "Farg those Jackals."

"They all escaped," Tak said gently. "You'll find them."

Even though she knew he was just saying that, his words somehow still helped. He was right. Most people, if not all, had left the station. She'd find them again.

"What's your name?" he asked.

"Daiyu, but people call me Dai."

"Pretty name." He seemed confused for a moment. "I think I used to know someone with that name."

"Thanks. It's from my dad's side of the family."

"Was he on the station?"

"No," she replied. "He died a long time ago."

He flushed and looked down. "I'm sorry."

"No need for you to say sorry all the time. You didn't do any of it."

"True. But I still feel bad that this all happened to you."

·"Well, it happened to you as well," Dai replied, feeling a flash of anger. "Stupid fargin' Jackals."

He looked at her for a moment before speaking again. "Any idea of how long until we land or crash or whatever?"

"No clue. The evac ships aren't designed for normal space-flight. They're all preprogrammed to head to a planet in the Central Worlds—though I totally forgot which one—and have single-use flex drives and only basic navigation systems. There's no way to know—" She stopped, an idea forming in her mind. "Actually, there may be a way to find out."

Dai gingerly removed her restraints. Since there was no arti-ficial gravity on the small craft, she had to push herself toward the cargo container where she'd dumped her gear. She grabbed her tool bag and used the handholds recessed in the hull to pull herself to the AI housing unit at the front of the ship.

"The ship's system must know its destination even if it doesn't display it," Dai explained as she removed the access pan-el. "It has to account for some of the elementary considerations of time and space to navigate. I may be able to get an idea of where we are and where we're going."

It took her almost a full standard, but Dai extracted both their location and intended destination from the system. Her mother would've been proud. Unfortunately, it wasn't good news. Dai double-checked her calculations, but they still pointed at the same bleak outcome.

"I've got good news and bad news," she announced.

"Okay." Tak took a small drag from a chempen.

Who used a chempen on an evac ship? "Good news is we're heading towards a planet."

"Wait, there was a risk we weren't?" Tak asked.

"Well, yeah. Frankly, it's a minor miracle that we are, considering the ship was malfunctioning."

"Well, what's the bad news?" Tak asked.

"We're heading towards Faltran."

He looked confused. "So?"

"It's a Fringe planet that's known to have Jackal camps on it."

Tak groaned and dropped his head into his chest. "We escaped the station just to die on some Jackal planet?"

"It's not a Jackal planet," Dai corrected. This guy didn't seem to know anything about life outside the Central Worlds. "It's unincorporated—like every planet in the Fringe. The Jackals don't own entire planets. But there are a few they're known to operate out of—like Faltran."

Tak considered the information, idly tapping his lip with his chempen. "I guess we just need to keep our heads down and find some way to get a ride to the Central Worlds."

"So, that's the other part of the problem. Since Faltran isn't part of the Central Worlds, our credits are worthless there."

"There's always a way." Tak placed his pen in a shirt pocket. "We'll find something to trade or find someone who's willing to receive payment on landing. If we can reach the Central Worlds, I may know a few people who might help us."

Dai nodded. "Sure, that sounds great. I'd help out, but all my *associates* just had their home wiped out and left in evac ships."

Tak shook his head and scoffed. "How long until we land?"

"'Land' is a strong word," Dai replied. In truth, she didn't know what would happen when they arrived at Faltran. She'd never been in an escape ship before, or any ship for that matter. From what she'd seen of the ship's systems, their landing was going to be rough. "I'd say we have about ten standards until we reach the planet. You can take off your restraints if you want to move about."

"Sounds good. If I'm going to crash-land on a Jackal-infested wasteland, I'd like to get my blood circulating beforehand." Tak fumbled with his restraints and finally released himself. "What I don't get is how they can even exist. Are we back in ancient times or in some holo?"

He sounded like some spoiled rich kid. The stereotypical Centraler coming out to the Fringe and looking down on everyone.

"Sounds like something that someone from the Central Worlds would say," she retorted.

He scrunched up his face. "What d'you mean?"

"Out here, we don't have everything handed to us. There are a lot of planets like Faltran that never had sentient life and never had enough resources to justify colonization. The people make do with what they can." She sniffed. "How many people died in the 'civilized' Central Worlds during the wars of unification? Millions? Billions?"

"Didn't they just destroy your home?"

"Well, that's true," she admitted, her anger ebbing. "It's only gotten bad in the past few rotations, according to my mom."

"I can't believe no one's done anything about it."

"I can," Dai snickered. "As long as they stay out of the Central Worlds, the Council doesn't care, and no one on the Fringe has enough firepower to take them on directly."

"We might land right in the middle of them," Tak said. "Any weapons on board?"

Dai looked around. "I didn't see anything." Each rotation, every person on the Triple-Deuce was supposed to attend an emergency-protocol training session. She hadn't gone to one since she was nine.

Whoops.

"Evac ships are supposed to have survival gear," Tak said confidently as he floated through the cabin, opening any storage containers and panels he could find. "There's got to be something here. We're about to land on a potentially hostile planet, and we'll need everything we can get."

Daiyu was a strange girl. It took Tak a few standards to realize she was actually seventeen rotations old. She seemed so much younger. She was a strange mix of complete naïveté and technical expertise, with a smidge of sarcasm thrown in. She'd never had her own home but probably could disassemble and reassemble the escape ship they were in. She seemed lost, and rightfully so, at the recent events. But she hadn't flinched at the realization of where they were going.

He'd been a few rotations older than her when his own world came crashing down. It had been a dark time in his life, and many of the details were still fuzzy, but he didn't remember handling it half as well as her. Mainly he remembered intense fear, despair, and a sense of doom. If it hadn't been for a few helping hands, he probably would have died.

They'd scoured the interior of the escape ship, eventually locating a small box tucked into the bulkhead that contained rations and several bags of water. It wasn't much, but it was something.

Once they'd located the supplies, Dai withdrew into herself. Without a purpose, she'd let the events of the past cycle catch up to her. He knew the feeling. She floated above the chairs in the back of the compartment, staring at the hull, murmuring softly to herself. Tak didn't disturb her. He had a good idea of what she was feeling and knew there was nothing he could do to help. If she wanted to talk, he'd be there, taking some hits from his chempen.

"So you're a chemer?" Dai asked, eyeing the metal cylinder perched on Tak's lips. Most of the time when people said something like that to him, it was with disgust. Instead, she was curious.

"Yeah," he said. "Been on the pen since I was seventeen. Got hooked at uni."

"What's it like?" she asked.

"What I'm taking now just calms you," Tak said. "This is a combo fill. Nothing heavy or illegal. Just enough to take the edge off."

She held out her hand. "Mind if I try?"

Tak was about to hand over the pen when Dai's combrace started beeping, alerting them that they were getting close to Faltran.

"Maybe next time," Tak said.

They climbed back into their seats and fastened their restraints. It was a precaution since they didn't know exactly when they'd arrive, and there might be no warning when they entered the planet's atmosphere.

As he waited, Tak began nodding off. He realized his head was bobbing up and down as he strained to remain conscious. His fellow passenger was wide awake and staring intently at the windowless bulkhead in front of them.

A small hum came from the back of the ship, and Tak felt the combination of nausea and disorientation that could only mean the flex drive had turned off and they were no longer warping through space.

Dai cleared her throat nervously.

"Wait," Tak said, turning to look at her. "Is this your first time on a ship?"

She blushed. "I've been on mining pods a bunch of times."

"But you've never left the asteroid belt around the Triple-Deuce before, have you?"

"No," she admitted.

"It's totally okay if you're nervous."

Her face grew even redder. "I'm not nervous... Well, not much. I just want to land so I can get back."

"Back where?"

"To..." She trailed off. "I need to get back to my mother and my friends and you need to get back to the Central Worlds." The words came out as a sort of mantra rather than a sentence. It was as if she was telling herself.

"We'll get there."

The small ship shuddered, and Dai let out a squeak.

"You okay?" Tak asked. "We're entering the planet's atmosphere. Not long now."

She nodded, tight-lipped.

"It can feel strange the first few times, but just remember, they've tested these things a hulluva lot more times than you or I."

She shot him an annoyed glance. "I know, I know. I helped test some of them."

The shudder grew into a gentle shake and the seats chattered slightly as they vibrated against the floor. It was a much rougher experience than Tak was used to. He was guessing their small ship was descending at a much steeper angle than the private luxury yachts he'd traveled in as a kid or the commercial liners he took now.

A roar sounded in front of them, and he was pitched against the restraints. "It's just the reverse thrusters slowing our descent," he said reassuringly. He had to admit he wasn't just saying it for Dai's benefit.

She started retching next to him. Tak opened his mouth to comfort her, but the stench of her vomit hit him at the same time. Instead of reassuring her, he ended up joining her.

"Tak! What the farg?" The entire front of her shirt was covered.

"I'm not the best passenger either," Tak admitted.

"Yeah, I would say that you're—"

The ship rocked forward, cutting her off. They were hurled back and forth against their restraints and the sound of metal grinding against stone filled the cabin. After what felt like an eternity, the screeching stopped.

Tak unfastened his restraints and stood up. Or at least that was what he intended to do. Instead, he slipped into the small pool of goo on the floor in front of them.

"We're here," he announced cheerfully from the floor. Dai grunted and kicked him in the ribs.

Chapter Four

Faltran

The evac ship had slid across the top of a rocky plateau and come to rest only meters from the edge. Dai hobbled around the outside of the ship, still recovering from their landing and ten standards of weightlessness.

For a moment, everything that she'd been through disappeared from her mind as she looked over the planet's surface and tried to take it all in. The azure sky was dusted with wisps of the purest white. A forest of green stretched to the horizon beneath her, ending in a hazy band of purple where it met the sky. As she stared into its depths, she could see the branches swaying in the light breeze and birds circling in the air above, looking for their next meal. The air smelled alive and fragrant, an almost endless collage of scents. She'd lived her entire life in the vast void of space but had never felt a sense of her own insignificance until now.

"Damn!" Tak had removed his formal coat and shirt and was wiping them on the rocky ground. "I'm not looking forward to wearing this through the jungle."

Dai felt a surge of annoyance. Who cared about that when all this was around them? She'd found the answer to a question she hadn't realized that she'd been asking. The galaxy was so much larger and more complex than she'd realized growing up on a tiny station in the middle of an asteroid belt.

"Any idea of where to go?" Tak brought the coat up to his face and sniffed. He immediately jerked his head away and threw the clothing over the side of the precipice. "You got like a tracker or anything in that bag of yours?"

Dai wanted to shake him. How could he look out at such beauty and throw his vomit-encrusted coat on it?

"No," she replied. "Your guess is as good as mine."

Tak frowned and then clambered onto the top of the ship. Holding a hand over his eyes to block out the sun, he scanned the forest.

"There!" he shouted, pointing. "There's a settlement over there."

At first, Dai couldn't see what he was pointing out. Then she made out dark, angular structures and small whisps of smoke among the dense foliage. "It might be Jackals."

"Maybe," he admitted. "But we won't know for sure unless we check it out. We won't be able to travel far in this jungle, anyway."

A bird called sweetly from a nearby tree, and Dai couldn't help but smile. She doubted it would be as bad as he'd said.

Dai couldn't remember a time when she'd been more miserable. Her knee stung and her shoulder ached. The trees were dripping with humidity, and the cool breeze she'd felt on the outcropping above was blocked by the seemingly impenetrable labyrinth of life that was the forest. She trudged through the thick underbrush a few paces behind Tak, his chempen dangling from the corner of his mouth. Every few secs, she flinched at the sound of crawling or scurrying nearby, imagining some creature leaping out to attack her. Tak pushed the underbrush away as he slowly made his way through the forest, trying to clear a path. But every time he pushed a branch aside, it snapped back and hit her in the face.

Dai pulled a clump of seeds and leaves from her mouth. "This is horrible. How much farther?"

"Beats the hell outta me," Tak said. "I don't even know if we're going in the right direction."

"What?!" *Why oh why am I following a Centraler?*

"I'm tryin' my best here, but I can't see anything in front of me."

"We're doomed."

"Very likely," Tak said casually as he pushed another branch aside and stepped over a mossy trunk.

"Don't you know—" The branch slapped Dai in the face. "Ugh. Don't you know any survival tricks or anything?"

He hooted. "I'm a city boy. Grew up on Hkar'Trush. The closest thing I ever came to being out in the wild was when we'd pick berries at a hydroponics farm."

Dai was quickly running out of ideas of what Tak actually *could* do.

"I've been looking at the shadows," he said. "They're going off to our left."

The foliage was too thick for Dai to see anything *but* shadows. She realized they were utterly and hopelessly lost. But they'd been going too long to change direction now.

"I've got a good feeling about this," Tak said. He'd seemed to have gained some measure of confidence since they "landed" on the planet. "We have any water left?"

"No," Dai replied. She wasn't sure how she'd ended up being the one to haul all their meager supplies.

"Too bad. I'm getting a bit parched."

Dai ignored her own dry mouth and continued to trudge forward. The man had drunk at least three-quarters of their water.

In the forest, everything looked the same. Dai couldn't tell if they were traveling forward or just heading in circles. She doubted Tak did either. But he continued to make his way with a cheerful sense of confidence, talking about what he'd do when they got back to "civilization," as he called it.

He abruptly dove into the prone position and waved her down. Dai dropped and lay still, trying to understand what had spooked the man.

Then she heard it, a voice faintly drifting through the brush in front of them. At first, she couldn't make out what it was saying. It was getting closer, and as it got near, she started to make out words.

"—hate walking through this jungle. Place gives me the creeps."

A grunt of acknowledgment.

Lifting her head, she could see two men walking carefully around a small clearing. Dressed in loose-fitting brown robes that fell in rolls from their shoulders, they paced in circles, staring at the ground, and periodically kneeled to dig things from the soil. They didn't seem like Jackals. But then again, she'd never actually seen one before.

"Hey!" Tak shouted, waving a hand above his head. Dai pressed her face against the ground. What was he doing?

The two men shouted in surprise, and the taller one pulled out a gun and pointed it in their direction. He didn't appear to know where they were.

"Don't fire," Tak said. "We mean you no harm. We survived a Jackal raid and crashed on your planet."

The two men looked at each other nervously. "Then show yourself," said the man with the gun, wiping his forehead on his sleeve to brush away the sweat-soaked brown hair that hung over his eyes.

"Okay, we're standing up." Tak looked at Dai and nodded.

They both slowly rose to their feet, their hands held far away from their bodies. Dai had already determined where she was going to jump if the man started shooting—a dense clump of bushes to her right.

"Step forward," the gunman ordered.

They both stepped into the small clearing, moving as slowly as possible.

"Where you from?"

"A mining station," Tak replied. "Jackals attacked, and our escape ship took us here. What planet are we on?"

"Faltran." The man slowly lowered his weapon.

"Great, great." Tak turned to Dai. "Good job on your calculations." He turned back to the two men. "Now, is there any chance that you could help us out? We *desperately* need to get back to the Central Worlds."

Both men grinned at Tak's request. "That's gonna be a tough one, but we'll do what we can," the gunman said. "But *we're* gonna need *your* help first."

The two men introduced themselves as Rog and Szan and explained they were members of a small commune outside of the forest. They were factures, which meant they built and repaired the tools and equipment in their small village and were gathering fungii for medicinal bandages. Rog, the one with the gun, seemed to be the leader and was the more gregarious of the two by far. Szan kept quiet, occasionally adding a word here or there.

The men refused to leave until they filled both of the cloth sacks they'd brought with them. It took several standards of crawling and stooping, but the four of them finally filled the sacks to the men's satisfaction.

"Stay close and do exactly what we say," Rog said after he and Szan had tied the bags shut and slung them across their backs. "We'll need to pass through the Jackals' patrol routes and sensors."

Tak felt a small flutter of fear at the words. In less than a cycle, Jackals had gone from being something children dressed up as at parties to a very real and deadly threat. He glanced at Dai, and judging by her wide-eyed expression, he guessed she was feeling the same way. He also realized that the settlement they'd seen from the plateau had almost certainly been a Jackal base. It turned out to be dumb luck they'd ended up getting lost.

"So, how dangerous is this?" Tak asked.

Rog smiled. "Over the long run? Less dangerous than if you stay in the forest."

"Still pretty dangerous, though," Szan added.

"So, we've got that cleared up," Tak said, feeling no sense of comfort. "Which is good."

"Can we go?" Dai tightened the straps on her tool bag.

Szan led the party through a small trail that cut through the dense brush. Tak guessed the two men had created it when they were entering the area. Occasionally, Szan stopped and motioned for them to kneel while he tilted his head, listening. Tak couldn't hear anything except his own breathing.

"Okay, we're in the clear," Szan said as he stopped and turned around to face the rest of the group. "We're past any real danger."

"Define *real* danger." Tak wasn't sure what imaginary danger they faced, but he wanted clarification.

"We're out of any known patrol routes or defenses," Rog explained. "Doesn't mean we could run into them by chance, but it's less likely."

Szan crawled under a large bush. "Hey," he shouted as his feet disappeared inside. "Help me out here."

Tak joined the others at the edge of the bush and tried to see inside. The purple-hued leaves were too broad for him to make out the interior. He could hear Szan's grunts of effort and the rustle of something being pushed through the dense branches. A curved plate of dull metal pushed its way through the leaves, and he grabbed one side while Dai grabbed the other. Together, they pulled, dragging what turned out to be a small vehicle from the bushes.

"Good job," Rog said. "There's one more." He seemed to relish his position as foreman of their little operation. Considering the two men were saving his life, Tak was more than happy to do a little heavy lifting—or pulling in this case—while he watched.

As soon as the second vehicle was clear of the bush, Szan crawled out, his mop of black hair peppered with dead leaves and small branches.

"What are these?" Dai asked, eyeing the two single-tracked vehicles.

"You've never seen a unitrack before?" Szan looked at her askance as he pulled twigs and debris from the vehicles.

"They're pretty common in the Central Worlds," Tak explained. He doubted Dai wanted to explain exactly *why* she'd never seen one. At least not at that moment. "Good for going off-road and that sort of thing."

"Let's get out of here," Rog said as he sat down on one of them. "You can ride with me." He held a hand out to Dai.

She shyly sat behind him on the narrow seat above the vehicle's track. As soon as she was on, he fired up the engine. After the steady quiet of the forest, the loud thrum was almost overwhelming. Tak glanced around nervously. If there were Jackals nearby, they would have heard that for sure.

"We gotta move," Szan said, sitting down on the other one. Tak sat behind him and grabbed the handholds on either side, imagining himself flopping off the end of the vehicle. As soon as he was settled, they leapt forward and tore after Rog and Dai through a small path in the jungle.

Chapter Five

Faltran

The noise of the unitrack's engine and the rush of the air made it impossible for Dai to understand a single thing Rog was saying. He didn't seem to notice and spent the entire time they were winding through the trees shouting things at her. At first, she tried telling him she couldn't hear, but her words were either lost in the wind or he just didn't care. After a while, she gave up and concentrated on the surrounding scenery.

She was stranded on an unfamiliar planet inhabited by murderous Jackals but couldn't help feeling excited. Compared to a mining pod flying through space, the unitracks were practically standing still. Yet she still felt like this was the fastest she'd ever gone in her life. The forest, which had seemed almost hellacious when she was walking with Tak, had become beautiful once again. The experience would've been downright enjoyable if she wasn't thinking of her mother and her friends the entire time. Had they made it to safety?

The forest gradually thinned, and the landscape turned into small gnarled trees, then a windswept prairie. Finally, only small wiry bushes dotted the area around them. As they made their way over the sand, the sun dropped low in the sky, casting everything in a purplish light and then giving way to a dark night sky. Rog and Szan strapped thermal goggles to their faces so they could see in the dark.

As the unitracks crested the top of a dune, Dai saw a sprinkling of lights in the gulley below. They descended the gentle slope, and she made out shapes moving among large tents that were set up underneath the glow of strands of lights. As they grew near, she saw crates and vehicles scattered between the tents. People walked through the area, carrying sacks and talking to each other.

Rog and Szan brought their vehicles to a stop at the edge of the encampment and cut the engines. Dai stepped off and almost fell. Her legs had fallen asleep after standards of sitting on the back of the unitrack and her knee still throbbed. As she looked around, she realized that what she'd originally thought were tents were buildings. Their curved sides were made from metal coated with peeling and cracked purplish-brown paint. The locals, dressed in the same baggy robes as Rog and Szan, didn't seem to pay them any mind as they walked through the area.

"Well, we're here," Rog said. "This is Nashoba." He made a sweeping gesture with his arm.

"It's lovely," Dai lied. She was a bit disappointed since it was the first town she'd ever been in.

"It's home." Rog walked toward a nearby building. Like all the others, it was vaguely circular in shape, with a tall central peak and raised sides. "Let's get inside. Looks like there's a storm coming." How he knew, Dai had no idea.

The interior of the building was a single chamber, lit by a light dangling from the top. Underneath the spartan chandelier, a dark gray box, decorated with silver scrollwork, radiated a gentle warmth. Squat chairs sat around the heater, and cots lined the edge of the building. Dai felt a sense of comfort and warmth in the dimly lit room; it reminded her of the Triple-Deuce's observation dome in that way.

"Take a seat," Rog said as Szan walked to a chest and began rummaging around. "Let's get some food in our bellies." Szan pulled out several sacks and tossed them to the others.

Dai flopped into one of the low-slung chairs and tore open her bag to find it filled with small five-legged creatures that appeared to have been dried out in the sun and seasoned with a salt and herb mix. She gulped and picked one up by its stubby tail, pondering how hungry she really was. Tak had already decided and placed his bag on the ground next to him.

"What is this place?" he asked, looking around.

"It's our guest house," Rog replied, crunching down on a tail. "It's for travelers and friends who come by the commune."

"We welcome all travelers," Szan said.

"I mean the town," Tak said. "Why are you all the way out here?"

"Ah, yes, our commune. Well, Nashoba was created over fifty rotations ago by our ancestors. They sought refuge from the Central Worlds so they could establish their own society, one free from the oppression of hierarchy and rulers. Here we operate as a collective. No leaders or followers, each person with a single vote. We contribute what we can and take what we need."

"But why here?" Dai asked, her mind on the desolate landscape outside.

"That was more a function of necessity. When our ancestors arrived on Faltran, they found the forests had already been settled and the occupants weren't the friendliest."

"The Jackals were cannibals before they started raiding stations," Szan added.

"Of course they were," Tak said dryly.

"To the north are the cities," Rog continued. "But their petty mayors didn't understand our ancestors' plans and cast them out. So they came here and began building Nashoba, an oasis where we can live in peace and tranquility."

"I gotta ask," Tak said. "What do you do out here?"

"What do you mean?" Rog looked confused.

"There's nothing but sand. Doesn't it get boring?"

"For outsiders maybe," Rog replied with a smirk.

"There's not always—"

Rog cut off Szan. "We've got plenty to do here, and we have everything we need. No, it doesn't get boring. Our ancestors removed all the problems that 'civilized' people like you face every day so that only the things worth experiencing in life remain."

Tak looked around doubtfully.

Dai realized Rog and Szan's commune wasn't much different from the station she'd grown up in. A small, isolated community that was almost completely self-sufficient, with the occasional traveler stopping by. She could appreciate their perspective that they had everything they needed. Tak had briefly mentioned his life as a consultant, continually flying between planets and mining stations, and she could also see how he'd think living a quiet life like theirs could be boring. But just a cycle ago, she would have agreed with Rog and Szan.

"It may not be for everyone," Rog admitted. "We're going to Capital tomorrow for supplies and can take you with us." The thin metal walls rattled, and Rog tilted his head. "The storm's almost here. We'll head out after it passes. You should stay inside until then."

The two men walked through the metal door and into the night. As they left, Dai could hear the wind picking up outside as the door slammed shut.

The wind screamed outside the building, rattling its thin metal skin against the frame. The furious storm, dim lights, and remote location made Tak feel like he'd been thrown back in time.

After Rog and Szan had left, both he and Dai plopped down on cots, exhausted. Despite all they'd been through, neither could fall asleep. Tak lay flat on his back, looking at the sloped ceiling, listening to the sounds of the wind and his traveling companion rolling around in her own bed. Images of their escape from the Triple-Deuce and the trauma of crashing onto Faltran flashed through his mind.

It reminded him of what happened four rotations earlier, when he graduated from university. Then, he'd been a completely different person. Since he'd never been much of a student, he'd barely been able to make it through the mid-level government school his parents had sent him to. His parents were loaded, and Tak saw little point in studying when he'd known from birth he was going to run the family business. He hadn't expected it all to come to a halt so suddenly.

He'd stepped out of the private aircar and onto the landing pad outside his family's penthouse on Hkar'Trush. What seemed like an entire platoon of security patrollers waited inside. They sat him down, gently telling him of his parents' deaths in an aircar accident. As they continued to talk, their reassurances gradually shifted to questions about his family's company and his involvement in it. That was when he realized you didn't need that many patrollers just to tell someone their parents died.

Much of that day—hell, if he was being honest, much of his life—was a haze, but he remembered the feeling of helplessness and despair as he ran from his family's home that night. He only remembered his previous life as if it were a story told to him long ago. The characters and the plot were vaguely familiar, but he couldn't quite remember how it all fit together.

A small light caught Tak's eye. He'd forgotten he still had an unread message on his combrace. After a few presses and gestures, a short message glowed above his wrist:

You've been found.

There was no signature, and the message had been encrypted and sent through an anonymous proxy, but there was only one person who could've written it. Had the attack on the Triple-Deuce been to kill him? Or had he been at the wrong place at the wrong time?

"You ever been out in a sandstorm?" Dai asked, breaking Tak's concentration.

He craned his head to look at her. "No."

"Wonder what it's like."

"It sucks, from what I can tell." He had no desire to leave the relative comfort of the guest house.

"I want to see," she said. "Might be our only chance."

"If Rog and Szan didn't want to be outside during it, I'm guessing we'd probably die." He was only *slightly* exaggerating.

Too late. The girl had already swiveled off her cot and padded toward the door. She looked even younger than normal under the harsh glare of the overhead light. He felt suddenly protective of her; she'd had her entire life upended. Tak never had siblings, but he guessed this was what it felt like.

"Dai, don't go out there."

"I just wanna see," she said.

With a groan, Tak stood up and followed her to the door. She pressed a hand against it, trying to push it open, but the wind and storm were pushing right back. She pressed her shoulder to the door and slowly shoved it open. The wind sounded like a ship's engine, loud and steady. When there was enough space for her to slip through the door, she planted her foot on the ground to prevent it from closing and looked back at Tak.

"Ready?"

Why the hell were they doing this? What was the point? It was like she was possessed. Walking into a howling maelstrom wasn't high on Tak's list of things to do, but he wasn't going to let her go out there alone. He looked her in the eye and nodded.

Dai stepped outside, and he followed. The sand was everywhere, stinging his face and arms, flowing down his throat, up his nose, and, most painfully, into his eyes. He closed them, tears leaking out. The sound of the storm was all around him, drowning everything out. Tak shouted, but his voice didn't even reach his own ears. He kept one hand on the door and reached for her. It touched something, and it took him a moment to realize it was Dai's clothing. He pulled her toward him and pressed her arm against the wall of the building.

Stay there, he thought.

He grabbed the door handle with both hands and pulled. It barely moved. It took every bit of his strength to open the door against the pressure of the wind. When he'd estimated it had moved enough for them to fit through, he placed his foot in front to keep it open and pushed Dai inside, rushing in after her.

Tak dropped to the ground, and the door slammed shut behind him. What was she thinking? He tried to open his eyes, but they were coated with sand. In front of him, he could faintly hear her crying. Her sobs were almost lost against the thrum of the wind against the walls.

"So, was that worth it?" Tak asked.

Dai's sobs stuttered and slowed into deep breaths. "Yes, I think it was."

"You are fargin' insane." He slapped the sole of her boot in front of him.

She just laughed bitterly, sand-coated tear tracks on her face.

Dai woke up to the sound of silence, her body aching. The storm had moved past, but sand still completely coated her body and the cot. Whenever Rog arrived, she'd ask if there was a cleaning bot around.

She didn't know what had possessed her to go out into the storm. At the time, she hadn't really been thinking, just feeling. She'd felt like it was something she had to do because it might be her only chance. Once she found her mother, they'd probably find lodging on another station and work as mechanics there. It wouldn't be the Triple-Deuce, but it'd be similar.

Her knee screamed as she stood up and walked to the chest of food in the center of the room. She rummaged around, found a bag of dried plant rings, and sat down by the central heater. Tak remained blissfully unconscious on his cot, snoring away. He reminded her of Max in many ways, funny and a bit silly, but Tak had an edge that her friend didn't have. Perhaps it was how he'd entered her life. She sensed an aura of mystery around the man.

"Hey! Wakey wakey!" Rog's booming voice proceeded him as he strode into the room. The thunk and yelp of Tak falling off his cot came from behind her. "We're heading out—" Rog did a double take as he looked at the sand strewn across the room. "What happened? You went out into the storm."

"Yeah," Dai admitted. "I couldn't help it. It was just something I *had* to do."

"Now Szan's going to have to clean this all up." Rog shook his head. "We don't have maids or cleaners like you Centralers do."

Dai wanted to protest. He knew perfectly well she wasn't from the Central Worlds.

"It's my fault. I'll fix it." She hated the thought of Szan cleaning a mess she'd made.

"Yes, it *is* her fault," Tak chimed in as he pushed himself off the floor. "I told her not to."

"As your hosts, Szan and I are responsible for you. There isn't time for you to clean it up yourselves before we head out. So, he'll need to get this situation resolved."

"I can clean it up myself."

Rog held up a hand. "Don't worry about it. He'll be happy that he can be of some assistance."

"No, really, I—"

"Please. Stop," Rog said. "I hate to be blunt, but you're in desperate need of some time in the showers. Szan is used to cleaning up sand. We live in a desert, after all." He clapped his hands together as if they'd settled the matter. "Now, let's get you sorted." Dai wondered if Szan would appreciate her offer.

Dai and Tak followed Rog out of the guest house. Dai had to shield her eyes against the mid-morning sun as they stepped out into the small village. People strode between the buildings, all dressed in the same flowing robes that Szan and Rog wore, or sat in the shade, resting or working on crafts. As they followed Rog between the metal-clad buildings, it surprised Dai that none of the inhabitants seemed interested in them. They continued to stroll through the area or focus on their work, not bothering to even turn their heads to look at the strangers.

"No one seems to care we're here," Dai observed.

"I'm guessing they get more than a few travelers," Tak said. "I mean, they have a building just for them."

Dai wondered why they'd have so many people coming through their relatively quiet commune. From what she'd been able to tell so far, there wasn't much out there.

Rog led them to a bathhouse filled with stalls created by cloth dividers hung from the ceiling. The stalls were divided into two sections: an area with a wood bench, where she could undress, and a vestibule containing only a pot filled with heavily scented water and a sponge. Her "bath" was heavenly. Dai hadn't realized how badly she'd needed to get clean. When she stepped back into the changing area, she found a set of robes, identical to the ones the residents wore, waiting on the bench. Next to it, someone had neatly tied her clothes in a roll.

She put on the robe and stepped outside, holding on to her old clothing. Immediately, she appreciated the difference between the robe and her previous clothing in the desert heat. Despite its bulky appearance, it was actually cooler than her pants and shirt, with its breathable, heat-reflecting fabric and hidden vents that allowed air to flow through. Tak stepped next to her, waving his arms as he adjusted to the outfit.

"Not bad," Rog said as he looked them over.

They returned to the guest building, which Szan had already cleaned, and headed out to a small level area at the edge of the camp, where several aircars were scattered. From what Dai could tell, they were older models with dinged fuselages and scrapes along their faded paint. Szan was standing next to a small six-seater with a large transparent bubble over the passenger cabin.

Soon, they were soaring over the undulating dunes, the engine making a worrisome whine as they went. The vehicle was so old Rog had to pilot it manually rather than use an AI.

Dai stared at the barren landscape flying beneath her. She could see the edge of the forest behind them, but other than that, it was desert from horizon to horizon. Occasionally, another vehicle would appear in the distance, but they were always too far for her to tell the make or model.

"Are you worried about Jackal attacks?" Tak asked.

"Nah," Rog replied breezily. "They only attack people who go into the forest. Other than that, they keep to themselves."

"But they're Jackals," Dai said. "They steal. I thought that was kind of their thing."

"Jackals still need things like medicine and food. Besides, there's not much on Faltran outside the cities for them to steal. There's an unspoken agreement around here. Everyone leaves them alone and they leave us alone. They come into the cities for supplies and stop by our commune when they're traveling through."

"Good guests too," Szan added. "They bring gifts."

"Yeah." Rog nodded. "They've got some good stuff."

"Remember when they gave us that crate of brandy?" Szan asked with a smile.

Rog laughed. "Old Cennie ended up streaking through the commune." The two men laughed at the memory.

Dai wondered whom the Jackals had stolen the brandy from. Had their victims survived? It all felt wrong. "Aren't you guilty, then?"

"Guilty of what?" Rog asked as his laughter subsided.

"I don't know, of helping them out. They're killing people out there."

"We can't stop them," Rog said. "If we even tried, they'd wipe us out."

"They didn't used to be so bad," Szan added. "A few rotations ago, it really picked up. Used to be they'd have a raid and then sit in their camps for a dec. Now they're back out before they've even sold the loot from the last time."

"Greed gets to everyone eventually," Tak said.

Dai wasn't sure about that. Most of the people she'd grown up with hadn't cared about credits. Rog and Szan didn't seem to either. She thought about saying something but let it slide. The Jackals *were* greedy scum, and that was all that mattered.

Chapter Six

Capital, Faltran

T ak was less than impressed by Capital. It had taken an almost comical back-and-forth between him and Rog until he understood the name of the city. He still held that whoever had named it suffered from a severe lack of imagination.

Rog landed the aircar in a large paved lot near the edge of the town. As Szan began to pull boxes and sacks out of the back and load them onto a small port-a-skiff, he explained that they had to stop by to deliver some materials to customers in the city on their way to the port.

The small Fringe town was a hodgepodge of prefabricated metal residential blocks with the occasional high-rise peeking through. Everything seemed to be at least thirty rotations behind the times, from the aircars to the fashion. Dai, who'd never been to a city of any sort, walked around with her head practically swiveling off her body and her mouth slightly open. Tak wanted to laugh but thought better of it. The last thing she'd want was someone pointing out her relative inexperience. The people looked to be a rough sort, mostly Human, with a few other species sprinkled in. More than once, a passerby growled at them or hurried past, shooting them a guarded look.

"What's going on?" Dai asked. "What did we do?"

"It's just ignorance," Rog replied.

"People think that we work for the Jackals," Szan explained quietly. "Nashobans don't turn away any travelers unless they're a threat. They don't seem to get that."

"When we met you, you were worried about the Jackals killing you," Tak said.

"Yes, because we were in their forest. We have an agreement, and we sometimes have to break it, knowing the ramifications if we're caught."

"They know we do it," Szan said.

"Yes," Rog agreed. "It's a bit of a game, really."

"A game?" Dai turned from the statue she was examining to look at him.

"Not a very fun game, I admit."

Rog and Szan took them on a circuitous route through the town, stopping periodically at shops along the way. Rog explained that the commune had an agreement with them to sell some of their handmade crafts and tools. They were all clearly high-end stores with exotic wood and stone facades and highly curated selections. Credits were no good out here on the Fringe; instead, the clerks passed Rog small metal coins, which they called chits, in exchange. By the time they reached the city's port, the man jingled like a bell.

As they walked along, Tak felt uneasy, thinking about the cryptic message he'd received. He doubted there was any way someone could know he was there, but there was no way for him to be sure.

Finally, they arrived at the port with the port-a-skiff, now empty, trailing behind them. The building was easily the largest in town. It was an enormous rectangle, with a glass facade facing the street. A few pedestrians trailed in and out, bypassing a rusty metal sculpture of an ancient rocket taking off.

"This is where we part ways," Rog said. "We'll be in town for another cycle in case you need us. We're staying at the Desert's Dawn, near where we parked the aircar."

"Thanks, Rog." Dai leapt forward and hugged him, clearly catching him by surprise. "You saved us."

Rog, for once at a loss for words, blushed.

"Thank you," Tak added. "If there's ever anything we can do for you, let us know."

"We will," Rog replied.

"Good luck." Szan opened and closed his mouth as if there was something else he wanted to say, but seemed to decide to leave whatever it was unsaid.

"Thanks."

Tak and Dai turned and stepped inside the port building.

It had seemed almost modern from the outside, but inside was a different story. The building was filled with spacers, old cargo bots, and piles of goods. Monitors hung from the ceiling, filled with ship names and departure times. It quickly became clear to Tak that this port was intended for small-time cargo-haulers rather than the space-liners and transports that they needed.

They walked through the large main atrium, and he scanned the area, looking for a passenger desk. There were several makeshift counters set up near the walls of the room, but they were clearly intended for people looking to haul cargo rather than passengers. The streets of Capital had been filled with Humans, but the port was a mix of species. Large Hkrum waddled past with their tails swishing behind them. Packs of Fergormi scurried by, chittering to each other. Tak even saw a Sworomo clunk by in an aerosphere, the suit filled with water so the creature could survive in the air.

Dai seemed overwhelmed by the chaos and sights of the port, her head swiveling back and forth with each new creature or sound. Tak could only imagine the culture shock she felt after spending her entire life on a quiet station with only Humans around except for the occasional alien. More than once he had to pull her back so she didn't run into someone or something.

After spending a standard futilely walking through the building, searching for a passenger desk, Tak began talking to groups of spacers and subtly asking if they had room for two stowaways. Many of the aliens didn't have translators, and without an earpiece, Tak couldn't understand the chirps and grumbles that made up their native language.

Just as he was giving up hope, a Yshri captain named Quen agreed to take them for an astronomical price. It would deplete most of the credits that Tak had saved, but they didn't have any other choice. Since he didn't have any credits on him, he had to find someone that would accept payment when they got back to the Central Worlds.

"Last thing, you got your documents?" Quen asked through a small device attached to the front of her vest that translated the low tones of her voice. She reached into a pocket with her translucent hand and pulled out a scanner.

Tak nodded and held out his combrace, and she ran the scanner over it. The device beeped a few times, and her skin shimmered as she studied its screen.

"I can't take you," she said. "Your interstellar travel permissions have been revoked and there is a note to detain you on sight."

Tak's heart stuttered. How could it be possible? He'd been so careful. He'd thought it was all behind him.

"What's going on?" Dai took a gulp of air and looked at him with wide eyes. "Why would you be tagged to be detained."

"I don't know," Tak lied. He turned to Quen. "Scan her." He gestured to Dai's combrace.

The captain ran the scanner over the girl's combrace. "She's good."

At least Dai could get out of here. She'd have to figure out how to get back to her mother, but she'd manage. As soon as she got to the Central Worlds, she could contact her, and they'd figure out a way to meet up.

"Okay, she'll go, then, and I'll—"

"Hell no," Dai interrupted. "I'm not going."

"This is your best bet," Tak said. "Take it."

"No." Dai grabbed the sleeve of his robe. "We'll figure something out."

Tak gently dislodged her hand. "There's nothing to figure out. Just getting a ride from the Fringe into the Central Worlds is hard enough. Finding one that'll take me with a detain order is damn near impossible. You've got an opportunity. Take it."

"No."

"Look, I appreciate your loyalty, but you need to get back to your mother. She doesn't know you're alive and she's gotta be frantic. I'll be fine. Believe it or not, I've been in tighter spots than this."

Dai studied the dusty tiled floor, biting her lip, then looked back up at him, her jaw set in a defiant manner. "It's not for you. It's for me. I can't. I just can't do this right now. Maybe in a few cycles. But for right now, it..." A single tear drew a jagged line down her cheek. "I need us to stick together."

Tak gave an exasperated groan. He couldn't force the girl to go.

"I'll be here for a few more standards," Quen said. "Pad thirty-one alpha."

As they watched the Yshri slink away, Tak sighed. He had no idea how they'd get off the planet, much less to the Central Worlds. There was nothing he could do about his documents here in the Fringe. They'd have to find a smuggler. The only problem was that they had no credits to pay, and smugglers weren't known for their willingness to perform without payment up front.

"Well, time to regroup," Tak said.

"Yeah," Dai agreed, nodding numbly.

"So, why do they have orders to detain you?" Dai asked as they made their way through the crowded streets.

"I don't know," Tak lied. "It must be a mix-up."

"Stop lying." Dai nimbly moved to the side to let another pedestrian move past. "What's going on?"

"These things happen," Tak said. "It sounds trite, but the galaxy is a big place and mistakes happen. I know a few people this has happened to. Normally you can just go into an admin office and get it fixed up. Unfortunately, that's not an option out here."

"You're still lying," Dai said. "What's so bad? Why won't you tell me what's going on?"

Tak stopped and turned to face her. "I don't know what's going on. You've spent your entire life on a small station on the outskirts of the Fringe, so you don't understand how things are in the rest of the galaxy. I'm here to tell you that they're messy and confusing and mistakes are made. We need to focus on the here and now."

"This *is* the here and now," Dai spat back. "We are stuck *here*, right *now*, because of something that's going on with *you*. Stop lying and talking down to me. I'm not a child."

"This is the first time you've ever fargin' stepped foot on a planet. We're not in a holo." Tak wished she'd just trust him and stop asking questions he couldn't answer. He wanted to get her to safety, and she kept asking questions that were none of her business.

Dai gave a shout of frustration and shoved him back. "Fine. I'm going to check out this city, then, and maybe I'll learn a few things. I'll find you later."

Tak grabbed her sleeve. "Wait, don't just go wandering off. You've never been in a town before. Don't—"

Dai grabbed his hand and spun, flipping him over her hip. He landed on his back, hard, the air knocked out of his lungs. Her almost angelic face appeared above him.

Gee, how'd she learn to do that?

"I picked up a few things about taking care of myself on the Triple-Deuce," Dai said with a smirk. "Don't look for me."

By the time Tak had sat up, she'd disappeared into the crowd. He dusted himself off, ignoring the looks from passersby, and trudged toward where they'd parked the aircar.

It took a standard, and stopping to ask for directions a few times, but he eventually found the Desert's Dawn. The squat building was painted to look like a sunrise, with deep reds at the base of the structure transforming into a light blue near the top. The lobby was a study in the Fringe's rustic architecture, with several balconies extending over a central atrium, which was empty except for a restaurant that took up the rear half of the space. A handful of tables were occupied by guests idly eating while watching their ocutabs.

Tak made his way to a large desk carved from a single piece of wood in the center of the lobby. He wondered how large the tree had been. At least as wide as the lobby, he guessed.

The attendant told him that no one matching Rog and Szan's description had arrived, so Tak decided to take a seat in the restaurant and wait. After a few sideways glances, the other diners paid him no mind. He was almost nodding off when he heard something that jolted him back to the present.

"—another attack on a station." It was a man's voice, a deep baritone.

"Where?" a woman asked.

"I forget the name. It's another one far out in the Fringe," the man replied. "That's been, what, three this dec?"

"At least. Why isn't the government doing anything about it? They're going to start attacking stations inside the Central Worlds soon."

"The Tryresh have the chair. They're pacifists. Even if you smack them across the face, they won't do a thing." Tak knew that wasn't true at all. The Tryresh were no more pacifist than most Humans. He didn't follow politics much, but he'd had his own dealings with the large creatures.

"I've heard they're getting a cut from the attacks." The woman's voice dropped to a whisper. "Using others' blood to line their pockets."

That also sounded extremely unlikely to Tak. The Tryresh were a rich species, which was one of the reasons they had ascended to chair the Central Worlds. Colluding with Jackals to conduct raids on the Fringe made no sense. What was even more curious was that they were having the conversation on a planet with a heavy Jackal presence.

"Doesn't surprise me," the man replied. "Can't trust a species that won't even stand up for what's right. There should be a full investigation."

"You know that'll never happen." A scoffing sound. "They don't care about their citizens. As long as the people stay in line, nothing'll change."

Tak *had* to see who these people were. He leaned back and tilted his head so he could study the table behind him. Their clothes, modern and relatively clean, marked them as Centralers, if he didn't know that already from the conversation. He guessed they were merchants, on-planet for a cycle before returning to the Central Worlds.

As his eyes darted over them, they returned the look with hostility.

"What d'you want, Muner?"

Muner? Tak had never heard that term before.

"The station. You know where the refugees went?" Tak asked.

They exchanged glances before the woman responded. "Why do you wanna know? What does a Muner care?"

"You just gonna crawl back and help your Jackal buddies?" the man asked.

"I'm not from the commune." Tak tried to keep his voice under control. "They took me in. I'm from the Central Worlds and I've got friends who work on mining stations."

"You? A Centraler?" The man looked dubious.

"Yeah, I'm from Hkar'Trush. What's wrong with you?"

"Wrong with us?" The man growled. "You're the one dressed like a Muner. Why don't you go back to the desert and leave us alone?"

He started to get up and move toward Tak, but the woman grabbed him by the shoulder and pulled him back. "Not worth it," she said. "Let's go."

The two stood up and brushed by Tak; the man made sure to put his weight into him as he walked past, knocking him into the table.

Tak stayed seated and let the two leave. He had to remain focused on one thing: getting back to the Central Worlds. Wherever Dai had gone, he trusted she'd return, and he needed to figure out what to do before then. But without any chits, he didn't even have a place to sleep for the night.

Chapter Seven

Capital, Faltran

D ai brushed past people in the street, not caring where she was going. Farg Tak and his stupid secrecy. They were stuck on this planet, and he wouldn't even tell her why. What did the man have to hide? The worst thing was she wasn't totally sure he *was* lying. She was pretty confident the detain-on-sight orders weren't a simple mix-up but couldn't say for sure. In holos, these types of mishaps happened all the time. Couldn't they happen in real life?

Either way, the man was certainly hiding something, and she couldn't stand the way he'd talked down to her when she'd questioned him. He acted like he knew so much more than she did, despite only being a few rotations older. Besides, he might've been to every single planet in the galaxy, but he still didn't know how to maintain a flex drive or how a sonic drill worked.

When she looked up, Dai realized she was completely lost. The crowds that had pressed against her earlier had thinned, and the dusty sidewalks were now made of a brilliant white stone.

Wherever she was, it was clearly a wealthy district. High-end aircars glided above the road, and the multi-level buildings practically shone with fresh paint while uniformed attendants stood in front, opening the doors for the patrons.

Dai's anger faded. What was she doing here? Why had she decided to walk around alone in a city after having been there for only a few standards? What would her mom say? She chuckled to herself, imagining what her mother's face would look like when she told her about this. She could practically hear the woman's voice. *You've got to be more careful, Dai!*

A small group of people entered a building across the street from her. She couldn't see any signs or markings on the outside, only a back-lit logo of a lightning bolt superimposed over a square that hung above a large multi-paned mirror. The same impulse that had gripped her the previous night and caused her to go out into the storm came back, and she made the split-sec decision to enter.

After she'd spent a standard walking in the sunlit street, the interior appeared almost pitch-black, and she almost ran into a large Kyrillian standing by the door, its opalescent eyes scanning each person who entered. The interior opened into the largest room she'd ever been in. It was at least twice the size of the Triple-Deuce's observation dome. Groups of people filled the floor in front of her and congregated on glass-bottomed platforms that hung from the ceiling at different heights. What she'd thought was an enormous mirror turned out to be a one-way glass window, and she could see a few people walking on the sidewalk out front. She was in a bar or recreation facility of some sort, based on the laughter and loud conversation, but she'd never seen anything like it.

Dai wandered around the floor, her head tipped back, watching the platforms. The people on them leaned against the side railings or stood in the middle, gyrating wildly.

What were they doing?

"Hey, you a Muner?"

Dai looked down to see a woman a few rotations older than her with blond hair tied back from her face. She looked at Dai with an expression that flickered between curiosity and confusion.

"Muner?" Dai asked, confused.

"Yeah, what're you doing here?"

"I'm not from Nashoba," Dai said. Now it was the woman's turn to look confused. "I'm not from the commune. I escaped a Jackal attack and my evac ship crashed on this planet."

A flicker of surprise. "Really? What station?"

"Station 222."

"Ah, I heard about that. How'd you end up wearing those?" She gestured at the robes.

"The people of Nashoba—the commune—took us in," Dai said. "They gave us these."

"Interesting... I heard they kidnap people and take them to the Jackals for ransom."

"They're not like that," Dai said with a flash of anger. "They *saved* us."

The woman held up her hands. "Sorry, just what I heard."

Dai gestured around the vast room. "What's this place?"

"You've never seen a stimbar?" the woman asked with a condescending smile. "This is the Dirty Stim."

Dai remembered the stimchip that Max had given her—it felt like a million rotations ago—which was in her pocket. Stims were chips that contained games or preprogrammed experiences. Put them into a stimpad, and you could experience almost anything. She'd heard of stims but never stimbars.

"Come with me." The woman beckoned Dai to follow and led her to a taut cable running floor to ceiling, next to a platform. The woman wrapped her hand around the cable and glided up to the platform.

Dai hesitantly grabbed the cable, expecting to be jerked upward. Instead, as her fingers closed, she felt a gentle pressure on her feet pushing her up. She relaxed her hand around the cable, using it to stabilize herself as she rose. When she was level with the platform, she stopped and easily stepped onto it.

"Put this on," the woman said, handing Dai a curved metal plate about the size of her palm.

It wasn't what she was expecting it to look like, but Dai knew what it was—a stimpad. She'd never seen one since they were illegal in the Central Worlds and their stations, like the Triple-Deuce. However, here in the Fringe, laws were whatever the locals made them. She eagerly placed the device on the back of her neck and felt it gently clamp on.

"You ever go on a ride before?" the woman asked.

"No." Dai felt a knot of nervousness.

"Well, get ready, then." She walked to a small panel at the side of the platform and began tapping on the screen.

The stimbar disappeared, and Dai was in... nothing. It was a complete void. No light, sound, or smell. She blinked and was soaring above a verdant green forest. Air rushed around her in a howl, and she could smell the sweetness of pollen coming from below. She tried to change her direction and realized she had no control over what was going on around her; this was a recording rather than something she could interact with.

She flew over the landscape, then suddenly dove, streaking through the green canopy of the forest. Underneath, the bottoms of the leaves were a mixture of reds, oranges, and yellows, colors so vivid they hurt her eyes. She darted between trunks and branches, flying over the sparse underbrush. Her heart leapt in her chest. Everything was so real. She felt as though she were there, even though a voice in the back of her mind reminded her she was not.

She dove through a hedge and burst into an encampment that filled a large clearing on the other side. People sat on the porches of the makeshift shacks that lined the edges of the area, talking to each other while children ran in the center, laughing and playing games. It was a heartwarming scene. Despite living in these humble shacks, they seemed to be a content and close-knit community.

Several of the adults noticed her and jumped up, pulling guns from their waistbands and holsters, and fired at her. She dove sideways, then sped forward and zoomed through the hedge on the opposite side. As she came out, an alarm wailed around her, and shouts erupted around the area. It was hard to tell, but it seemed like there were several clearings, just like the one she'd abandoned, scattered around the area. A ship, several times larger than the evac ship she'd used to get to Faltran, sat on a hard earthen pad in front of her. It looked like it had originally been a merchantman—the size and large cargo area in the back were clear giveaways—but had been modified for battle. Armor was affixed to the outside, and several missile and weapons arrays had been bolted to the bottom of its stubby wings. Mechanics, dressed in ragged, grease-stained coveralls, crouched on makeshift scaffolding, their arms immersed in open access panels on the hull.

When they noticed her, the workers shouted and pointed, and some even threw their tools at her. She easily evaded their attacks and continued to fly around the ship. Dai suddenly realized what she was looking at; it was a Jackal ship. It was a Jackal camp. This was a stimvid of a drone that had somehow made it through their security. Why would the woman show her this?

Below her, kids ran on the ground, following her, shouting with glee and pointing. Children, even Jackal children, would always be the same. Cracks of gunfire burst out next to her and she fell to the ground. She felt a moment of terror as she stared into the barrel of a long rifle pointed at her, and then she was cast into blackness once again.

Dai blinked as she pulled the stimtab from the back of her neck. "Why'd you show me that?" She was disoriented and more than a little sick to her stomach. The last secs of the stim had been unsettling, to say the least. Still she felt a faint pulse of pleasure radiating through her body. It was the reason so many people became hooked on stims.

"I thought... I dunno. I thought maybe it's something you'd want to see." The woman looked younger and less certain of herself—she might actually be Dai's age. She laughed and traced her finger down Dai's arm, sending chills through her body. "Come on, follow me."

Dai followed her down the cable and toward a booth filled with people in a far corner of the bar. She could instantly tell the three in the middle were Centralers. They looked like something out of a holo with their trendy clothes, surgically perfected features, and expressions that somehow were both condescending and unconcerned. What were they doing out here? These weren't merchants. They were young adults, not much older than her. The other people at the table, the ones seated on the outside, seemed to be natives, and based on their body language, Dai thought they were clearly not comfortable.

"What's your name?" the woman asked Dai with a giggle as they made their way across the floor. "I forgot to ask."

"Dai."

"I'm Riya." She giggled again and waved at the table. "And this is the crew."

"Hey, meet Dai," Riya shouted to the table as they walked up. "She looks like a Muner, but she's actually an Orbiter."

"You're a strange one, Dai," said a man with a single line tattooed down the center of his face. He cocked his head. "Why would an Orbiter want to be a Muner?"

"Don't answer any of his questions," said a woman next to him as she pushed the man to the side. "You may implicate yourself."

"Your paranoia is becoming tiring, Rocious," the man replied. "I think you may be under the influence of something."

The three Centralers laughed uproariously while the Faltrans around them shifted uncomfortably. Dai had seen enough Orbiters high on chems to know the signs almost instantly.

"Maybe I should go," she demurred.

"Ah! No! Stop her! My kingdom to anyone who apprehends this lovely creature," the tattooed man said. He seemed innocuous, but his words sent her hackles up.

"They can be a little much," Riya admitted. "We *might* have been enjoying some of the local chems."

"I can tell," Dai said dryly. This wasn't the same stuff as in Tak's pen.

Rocious laughed at Dai's words and stood up on the seat, her hands raised high. "Yes, we've drunk the nectar of the gods. Our vision is clear, and our hearts are pure. We've come seeking the truths of the galaxy, here in this nest of Jackals."

"Don't expose our mission, scum," the man said. He roughly pulled her down and looked at the other Centraler woman next to them, who quietly observed the conversation. "Mujin, what do you make of all this?"

The woman pursed her lips and tapped her cheek thoughtfully. She leaned forward, her rainbow-colored hair forming a curtain that blocked her face. "This is most peculiar. This woman may be the one that has been foretold. We should welcome her and learn the secrets of the Orbiters. If we do not understand the truth, then we shall be cast permanently into the Fringe."

The conversation was beginning to bore Dai. They clearly thought they were witty, but nothing they said made any sense. There wasn't animosity in their words, insanity perhaps, but the three Centralers seemed to be oblivious and drugged more than anything.

"We need everyone else to depart forthwith," the man shouted. "So that we can focus on this visitor." He waved the locals sitting on either side of them away from the booth.

"I'm going to take off," Dai said, looking back toward the doors on the far end of the chamber.

"I know we're a little crazy, but maybe we can help," Riya said. "You can leave. But if you stay, I'll wrangle up some food for you."

"Well, maybe for a little bit." Dai hadn't eaten proper food in way too long. If she could get a meal, well, then she'd put up with a *lot* of crazy.

One thing became immediately clear to Dai: whoever these people were, they were rich. Servers made regular rounds to their table with platters filled with food and drink. Each time, one of the Centralers would hand over a pile of chits without bothering to count.

Between the eating and drinking, the conversation was, at best, fragmented. Whatever chem the Centralers had taken, it rendered them unable to stick to a single subject for very long.

Riya, although odd, seemed to at least be rational and helped Dai as she navigated the conversation and fielded random questions from the group. From what Dai could gather, the four Centralers were on a vacation of sorts. When she asked why they were on Faltran, they talked of finding universal truths and expanding their mental horizons. However, she suspected the lack of laws regarding stims and chems was the real reason they were out in the Fringe.

The good news was they were happy to let her choose whatever she wanted from the menu. As Dai fielded questions around subjects as diverse as Fringe politics, mining, her family, and when she first kissed someone, she inhaled so much food that she had to slouch in the booth to be comfortable.

"So, we'll assume that Dai is your real name," said Rat, the man with the tattoo.

"Actually, it's Daiyu. People just call me Dai."

He groaned. "Your story changes every time you tell it."

"No, I just told you—"

"You're looking for a way off this planet, though?" Riya asked.

"Yeah," Dai admitted. "We need to get to the Central Worlds."

"*We?*" Mujin asked. "Who's we?"

"There's another person stranded here with me," Dai said. "He's a Centraler, like you."

"There aren't many Centralers like *us*," Mujin retorted with a giggle.

Dai raised an eyebrow. "How so?"

"We're not your average travelers," Rat said. "In case that wasn't already apparent."

"Yeah, that part's pretty clear," Dai said. She didn't mean it as a compliment. They seemed to be pure fluff, rich kids on a joyride with their parents' credits. But they'd somehow arrived on Faltran using a private ship and might help get her and Tak back to the Central Worlds without going through customs. If she had to entertain them, then she would do it.

"We'd need to meet this gentleman—I assume he's a gentleman—before we could discuss this further," Mujin said.

"I'm sure he'd be fine with it," Dai said. "When are you going to return to the Central Worlds?"

"When it's time." Rat languorously leaned back in his seat. "We're not on a schedule. Certainly not on yours."

Dai bit down on her response. She needed these people, no matter how obnoxious they might be. "You hang out here every cycle?"

Rocious leaned over the table and stared at her. "Why're you askin' questions like that?"

"So I know where to find you."

"Stop being so paranoid." Riya glared at her friend, then turned to Dai. "We're either here or at the hotel across the street."

"You want a little something else?" Rat asked, wiggling his eyebrows suggestively. He pulled out a chempen that was identical to Tak's. Except Dai was confident it wasn't filled with the legal low-grade stimulant Tak used.

"I'm good," Dai said. "Perhaps later." More like never. She'd seen people strung out in the hallways of the Triple-Deuce many times. She wasn't going down that road.

"Suit yourself." He seemed disappointed. "How 'bout we fire up some stims? There're some multiplayer games."

"Yes." Finally, something Dai could agree to.

Chapter Eight

Capital, Faltran

T ak remained at the Desert's Dawn with his eyes glued to the door of the hotel, imagining all the things that could happen to Dai. He knew she was smart and capable, but she was still young and had never left the relative safety of the Triple-Deuce. The rest of the galaxy operated by rules that would be foreign to her.

After a standard, Rog and Szan strode through the entrance, several large crates precariously balanced on the cargo skiff trailing behind them.

"Hey!" Tak stood and waved them over.

"Ah, Taksh, we wondered if we'd see you again," Rog said. "Where's Dai?"

"I'm not sure," Tak said sheepishly. "We had a bit of an argument."

"Well, she'll return. She doesn't have any chits." Rog shook his head sadly. "In the cities, you can't do anything without chits."

"That's part of the problem," Tak replied. "We're stuck here with no chits and no way to get out."

"There may not be any ships available today, but they're always coming in and out of Capital's port."

"I'm not allowed to travel to the Central Worlds," Tak said. "There's a detain order on me."

Rog raised his eyebrows. "Forgive me, I've never been to the Central Worlds, but that seems odd. Aren't you a citizen? Have you been doing anything... illegal?"

"No," Tak said indignantly. "I've been minding my own business."

"Hmm. Very strange, then," Rog said. Szan nodded in agreement.

"I don't know why I'm not allowed to return, but I can't find out until I get back there, and I'm certainly not going back in restraints."

"Probably a good idea." Rog nodded. "It's a lot easier to be put in restraints than get out of them." He patted the pile of crates on the skiff behind him. "We need to get these put away in our room. You're welcome to join."

Tak followed the two men up to their room. It was a simple affair: two beds, a small food prep area, and some seats. Even though Capital was outside the desert, there was a coating of fine dust across everything. It probably wasn't intentional, but it did go with the hotel's desert theme. He guessed the room was considered the lap of luxury for a planet like Faltran, but to his Centraler eye, it was a pit.

After maneuvering the skiff into a corner, the two men lay down and were soon fast asleep, after reassuring Tak that Dai would be back shortly. As they started to snore, Tak could barely sit still. He was worried about Dai. The girl had given up her chance to be with her mother so she could remain with him. He owed her, whether or not he wanted to.

Perched in one of the tattered chairs, staring out the small window for a standard, Tak couldn't wait anymore. He wouldn't just sit there and wait for things to happen. He left the two Nashobans sleeping in the room and started patrolling the streets around the hotel. Capital was clearly a Fringe town; there was a sense of lawlessness and disorder that he hadn't seen in the Central Worlds. Street vendors sold their wares out of small carts crudely attached to skiffs. Private mercenaries, clad in a mishmash of protective gear, walked through the area with their stun batons at the ready, seemingly anticipating violence. Tak knew the Central Worlds could be violent as well—in some ways *more* violent—but they hid it behind a veneer of civility.

He stopped in his tracks when he saw a small column of sleek skiffs passing in front of him. Guards strode easily in front and behind, their weapons casually slung across their backs. They wore body armor, and some even had augmented exoskeletons bristling with weaponry.

Jackals.

"You gonna go say hi to your friends, Muner?" asked a petite woman standing next to him.

"I'm not a fargin' Muner," Tak said heatedly. "Besides, if you're so great, how come you Fringers let them trade here?"

The woman sneered at him, spat at his feet, and stalked down one of the side streets.

As a Centraler, Tak was used to looking down on the Fringers. On Hkar'Trush, they called Fringers lazy and lawless. He'd believed that himself until he started traveling out to stations in the Fringe. Were they lawless or lazy? Not really. They didn't have the institutions and the security the Centralers had, so they got work when they could, and they protected what they earned.

It was interesting, and a little disheartening, to see that the Fringers looked down on the Muners. He hadn't heard Rog or Szan talk badly about anyone but wondered if there were people they disdained as well. Perhaps it was all a big cycle of condescension and ignorance.

"Bastards."

Tak turned to see Dai glaring at the column of Jackal skiffs, a look of pure hatred in her eyes. They stood next to each other silently, watching until the column had completely disappeared.

"Where'd you go?" Tak asked.

"I wandered around," Dai replied casually. "Saw the sights." She paused. "I think I have a lead on a way off-planet."

When Dai saw the procession of Jackal skiffs laden with stolen supplies, she'd felt a depth of hatred she'd never known was in her. After leaving the Dirty Stim, she'd wandered the streets, trying to orient herself, when she'd come across the line of skiffs. When she realized Tak was standing next to her, she'd felt a wave of relief. They'd known each other for only a couple of cycles, but she already thought of him as a friend. More than a friend. A brother. Albeit a know-it-all, annoying older one.

It turned out that they were a lot closer to Rog and Szan's hotel than she'd realized. Tak led her through a few streets and soon they were walking into its spacious lobby. As they'd walked past the food carts, she felt the urge to apologize. He'd kept things from her, but that didn't mean she had the right to know them. She couldn't demand answers after they'd known each other for two cycles. And despite everything, she somehow still trusted him.

When she and Tak entered the room, Rog and Szan were sitting on their beds, clearly having just woken up. She reflexively returned their grins as she walked through the door. Seeing how the people from Nashoba were treated here in the city, she was even more appreciative of their friendliness and optimism.

"Enjoy exploring?" Rog asked with a wink.

"Yeah, I did," Dai said. Honestly, she had. Despite everything going on, she'd enjoyed walking through a *real* city and seeing things she'd only heard about.

"Where'd you go?" Szan asked, surprising her.

"I don't know. I mainly wandered around the streets after Tak and I... split up. I walked into a stimbar and—"

"A stimbar?" Tak asked with alarm.

"Yeah." Dai fixed him with a glare. "A stimbar."

"You understand they're illegal?"

"Not in the Fringe," Rog said.

"Exactly," Dai said. "Not here. Besides, I didn't know what it was when I entered."

"You know *why* they're illegal in the Central Worlds? You get a bad stim and it'll fry your brain." Why did he think he could sit there and tell her what to do?

"Yes, I understand that," Dai replied. "Like I said, I didn't know what it was when I entered. Besides, I met some people there. People who might help us." Using a stimpad had been amazing, though. Wasn't life just a series of risks anyway?

"Who?" Tak asked.

"A group of rich Centralers," Dai replied. "They were hanging out, and I got to know them. I told them about our situation, and they said they might help."

Tak looked at her wearily. "Going up to strangers and asking for help is a bad idea." He seemed to forget he'd basically done just that earlier in the same cycle. "You don't know what they want or where they're coming from. I'm guessing they were young, about my age, either smashed on chems or coming down from a high."

Dai could tell her lack of a response was all Tak needed to know that he was right.

"Rich Centralers take their private yachts out to the Fringe for the drugs and stims," he continued. "They spend a few decs out of their mind and then return to their privileged existences. They're flakes. Leeches."

He spoke as if he had firsthand knowledge, and his description fell neatly in line with Dai's own impressions. Still, she was annoyed that he seemed ready to dismiss them out of hand when they were the only lead that they had.

"Well, maybe. But if they have a yacht, then they can sneak us past customs," Dai said hurriedly. "They're the only option we've got. What else can we do? Hang out around the port and hope to find someone who's willing to smuggle us out? How's that any better?"

Tak pinched his lips together. She already knew him well enough to know that meant she'd won. He didn't have a response to that.

"They want to meet you, though," Dai said. "They seem to have some trust issues."

"Often people under the influence do," Rog said philosophically.

"When are they leaving?" Tak asked.

"They didn't say."

Tak looked at Rog and Szan. "When are you leaving to go back to Nashoba?"

"We'll leave in the morning," Rog said. "We try to stay in Capital for as little as possible."

"I can understand why," Tak said. "The looks I got wearing these robes." He shook his head.

"They don't understand the values we live by," Rog said. "They think because we welcome all travelers and don't accept payment that we're somehow in league with the Jackals."

"Ignorance," Szan murmured.

"I hate to ask this," Tak said diffidently. "But any way you can help us with some chits? Just enough to get our bearings?"

"We don't have much, but we can give you what we have," Rog said. Dai was impressed and grateful he didn't even hesitate to respond. "But we're allowed to stay here at the hotel for free due to an agreement with the owner, so I'm not sure where you'll be able to find lodging when we leave in the morning."

"If I remain, we can stay in this room," Szan said.

Rog turned to look at his friend, his eyes wide. "What? Are you sure, Szan?"

The other man nodded. "Yeah, I'm sure. They need help and you don't need me back at the commune anyway. Hendrick's gotten pretty good with tech and—"

"It's whatever you want, Szan."

There was an emotion behind the words that Dai couldn't place. She wasn't sure what had happened, but by the way the two of them were acting, it was significant. She could tell Tak felt it, too, by the way he watched the other two men's faces without saying a word.

"Well, if you're going to stay here, we'll need some new clothes at least," Rog said reluctantly as he slowly stood. "Let's go before the shops close."

"What d'you think?" Dai asked, feeling more than a little silly. She knew she sounded inane but couldn't help herself. It was the first time she'd ever picked out her own clothes. On the Triple-Deuce, she'd either worn a work jumpsuit or whatever the older kids had outgrown. To have her own clothes, ones she'd picked out herself, was something special.

Tak was nice enough to play along. He hummed softly to himself, hand under his chin, as he walked around, studying her.

"Hmm. Very nice. I think it fits you just right," he said admiringly. "Yes, perfect."

Szan grunted in agreement and nodded.

Tak was already wearing a simple gray and blue shirt and slacks. Dai hadn't even finished looking at all the options before he'd found the outfit and changed. Szan took almost as long as her. The man clearly had worn little besides the typical Nashoban robes. She was pretty sure he'd ended up copying Tak since his outfit was almost identical except for some slight silver piping along the collar and cuffs of his shirt.

Rog watched them apprehensively and only spoke when spoken to. The discussion with Szan had clearly shaken him, and he seemed lost in his own thoughts.

After they'd paid, they headed to a restaurant that Rog claimed was the "best in town"—that they could afford. The food *was* delicious, the company was friendly, and the night was magical. As they sat around the warm glow of the table light, Dai laughed as Rog told them about life on the commune and some of the crazy characters that lived there. It made her wish that she'd had more time to get to know the people before they left. Szan listened quietly with a small smile on his face, adding an occasional clarification if Rog's version of events drifted too far from reality.

"How long have you two known each other?" Dai asked.

"Well, we met when we were in crèche together, over twenty rotations ago," Rog said, smiling. "Szan was a rotation older, and when we first met, he never let me get a word in edge-wise." He laughed. "I've been getting revenge on him ever since."

Szan smiled and placed a hand on his friend's shoulder. Rog looked at him for a moment, then gave a slight nod.

Szan cleared his throat, then turned to look at Tak and Dai. "I'd like to come with you," he said. "If you're able to find a way to the Central Worlds and bypass customs, then it means I can, too."

Dai had expected this based on the way the two men had been acting, but she was still surprised. What would make someone who'd grown up in a commune in the Fringe want to go to the Central Worlds?

"Szan was always the dreamer." Rog leaned back in his chair with a sigh. "He won't be truly happy in Nashoba. And, well, the rest of Faltran isn't any better."

"Are you sure?" Tak asked, staring at Szan. "There's not really any going back from this. If we're able to get into the Central Worlds, you'd almost certainly not be able to return. Not for several rotations, at least."

"Yes, I'm sure," Szan replied evenly. "I've thought a lot about it, even before you came, and now that the opportunity is here, I don't want to miss it."

There was, of course, the added trouble of having another person with them. But Szan and Rog had saved them and shared everything they had. There was no way Dai would say no, and she knew Tak would agree.

"If you want to come with us, we'd love to have you," Dai said, smiling. "I don't know if these Centralers will help us out or not, though. It may take a while to find a way off-planet."

"I can help you while you're here in Capital," Szan replied. "I have some chits to pay for food, have connections so we have lodging, and don't mind waiting until we find a ship." He smirked. "You get very good at waiting on a commune."

"You're always welcome with us, Szan," Tak said, still looking intently at the Nashoban. "I just want to make sure you know the stakes. Once we leave, there'll be no coming back."

"I'm not concerned about coming back, only about going forward."

Chapter Nine

Capital, Faltran

Their meal continued for another standard. Then Tak and Dai returned to the room to give Rog and Szan some privacy. There was a lot for the two men to talk about, and they were in the way. Tak had never had a friendship like that. The people he'd grown up with had been acquaintances more than anything. He'd crossed paths with them because they went to the same academy or their parents traveled in the same circles. His relationships had been based on nothing more than proximity.

The next morning, they helped Rog take the supply-laden skiff back to the aircar and watched quietly as it lifted off and headed out of town. Szan remained impassive the entire time, except for a few secs when he gave Rog a final goodbye embrace. Tak didn't think Dai saw Szan's face collapse and tears drip from his eyes and onto his friend's shoulder.

When the aircar had disappeared, they returned to the Desert's Dawn. Szan and Dai flopped onto the two beds, while Tak lay down on the cot he'd retrieved from the front lobby the previous night. As he stared at the off-color white ceiling above, he thought of the message on his combrace. Was he being hunted? Did whoever was following him know where he was now? He doubted it. Otherwise, someone would have already tried to grab him from the hotel. He took a deep breath. It was time to tell the others what was going on. If there was a risk to their lives, they deserved to know.

"So, what's next?" Dai asked with mock levity.

Tak abruptly changed his mind. If he told them about his past, then he was putting them in danger. They just needed to get back to the Central Worlds, and then he could see Dai safely to her mother and help Szan get settled. After that, he'd figure out what to do.

"I think we should talk to your new friends at the stimbar," Tak replied, sitting back up. Although they were Bingers, they were the best lead they had.

"You're *all* my new friends," Dai said with a chuckle. "They're just my *newest* friends."

"We're friends now?" Tak gave her shoulder a playful shove. "I was thinking acquaintances."

"Business associates, perhaps," Szan added, straight-faced.

"My newest friends told me I could find them at the Dirty Stim," Dai said. "As my two colleagues, you can join me."

The streets of Capital were already much more crowded than a standard earlier. Food skiffs on the sidewalks emitted wispy clouds of savory steam. The dense crowds of partiers and paid muscle Dai had told them about from the previous night were gone, replaced with men and women striding purposefully down the sidewalk and public aircars filled with people coasting over the streets.

The Dirty Stim wasn't too far from their hotel. In less than a quarter standard, they arrived at the entrance. The sign above the one-way window was off, appearing only as a dark square against the tan facade of the building.

"It's too early," Tak said, looking down at his combrace.

"They're staying at the hotel across the street." Dai pointed to the ornate structure. If it wasn't the nicest building in the city, it was close.

"I doubt they're awake yet," Tak said. Rich kids who were on a Fringe Binge weren't on Faltran for the scenery. They'd stay out until the early morning and then head back to their hotel to sleep off the effects of whatever chems they'd taken. It hadn't been that long since he'd been on his own Binge, and he remembered the mentality.

They headed back to the port. Waking up a bunch of kids coming down from chems was not a good way to get into their good graces, and there was always the off chance they might find a ship that was traveling to the Central Worlds.

Ports never followed the same circadian rhythm as the city they were in. Spacers operated on their own cycles and were rarely on a planet long enough to justify changing them to align with the locals' cycle, so ports became a constant hive of activity, day and night. Tak led the other two through the building, trying to casually eavesdrop on conversations and looking for anyone who seemed unsavory enough that they'd be willing to take on some unlicensed passengers.

Szan was a few rotations older than Tak, but he looked even more lost than Dai amidst the hustle and bustle of the aliens, stevedores, and cargo-laden skiffs. He'd clearly never been in the building and walked a few paces behind Tak, whispering questions to Dai. She seemed to relish her new position, and Tak could hear her answering with the tone of a seasoned expert.

Although the facility was busy, none of the captains or crews they talked to had any interest in taking them on. The few people who seemed willing to bypass the Central Worlds' strict customs process demanded payment in credits up front, something they didn't have. The message on Tak's combrace continued to hover at the edge of his mind, making him jumpier than usual. He didn't think there was any way to find him on the planet, but his enemies, whoever they were, would have a perfect opportunity to attack him in the port.

By midday, they were all exhausted and ready to leave. Even Szan had seen enough of the port. They returned to the Dirty Stim to find its sign illuminated and its doors open. The enormous chembar was almost completely empty. A few people lounged against the counters at the edges of the room or stood on the platforms above, jacked into a stimpad.

Dai scanned the room. "I don't see them. They must be back in their hotel."

"Let's wait," Tak replied, taking a puff from his chempen. Barging into the Centralers' hotel was not a good idea if they wanted their help.

They sat around a table in a corner of the bar and watched as people slowly trickled in. Looking at their outfits, he guessed everyone in there was a local; the Bingers wouldn't arrive until later. Dai and Szan—to Tak's surprise—glanced at the platforms hung above the room, clearly eager to use a stimpad. Tak knew they wouldn't be so eager if they'd seen what it looked like when someone got a bad stim.

Before university, he vaguely remembered spending most of his time in places like the Dirty Stim. He and his "friends"—a group of kids with more money than brains—would meet up in the Undercity whenever they could. It was the dangerous part of Hkar'Trush, filled with illicit chem joints, criminals, and back-room deals. Often Tak could remember heading out, but rarely could he remember what happened on those excursions. In the Central Worlds, the children of the ultra-rich were independent from a young age since their parents were too busy working or attending "events," as they called them. Most days, Tak would leave after crèche and stay out until the middle of the night.

"Don't even think about it," Tak said, grabbing Dai's hand.

"This place was filled with people on stims last night and there wasn't a problem," she said, snatching her hand away. "You're worrying over nothing." She eyed his chempen on the table. "Besides, it's not like you're so pure."

"It's not about being pure," Tak said, annoyed at her misplaced confidence. "And sure, you *probably* won't have anything happen to you. But I can tell you that a bad stim will ruin your life."

Dai shook her head, clearly unimpressed.

"I had a friend when I was younger than you. His name was Fez." Fez had been the quiet one in their little group, along for the ride but never taking the lead. His parents owned a hotel chain and spent most of their time on a different planet than their son. Fez had once confessed he wasn't sure if they remembered he was alive sometimes. "We used to head out to places like this back on Hkar'Trush."

"I thought stims are illegal in the Central Worlds," Szan said.

"They are," Tak said, "but we didn't care. We were kids and wanted to see the galaxy. Back-alley chem joints were the closest we could get. We'd take whatever chems we could get and use whatever stims we could find. Well, bottom line was Fez got a bad stim. It wasn't even a dodgy one. It was supposed to be one of the mainstream ones that was popular out here in the Fringe. I don't know if it really was, but I do know that blood started dripping from his ears and he fell to the ground when he attached the stimpad." Dai shuddered. "We took him to a medcenter, but they said there was nothing they could do. Damage was done. He was there for a dec before he could return home, and he hasn't left since."

Fez's parents had bought him the best medical staff money could buy. Tak had heard that they still went on all their trips and to the same events, and let their son sit in their enormous penthouse, alone. He'd probably spend the rest of his life sitting in an expensive room, unresponsive and mute.

What a life.

Szan nervously eyed the people taking rides on the platforms above while Dai's gaze darted between the platforms, as if she expected someone to pass out before her very eyes.

"What about chems?" Szan asked.

"What about them?" Tak took a small hit from his pen.

"Are they okay?"

"Depends on the chem." Tak held up his chempen. "We need to be somewhat on our game when the rich Centralers get here." He raised an eyebrow. "But there's no reason we can't relax while we wait."

With Tak's help, Dai tried a few items from the Dirty Stim's chem menu—or chenu, as their server called it. As they perused, Tak explained their effects and told her which ones to watch out for. The man clearly had an extensive knowledge of, and a fondness for, chems. Dai wondered if that was why he sometimes seemed so foggy and forgetful. She doubted her mother would have approved, but she was an adult—at least technically—now.

Dai wasn't sure how long they'd been sitting at the table, chempens in hand, when she noticed the four Centralers from the previous night across the room. The chems must have had more of an effect on her than she realized.

"That's them," she whispered to Szan and Tak, trying to motion subtly with her eyes.

They glanced over at the table on the far side of the room. "No need to whisper," Tak said. "They can't hear us."

"I know." A warm flush ran up her face.

"Let's go meet your friends." Tak stood up and held out an arm. "After you."

Tak and Szan followed Dai as she zigzagged through the dense crowd toward the Centralers. They were seated around a table, their heads close together, clearly embroiled in an argument.

"Hey!" Dai said with a small wave, attempting to appear casual.

Only Riya seemed to recognize her. "Dai, right?"

"Yeah." She'd hung out with them for standards. That Riya wasn't sure of her name was not a good sign.

"Who's this?" Rat asked. "We know her?"

"Yeah," Riya said in a frustrated voice. "She hung out with us all of last night."

"How's it going?" Dai asked.

"Now's not a good time," Riya replied. "We're having a bit of a problem here."

"She wants us to leave," Rat said. "But we've got unfinished business."

"The Gauntlet is not just unfinished business," Mujin said. "It's the *only* business."

The Gauntlet was the premier menu item at the Dirty Stim. It was a flight of chems and stims that was intended to "bring you closer to true enlightenment." When Tak had read through the ingredients, he'd told Dai that whoever ordered it was either suicidal or a complete idiot.

"Oh, I've heard you got to try that," Tak said with a conspiratorial smile. "You can't tell your friends you've been to Faltran without Running the Gauntlet."

"That's my man," Rat said, raising his fist. He turned to Riya. "We hung with them last night?"

"Not all of them," she replied. "Just Dai—the girl." She looked at Dai. "I thought you only crashed here with one person."

"I did. He"—she gestured to Szan—"is a Muner. A real one."

Mujin twisted a purple strand of hair around her finger. "How come he ain't wearin' the robes?"

"I'm incognito," Szan whispered as he slid next to her in the booth.

The four Centralers burst out laughing, and Dai felt the barrier between the two groups disappear. Rat called for a server and ordered the Gauntlet, plus a variety of other chems, and told him to "keep 'em comin'." Time passed, and soon three of the four Centralers—Riya declined any chem offered to her—were back in the same state as the night before. They oscillated between laughing with each other at the table and taking the cables up the platforms to ride a stim.

"Finally, we meet some *real* people out here in the Fringe," Rocious said as she put down her chempen, vapor still trailing from her mouth.

"There's nothing out here except chems and stims," Rat added after he took an enormous hit from his pen.

"Isn't it great?" Rocious asked with a laugh.

"What're you doing out here?" Szan asked. As the time passed, he'd gradually left his shell. He'd avoided the hard chems and stims, but the atmosphere seemed to have unlocked a part of him that Dai hadn't seen before.

"Who knows what we're doing?" Riya sighed.

"What d'ya mean 'who knows'?" Rat stared at her. "We're here finding truth."

Mujin nodded. "We were prisoners on Byrzyrk, maybe not in jails, but in our homes. Bound by the conventions of a society that didn't understand us and imprisoned us in gilded cages created by our families' wealth. But now, we have a chance for real freedom."

"You're convicts?" Szan raised an eyebrow.

Riya scoffed. "No. We're not convicts. We weren't imprisoned." The other three looked at her in surprise. "We're just rich kids on a Fringe Binge."

Tak flashed Dai a look that said, *I told you so.* Dai ground her teeth. The man could be *so* annoying.

"No, that's not true at all," Rocious said. "We're different. We're not here for chems." She took another hit off her chempen. "We're here to *understand* the Fringe so we can better understand and appreciate our own lives. So when we return to our penthouses and the drudgery of reality, we can remain free through the enlightenment we've gained."

"I can tell you're different," Tak said soothingly. "You've got an understanding, a maturity, about you."

Dai wanted to roll her eyes. He was laying it on thick. The Centralers, except maybe Riya, were too high to notice, though.

The night continued in the same fashion. The three of them listened to the Centralers spout pseudo-mystical theories and complain about their lives of stifling wealth. Szan seemed to drink it all in, and Tak was clearly more than willing to agree with whatever ridiculous thing they said. Dai felt like she should be enjoying herself but couldn't. Perhaps it was Tak's story about his friend, or maybe she wasn't cut out for a life like this, but either way, it all felt cheap and tawdry to her.

"I'm gonna go check out a stim," Riya said. She looked at Dai. "Wanna join me?"

"Sure," Dai said as she stood up from the table. She could see the streetlights shining outside the windows in the front of the bar. Time had flown by.

"I figured you would want a break from them," Riya confided as they walked away from the table. "They're my friends and even *I* need time away from them. You're a fargin' refugee and have to listen to them complain about having homes that are too big. I applaud you for not killing us all."

"They're fine."

"No, they're narcissistic jerks," Riya said heatedly.

"Why do you hang out with them?" Dai asked.

"What else am I gonna do?" She shrugged. "This was my chance to get off Byrzyrk and have some fun. If I have to babysit a few emotionally stunted rich kids, well, that's the price I pay."

"So, what do your parents do?" Dai asked. She knew that Rat's family was into nanomeds, but the others hadn't shared anything about their families.

"Various things," Riya replied airily. "They've got their fingers in a lot of pots."

If she didn't want to say, Dai wasn't going to press.

"My mother's a mechanic," she said.

"Very cool." Riya grabbed a cable and floated onto the platform above their heads. After she'd let go, Dai followed.

"That's an *actual* job," Riya said once Dai had stepped onto the platform. She leaned against the railing. "I don't really want to use the stimpad. You're welcome to, but I'm guessing you'd rather not as well."

"Yeah, I just..." Dai trailed off. She felt stupid saying she was *afraid* to try the device again because of Tak's story.

"It's cool." Riya smiled at her. "I feel the same way. Faltran's the fourth planet we've been to on this trip. I've had enough chems and stims to last a lifetime."

Dai looked across at the other platforms, which were now filled with people. When she looked down, she saw that the tables below were also filled with people, laughing and shouting at each other as they took drags from their chempens. As she studied them, she realized almost all of them were tourists, people from the Central Worlds who'd come to the Fringe just for this. It was a far different crowd from the one that had been there when they'd entered.

"Is this just a break, an escape from reality, for you?" Dai asked, still looking out at the crowd. "Are we just another stim for you? A fantasy, and then you go back to your *real* lives?"

"Yeah." At least she sounded sorry.

"You mentioned us coming with you when you leave. Is that real?" She prayed it was.

"I'll be honest, maybe. Last night, we all liked you and were already high. It's easier to say what you know the other person wants to hear, right? You want the party to keep going."

"This isn't a party for us," Dai replied, turning to look at Riya. "I barely survived the attack, and my mother doesn't know I'm alive."

"Look, I get it." Riya looked down. "But it's not my opinion that matters. You gotta get Mujin on your side. It's her family's yacht that brought us here. She decides."

"Well, at least I know where we stand," Dai said, disheartened.

"I'm on your side. Maybe you hang out with us enough, and they'll take a real liking to you. I'm trying to help with that." Riya sidled next to Dai. "I can't promise anything, but I will say I'm pretty sure we're your best chance."

That was what Dai was afraid of.

Chapter Ten

Capital, Faltran

Tak woke with a groan. He wasn't that much older than the four Centralers, but trying to keep up with them was going to kill him. They'd been going to the Dirty Stim every night for the past four cycles and he couldn't go on for much longer. Although he, Dai, and Szan were staying away from the hard chems and stims, continually staying out until dawn was draining. Dai felt the same way, but Szan seemed to be too happy watching everything going on to be tired.

When he wasn't stroking the egos of the Centralers, Tak's mind wandered to the message he'd received. Whenever he was on the street, he felt needles creeping up his neck, the sensation of unseen eyes spying and watching him. It had been rotations since his parents had died, but he still didn't know who had killed them and who was trying to track him down. All he knew was they were powerful and determined. Powerful enough to infiltrate one of the richest families in the Central Worlds and determined enough to keep after him all this time. There wasn't much he could do about it, though. They needed to find a way off the planet, and the only way to do that was to hang out at the port during the day and ingratiate themselves with the four Centralers at night in hopes of getting a ride.

"Ugh, what time is it?" Dai groaned. She stretched across her cot with an arm dangling down, touching the floor.

"Too early." Tak pushed himself up in the bed and leaned back against the wall. He grabbed his chempen from the bed-side table and took a deep drag. A nest of blankets topped the unoccupied bed next to his; Szan had already gotten up.

"How does he do it?" Dai asked as she saw where Tak was looking. Szan got up before them every morning. He said he went on walks to admire the town before the crowds arrived. He always cheerfully came back to the room, bearing kaf and something for breakfast.

"No idea. Must be a commune thing."

Dai rolled onto her back and sighed. She seemed perfectly content to remain on her cot, so Tak grabbed a quick shower. By the time he strolled back into the room, dressed and some-what alert from the steam and decontaminants, Szan was back, cheerfully munching on some sort of roll.

"Have you tried these?" he asked, his mouth full. "So good." He held out one to Tak.

It *was* good. A rich, buttery flavor saturated the flaky crust and complemented the zing of the spices that dusted the out-side.

"Throw me one," Dai said, holding up a hand. She'd sat up at last.

She caught the roll Szan tossed in her direction and took a large bite, letting out a small sigh. They sat quietly for several tics, enjoying their meal and the peace of mid-morning. Tak realized he was content in that moment; despite everything, he was enjoying himself.

"What about your parents, Szan?" Dai asked, breaking the silence.

"What about 'em?"

"Do they know you're gone?"

"By now? Probably." He shrugged.

"I'm surprised they haven't tried to find you," Tak said. "Or did you leave a note or something with them?"

"That's not how it works on Nashoba. We're children of the commune." He took a small sip of kaf.

"What's that mean?" Dai asked as she licked the spices from her fingers.

"Our biological parents are no different from any other adult. We are raised by the community." He seemed to notice the expression on their faces. "I guess that sounds strange to you, but it helps us keep our community strong. Think about it. If adults give preferential treatment to certain children, they do it to the detriment of the others. The only way to make sure that every child is truly equal is to treat them the same. It also makes things easier for the adults, as they can take turns raising the children."

To Tak, it sounded like trying to strip the humanity from Humans. But he'd seen enough things in the galaxy that he didn't understand or didn't agree with, so he wasn't going to raise a fuss. If Nashobans wanted to raise their kids without parents—or with a *lot* of parents—well, that was their business.

"That seems so... cold," Dai said. "Like, do you feel loved?"

"We all love each other," Szan said simply. "You had two parents who loved you. I had hundreds. How is that not being loved?"

"I guess." She grabbed another pastry and took a bite.

A buzz sounded from near the door, causing a shiver to crawl up Tak's spine. Had they found him?

Szan stood up and moseyed to the door, not bothering to check the small view screen before opening it. Riya stood on the other side, her long blond hair in a tangled mess around her face.

"If you want off this rock, we gotta get to the port right away," she said. "We're taking off. The others want to leave you. You've got a chance to change their minds if you come now."

Tak swore under his breath. Just like spoiled Centralers to promise to take them and then run off without a word.

"Thanks," Dai said.

"I tried to stop them." Riya bit her lip. "They wouldn't listen to me. I hope you can get through to them."

Tak took the final bite of his roll. "Let's go."

They jumped onto the transport skiff Riya had waiting outside the hotel. The vehicle glided through the empty streets and arrived at a nondescript door on the side of the port, which slid open noiselessly as they approached.

"I didn't know this was here," Szan said.

"You're not supposed to," Riya replied nonchalantly. "It's for high-priority visitors."

They flew down a well-kept corridor and arrived in a small waiting area. Plush seats lined the walls, and a heavily embroidered rug lay across the floor. As the skiff stopped, a uniformed attendant walked toward them with a perfunctory smile.

"Ladies. Gentlemen. Which vessel will you be boarding today?"

"The *Nero*," Riya said quickly. "No need to escort us. I know where to go."

"Of course." The man faded backward to a small wooden desk near the corner of the room.

The secret entrance, obsequious servant, and high-end finishes reminded Tak of his past. He'd known nothing but this for most of his life. Now it felt phony and offensive. Why should these four kids who'd achieved nothing warrant this type of reception when people like Szan and Dai—hardworking and moral people—had to stand in lines and deal with the byzantine administration of leaving the planet?

They followed Riya down a carpeted hallway lined with glass windows and small doors. Expensive private ships sat on pads on either side of them; these were pleasure craft, polished and maintained to perfection. Their white hulls sparkled under the light and were adorned with airy names like *Day Tripper* and

Galaxy Adventurer. Riya led them out a sliding glass door to where a sleek yacht rested, a low hum emanating from its engines. It looked like two cylinders fused down the middle, with a single aerodynamic nose cone and swept-back delta wings. Tak guessed it was a Yiloran model, but it was hard to tell; they built ships of this size to order and no two were alike.

"Riya, there—" Rocious stopped mid-sentence when she saw Tak and the others file out with her friend. "What're they doin' with you?" Her face grew red. "We told you we're not takin' fargin' refugees."

"I know what you said," Riya said. "But it's not your ship. I want Mujin to at least hear them out."

"You're a piece of work," Rocious spat back. "You're lucky we even let you come, and now you're tryin' to take in strays."

"Rocious," Tak said. "At least hear us out. I thought we were friends."

"Everyone's a friend when you're on chems. I don't know who you are or if you're even really from the Central Worlds. But if you are and they're not letting you back in, there's probably a good reason."

"What the hell?" Rat came down the portable set of stairs that descended from the ship's entrance to the ground. "What're they doin' here?"

Tak shouldn't have been surprised or disappointed by their reactions, but he couldn't help himself. They'd spent countless standards with these people, and promises had been made. Now Rocious and Rat were treating them like nuisances. He knew what they were thinking. They'd come to the Fringe to party and now it was over—back to real life. Whatever happened in the Fringe should stay there.

"You said you'd take us with you," Dai pleaded.

At least Rocious had the shame to look away. Rat didn't seem to feel a single bit of guilt. "That's just the stuff you say when you're high," he said. "You got your problems, we got ours. Don't be such clingers."

Before anyone could react, Dai bolted forward and pounded Rat with a vicious right cross. He fell to the ground with a cry, clutching his face with his hands. "What the hell?"

"Screw you, Rat," Dai shouted. "Clingers? We needed help, and you said you would. Now you act like you don't know us? Your family's right. You *are* a waste."

"I'm starting to change my mind," Mujin said with a grin as she strode down the stairs from the ship. "I would've paid credits to see that."

"Mujin." Dai clasped her hands together. "We told you all about what was going on with us. My mother doesn't know I'm alive. I need to get back to see her."

"It's not you I'm worried about. It's him." Mujin pointed at Tak. "I bring in someone who's on detain orders and they'll impound my parents' yacht."

"Look, we need to stay together," Dai said. "We've come this far. I can't leave Tak."

"Why?" Mujin asked, her head tilted. "You've known him, what, five cycles? He's holding you and Szan back. I'll let you both aboard. But I can't risk it with Tak."

Dai protested. She was a good person, but Tak couldn't let her continue to sacrifice herself. He'd been alone for a long time and could take care of himself. She missed her mother. She might not show it, but he couldn't imagine her not missing the woman she'd lived with every cycle for her entire life.

"Dai," Tak said. "You and Szan go on without me. We've tried to stay together, but I'm holding you back. Take advantage of this opportunity and get to the Central Worlds."

"You shouldn't let any of them on," Rat spat, holding his jaw. "You saw what she did."

"She just did what a thousand other people have wanted to," Mujin replied with a smile. "Only this time you didn't have mommy and daddy's staff there to protect you."

Dai looked Tak in the eye. "I already told you at the port. I'm not leaving without you."

"What about your mom?" Tak asked. He knew enough about Dai to know she was loyal to a fault. "She doesn't know you're alive. The longer you wait to return, the more she suffers."

"She knows I'm alive. I'm sure of it." She spoke the words with such conviction that Tak didn't doubt it. "Besides, what'll I do when I get there? We don't know where the other evac ships went. I need your help to find her."

"You need to get out of here." The one thing he wouldn't say, *couldn't* say, was that she was in danger just by being near him. Whoever was trying to find him would cut through her like butter if they needed to. "I'm good here. I'm in no hurry."

"You *seem* to be in a hurry," Szan observed.

"Well, I'm not." Tak shot the man an annoyed glance.

"Tak, look at me," Dai said. He felt a sting on his cheek as she lightly slapped him. "I. Am. Not. Leaving. Without. You." She turned to Mujin. "Look, you came out to the Fringe for fun, for adventure, right? What's a better adventure, better story, than smuggling two Fringers and a Centraler that's wanted by the authorities?"

"Think how your parents would react," Riya added.

"All three of them would flip their lids." Mujin smiled wistfully.

"You're not actually thinking about it?" Rat asked.

"I dunno, man," Rocious said. "Now that they mention it, it would make a helluva good story."

"I can help with getting past customs," Riya said. "I know people."

"I bet you do, Riya," Mujin said. Tak could feel the scales balancing as she considered it, staring at each one of them in turn.

"Fine. Let's do this." Mujin made a sweeping gesture with her hands. "Welcome aboard the *Nevo*. My valet will get your bags."

Chapter Eleven

The Nero

Mujin led them on a tour of the *Nero* as the crew prepared for liftoff. Dai quietly followed along, still drained from the earlier confrontation. It was a blur. She didn't know what had come over her. Punching Rat like that. Standing up to him and the others and making them take Tak. These were things she wouldn't have thought she was capable of. But she'd done them.

Mujin casually explained her family was in the shipbuilding business and the *Nero* was their crown jewel. It was every bit as sumptuous inside as it was out. Every bit of the gorgeous vessel was made from ultra-high-end materials and maintained to perfection. The enormous yacht contained over twenty staterooms and had more recreation areas and activities than the Triple-Deuce. There were holo theaters, simulation rooms, several dining areas, and a staff who outnumbered the passengers at least five to one.

The tour gave Dai a glimpse at how different her life was from these other people's. She'd never considered herself poor or unlucky. Growing up, she'd always had food, shelter, clothing, and friends. Sure, she'd had to work hard, even from a young age, but so did everyone around her. Touring the *Nero* was a peek into a world that made everything she'd ever had seem pitiful by comparison. The furniture in any of the staterooms was probably worth more than everything her mother had owned in her life. To the four Centralers, this was all normal, just a regular ship they used on vacation.

Mujin concluded her pompous tour at their staterooms. Each one was enormous and lavishly furnished. Her parents had each room decorated in the style of one of the member species of the Central Worlds.

Dai's stateroom was supposed to be a Pkorah temple. The room radiated a sort of primitive stateliness. It seemed unassuming at first, until she noticed the mirror polish and complex grain of the wood, the sophisticated way the electronics had been woven into the desk and furniture so they were almost invisible. The pieces were low on the floor, with deep green and blue pillows covering the seating areas.

She checked out a small control panel on the wall. It blended so perfectly with the style of the room that she hadn't noticed it at first glance. After a few experimental presses and flicks, she discovered that one wall of the room was a curtain that could be raised to reveal a massive window.

Dai looked outside. They'd already left Faltran, and the planet was rapidly dwindling in size. From this distance, she could see the four distinct belts of the planet. A temperate zone to the north, a desert, an enormous green forest, and finally a cap of ice on the southern pole.

"Nice digs," Tak said as he strolled into the room.

"We've already lifted off. How's that possible? I didn't feel a thing."

Tak chuckled. "Ships like this one have some of the best gravitational and inertial dampeners money can buy. You won't be able to feel the ship moving at all."

"This is ridiculous," Dai said. "I knew they were rich, but not *this* rich."

"And there are families out there that make them seem poor. Families with more money than some planets."

"Maybe the Nashobans have it right." Dai thought of Rog's and Szan's stories about growing up on the commune. "This is disgusting. The money it took to build a ship like this could feed an entire planet for a rotation."

"Well, depends on the planet." Tak flopped onto a low-slung mound of pillows. "Hkar'Trush, no. But maybe Faltran. Also depends on the food, too. I mean, if you start with your basic grains, then—"

"I'd thought Humans were all relatively similar," Dai interrupted. "Ya know? We eat, drink, all that. But actually, we live in very different galaxies."

Tak gave a small nod of agreement. "Yeah, there's a big difference between what these people are used to and what you had growing up." He smiled. "Thanks for sticking up for me back there. You didn't have to fight for me. But you did. Literally."

"Sure, uh, no problem." She could tell that Tak thought she wanted nothing more than to see her mother, and that was partially true. But she also realized that she couldn't go back to being the person she'd been. Back on the Triple-Deuce, she'd known that she wanted more; she just hadn't known what that meant. Now she knew it meant an enormous galaxy filled with thousands of species. And she wanted to see it all, even if her mother didn't. Her mom wanted to stay in one place, away from the galaxy that had taken her husband from her.

"It's no problem," Dai said. "You would've done the same for me."

"Well, I'm not sure that's true." Tak smiled but Dai couldn't help but detect a hint of honesty in his words. Would he have stood up for her in the same way?

"If you wanna repay me, I'd love to know what's really going on. Like all the things you're not telling me. We haven't known each other for that long, but you owe me."

Tak rubbed his hands together and looked out the window. The *Nero* had turned and Faltran wasn't visible anymore. He turned back to look at Dai.

"Fine," he said. "I *want* to tell you more, but... well, we're going to split up eventually, and the less you know, the better it'll be for you." He sighed. "For the last five rotations, someone or some group has been hunting me. I'm not sure who they are or exactly why they're doing it, but they found out that I'm out here in the Fringe. They're most likely the ones that put the detain order out on me. I know they're powerful and I know they're ruthless. I've got to get to my friend back home—"

"On Hkar'Trush?"

"Yeah." He nodded. "I think my friend may have information on what's going on. I'd thought I'd been able to disappear, but they've found me."

A thought occurred to Dai. If whoever was trying to get Tak was really so ruthless and powerful, perhaps they'd been behind everything that happened to them.

"Do you think they caused the attack on the Triple-Deuce?" she asked.

"Maybe," Tak admitted. "I'm not sure. Probably not. Well, maybe." He looked upward. "Jackal activity has been increasing on the Fringe and the Triple-Deuce was a prime target. But I can't rule it out."

Dai felt a surge of anger. She wasn't sure if it was directed at Tak or the Jackals—but she suspected both.

"Still—" Dai was overcome by nausea, which meant the *Nero*'s flex drive had activated. She stopped talking as she saw the stars outside the window stretch and elongate into glowing white lines.

"You've never *seen* a ship warp before, have you?" Tak asked.

Dai shook her head.

"Pretty interesting, huh?"

She nodded.

"Since the drive transforms the space around the ship, it affects how we view the stars. We're peering through the warp in space created by the drive."

"I know how it works," Dai said. "In case you forgot, I've repaired flex drives."

"Just not seen them used."

She ignored the twinge of annoyance. "When will we get there?"

"Byrzyrk's normally about three cycles away—seventy-five standards," Tak said. "I'm guessing this thing has some of the best engines on the market, so I'm guessing we'll take two."

"What'll we do when we get there?" Dai had been so focused on just getting off of Faltran that she hadn't even thought about what the next step would be. "We've got no idea where the other survivors went to."

Tak sighed. "I'm not sure. We need to figure that out, get you to your mother, and then I need to disappear. That's gonna be a pain."

At the mention of her mother, a wave of guilt crashed into Dai. She'd been so focused on herself that she hadn't had much time to think about her mom. She must be beside herself with worry.

"There's Szan, too."

Tak rolled his eyes. "I forgot about that. Just add him to the list of crap I've got to worry about."

"You have no idea why someone's hunting you?" Dai asked. She couldn't imagine living with a blade hovering over her head.

How could he not know who was looking for him? But then again, Tak was like that. She wasn't sure if even he'd noticed it yet. There were holes in his story—giant holes—and he honestly didn't seem to know what went in them.

"No," Tak said, clearly uncomfortable. "When this all started, I had to decide whether to run and live or risk death to figure out what was going on. I chose the first option."

"Can you tell me *anything*? Like what's your real name? If you're on the run, there's no way it's Taksh. Unless you're really, really dumb. Are you?"

"Fine." Tak sighed. "It's Rishi. You can't tell another soul, though. And I think the jury's still out regarding my intelligence."

"Last name?"

"I've told you enough for now." He stood up. "We're going to need to figure out how to get off this ship and get through customs when we get to Byrzyrk. I have no idea how we'll do that, but we need to talk with Riya and figure out how to do it, fast."

The trip exposed Dai to a universe she'd never known existed, a whole other strata of extravagance. Each meal was equal parts performance, art, and nutrition. The ship's crew was omnipresent and gratified her every wish immediately. Mujin's extensive tour had only scratched the surface of the facilities. Dai particularly enjoyed the holo theaters—there were several. At first, the plain white rooms seemed like nothing special. But once activated, the projectors, scent emulators, and speakers could replicate almost any environment. It wasn't fully immersive, like a stim, but it was close. She also enjoyed the ship's pool; Dai'd never swum before. Stepping into the warm, shallow water was amazing, though. She learned to lie back and let the water reach her neck while she rested against the steps leading into the pool.

The Centralers seemed to get a kick out of her and Szan's reactions to the opulence they took for granted. They laughed at the two Fringers as they eyed the complex dishes the ship's dining staff had created or tried to play on the sports sims. Thankfully, Tak didn't laugh and tried to be helpful since he was right at home on the enormous yacht—much to the others' disappointment.

"We're within range of the system's sensor array," reported a gray-haired pilot sitting behind a console.

"Two rotations," Dai said. "You were right on." Clearly, Tak knew quite a lot about high-end yachts like the *Nero*.

"I've been traveling the galaxy for a while," Tak said. "You can't be a consultant without learning a thing or two."

They were standing next to Riya on the *Nero*'s bridge. The ship's watch sat in front of immaculately polished consoles, going through a landing routine that was clearly second nature to them. Everything in the bridge was cutting-edge. Rather than the simple digital and two-dimensional displays Dai was used to, the *Nero* had holographic displays, ultra-precise sensors, and enough computing power to rival the Triple-Deuce itself. The crown jewel was the enormous screen at the center of the bridge, which showed a live video feed from outside with sensor read-outs and key aspects highlighted.

"Okay, I'm activating the signal." Riya stepped next to one of the crew members, plugged a small device into a port in the console, and tapped on an adjacent screen. "That's it. Now we wait."

"How long?" Dai asked.

"Depends on who's here," she said. "Shouldn't be too long."

Riya had told them her family had experience in what she called "other-than-legal shipping" and could help get them through the planet's customs. She'd instructed the ship's crew to hold position once they were near the planet and call for her. When Dai had asked what was going to happen, Riya had only said she would get them a ride and to say her goodbyes before they headed to the bridge. Considering the way the others had acted, there wasn't too much Dai wanted to say to them. After giving Mujin a sincere thank-you, she was ready to go. She was apprehensive; Riya's willingness to help seemed a little out of place. She didn't seem like the type of person who would go out of her way for a friend, much less relative strangers.

They walked to the back of the bridge, sat down in the cushioned seats that pulled out from the bulkhead, and waited silently. A standard later, one of the crew called out, "We're being hailed on an encrypted frequency."

"Patch it through to the private line," Riya ordered, pointing to a small earpiece near her seat.

"We can broadcast it over the bridge speakers if you'd like, ma'am," the captain said.

"No," Riya snapped. "Patch it through."

She draped the small headset over her ear, and secs later, Dai could see her lips moving as she talked. Whatever she was talking about, it was brief and relatively cut-and-dry. After a few moments, she set down the headset and turned around. "Captain, open the guest bay." She stood up. "Follow me."

The *Nero* had several landing bays, mainly filled with small pleasure craft that were used for quick planetside jaunts when a port was full or unavailable. Riya led them past the occupied bays to the guest bay, intended for visiting craft, and told them to wait outside. A ship entered and they watched as the atmosphere was cycled back into the chamber. Finally, the light above the door turned green, and it slid open with a quiet whoosh, revealing a small matte-black ship, perhaps twice the size of the mining pods on the Triple-Deuce. A small hatch on one side of the teardrop-shaped vehicle popped open with a hiss, and a man climbed out and strode toward them.

"Ms. Kelly," the man said with a curt nod toward Riya. He was short but appeared to be made of solid muscle. His shirt barely contained his broad chest and thick arms. Small silvery threads coursed along his neck, disappeared under his shirt, and appeared again on his forearms. They looked to be tattoos of some sort, but Dai hadn't seen anything like them before.

"Fix, how's it goin'?" Riya asked. "You think you can help?"

"Sure as fargin' gravity, ma'am." The man cracked his knuckles. "But who are these shrag blankets, anyway?"

Riya laughed. "They're friends. Friends who need our help."

"You're startin' to pull from the bottom of the parts bin, ma'am. I thought those other three airbags were bad, but these seem worse." He looked at them like he'd found them in a toilet bowl.

"You never seemed to need an excuse to bend the rules before, Fix."

He grunted. "True. Guess I just don't care for seein' you slummin' around with the likes of these."

"We're right here," Tak said in an annoyed tone.

Fix sidestepped past Riya and sauntered forward until his nose was almost touching Tak's chest. Before anyone could say a word, Tak had fallen to his knees with a gasp. Fix looked down at him, a sneer on his face.

"Yeah, there you are," Fix said. "And I'm right here. Glad we got that figured out."

Dai'd had enough. She would put up with a lot since it seemed like Fix was there to help, but there was a line. She dove at his waist, her feet leaving the floor. It was like running into a support beam. He let out a small "oof" as she struck his side. His feet remained planted on the floor, and Dai felt herself flying, her legs somehow above her head. As she landed, she felt a sharp pain on the same shoulder she'd injured only a few cycles ago.

"Better watch yourself, kid," the man growled. "You try that again and I'll do more than just throw you."

"You touch my friend again and I'll do more than just tackle you," Dai spat back as she pulled herself off the floor.

"Fix. Dai. Stop it," Riya scolded. "We don't have too much time before Byrzyrk's orbital sensors notice us."

"You *really* sure?" Fix asked, arching a ginger eyebrow at Riya.

"Yes. Stop tryin' to be a shrag and help us out, now." Riya fixed him with a glare, her earlier good-natured smile gone.

"Fine." The man ambled back to the small ship and motioned to its hatch with a grandiloquent roll of his hand. "All of y'all get in. I gotta be the last one."

Dai shot him a glare, walked forward, and climbed through the small entrance. The cabin was dark and relatively sparse, with three rows of tan seats taking up nearly all the space. They were almost parallel to the floor so that the occupant would have to stare at the ceiling and so tightly packed that Dai had to climb over the first two rows to make her way to the back.

After everyone had entered the ship, Fix closed the door and the rows of tiny lights on the ceiling illuminated the small cabin. Small portholes in the hull allowed Dai to watch as they disengaged from the *Nero*.

"We've headed out," Fix said. "Make sure you're strapped in. It'll get bumpy on entry."

Dai could hear Szan's breathing, fast and ragged, as the ship lifted from the pad and left the *Nero*. She knew it was only the second ship he'd ever been in, and the first had been an immense yacht. She could tell he was terrified.

"Don't worry," Dai whispered. "You're perfectly safe. This thing is small, but it's sturdy. You can tell whoever built it knew what they were doing." She hoped so.

"It's just a lot," Szan whispered.

"I know. But you wanted to experience life off Faltran, right?" She turned to smile at him. "This is it."

"I'm questioning that decision." Szan returned her grin with a weak one of his own.

Riya, who was sitting at the front next to Fix, called out the time until they'd reach the planet; it wasn't long. Covers slammed down over the portholes, and the ship started to shimmy and was buffeted side to side as they entered Byrzryk's atmosphere.

Dai turned and gave Szan what she hoped was a reassuring smile. "You got this."

He smiled back at her weakly.

A gentle thud sounded through the cabin as they touched down, and Riya reached over and opened the cabin door.

"We're here," Fix announced. "Now get the hell out."

Chapter Twelve

Byrzyrk

Tak climbed out of the small smuggler-class ship and took a deep breath. Despite the relatively cramped quarters, the ride had been remarkably smooth and comfortable. He'd even fallen asleep for a few secs due to the cabin's dim lights and his body's internal clock being completely out of whack.

They'd landed inside a shadow-covered courtyard surrounded by large industrial-looking buildings. Networks of pipes climbed along the walls like metallic vines and small bits of debris littered the hard-packed gravel beneath their feet.

"We've gotta move," Fix said, closing and locking the ship's door with a wave of his combrace. "Follow me."

He led them into one of the buildings facing the courtyard. Based on its exterior, Tak had expected it to be dark and cramped like the Triple-Deuce. Instead, they entered a large, brightly lit room filled with waist-high data processing units, each one emitting the static-filled hum of a machine at work. They wound their way through the machines and exited the other side to find a sleek black aircar waiting for them.

"Get in," Fix commanded as he opened the rear door and waved them in.

Tak hadn't been in a luxury aircar in a long time. He admired the plush seats that lined the cabin, surrounding a small table with a chembar embedded in the base, as he climbed inside and slid along the seat to leave enough room for the others. Once they were all in, the aircar lifted off.

"So where are we going?" Tak asked. "You know a good place to drop us off?"

"Depends. You got credits?" Riya asked. "You're not gonna make it far on Byrzyrk without them."

"I've got some. Enough for us to find a way off-planet."

"Won't the detain order be a problem?" Szan asked. "Or don't they check that kinda stuff within the Central Worlds?"

Both Tak and Riya scoffed. "They're *supposed* to," Tak answered. "But they rarely do."

"And there are ways around it." Riya looked at Tak appraisingly. "I'm guessing you've got someone to help with that."

Tak nodded. "Yeah, I have some connections." Really, he had one who might be able to help, an associate named Syn. But Syn was on Hkar'Trush, which made it awfully hard to help when they were on a completely different planet. He did know at least one person on Byrzyrk, though.

"Good," she said. "We're in Erd, the largest city on the planet, already. I can drop you off at a hotel."

"Thanks," Dai said. "That'd be great." Tak looked at her earnest smile. She seemed so young right then. She probably believed that Riya was just trying to be helpful. Tak didn't trust Riya—couldn't trust her. She had an angle. He just didn't know what it was yet.

Erd was enormous and densely packed. Byrzyrk was the homeworld of the Yoorkray, one of the founding members of the Central Worlds. Now it was one of the richest and most cosmopolitan planets in the galaxy, and its densely populated capital reflected that.

Tak had forgotten what it was like to be in a *real* city after spending so long in the Fringe. As the vehicle climbed up an elevated freeway, he chuckled to himself while Dai and Szan stared open-mouthed out the aircar's windows at the gleaming skyscrapers that towered around them, their tops lost inside the thick clouds. As he watched the wisps of mist floating between the ribbons of roads, he wished he could have that same sense of wonder for just a few secs.

They glided down an off-ramp and came to a stop on a large platform that extended out halfway up a tower. A Yoorkray attendant glided out of the building and opened the aircar's door. Tak followed Dai and Szan out of the vehicle. Large glass barriers surrounded the parking area, blocking much of the wind, but Tak could still hear it whistling above their heads. It was almost loud enough to drown out the hum of the traffic.

"Thanks for everything." Tak extended his hand to Riya, who gave it a firm shake while studying him intently.

"No problem," she said. "Look after them." She nodded at Szan and Dai. "I don't think I need to tell you this city will eat them alive unless you're careful." Both Fringers gave an annoyed grunt at her words.

"We're right here," Dai said with a peeved tone.

"I'll make sure they stay safe," Tak said, eliciting a second set of grunts.

"I'll pay for a few cycles here at the hotel. It should give you enough time to do whatever you need." She tossed three earpieces and matching bracelets to them. "You'll need these."

"Thanks," Tak said as he placed the earpiece behind his ear and put on the bracelet. The intellingua allowed the wearer to hear and speak in all the Central Worlds dialects. Szan watched Tak put on the device and followed suit, while Dai had clearly used one before.

"My dad's loaded, as you know already," Riya said. "It's nothing. You mind if I have a moment with Dai? You can go inside and get the room situated. Just tell 'em to put it on the Kelly account."

"Sure." Tak didn't trust her, but there wasn't much else he could say. She'd saved their lives. Besides, if she wanted to harm Dai, she'd have done it already.

Tak and Szan walked into the hotel's lavish foyer, leaving the two women to talk. The interior was decorated in classic Yoorkray style. A red runner embossed with silver threads ran down the length of the oval lobby. Large chandeliers jutted from the walls over the center of the room. The furnishings, even the chairs, were ornate webs of metal and glass.

They walked up to the reception desk at the end of the room. Two Yoorkray stood behind it, their feathers dyed deep black to signify their status as service workers. Their intelligent, almost reptilian faces peered up from their monitors as he approached.

"How can we help you today, sir?" one of the Yoorkray asked. The small device behind Tak's ear instantly translated the high-pitched squawks.

"Hey ya!" Tak said, trying to project an air of casual indifference. "We'd like a room for five cycles. It's courtesy of Riya Kelly. She's asked for it to be put on her family's tab."

"Ah, yes." The attendant looked past him, toward their aircar. Tak turned around but couldn't see anything except Riya and Dai talking outside. "Are you comfortable with a bio-encrypted lock?"

Considering he was being hunted, Tak was most definitely *not* comfortable with providing his fingerprint, DNA, and retinal scan.

"No, that's okay. We'll just use cards."

"Of course," the attendant said soothingly. It tapped on the screen in front of it and three small cards, about the size of Tak's thumb, popped out of a small machine on the counter. The Yoorkray handed Tak the cards, and he put two in his pocket and gave Szan the third.

"Dai's still outside with Riya," Szan said, looking at the aircar outside.

"No worries." Tak kept his voice light but wondered what they could be talking about. "Might as well check out the place."

They strolled through the crowded lobby, examining the layout. After Faltran and the Triple-Deuce, Tak had gotten used to being surrounded by Humans. It would take a bit of time to readjust to living alongside the varied species of the Central Worlds. Core planets, like Byrzyrk, were a mélange of the hundreds of different Centraler species. Every common area, vehicle, and machine had to adapt to all of their varying physiologies and tastes.

"It's all so strange." Szan touched a small plate with raised symbols on a wall next to a nondescript metal door. "What's this?"

"Touchplate," Tak said. "Not all species have sight." He pointed to the dotted lines etched into the floor. "They can follow the lines and use the touchplates to know where they're going. There're also ultrasonic speakers that some species use to navigate as well. You just can't hear it."

Szan gave a small grin. "It's all so different. Not at all what I imagined."

"What'd you imagine?" Tak was honestly curious. He'd spent his entire life on Hkar'Trush, the capital of the Central Worlds. It was even more diverse and populated than Byrzyrk.

"I don't know," Szan said. "But not giant towers that reach into the sky. It's like a story or a holo come to life. Feels weird."

They reentered the main lobby to find Dai standing in its center, her mouth open and her head darting back and forth, looking exactly like the new-to-the-planet Orbiter she was.

"Whatd'ya think?" Tak asked.

"It's like a holo." She sounded a little breathless. "All of this. It's just so... much."

"Yeah, Szan said the same thing. What did Riya tell you?"

Dai glanced at him and scrunched up her mouth. "Nothing. Just a goodbye."

There was something more she wasn't saying. But Tak had secrets of his own and he didn't have the time or inclination to pry information from his friend. He turned toward the banks of lifts. "Let's head up to our room."

Their suite was every bit as opulent as the hotel's lobby. The sitting area was in the center of three bedrooms, each with panoramic views of the city. To Dai's dismay, the furniture was designed for Humans instead of the adaptable type she'd seen down in the lobby. Tak explained they maintained rooms for different species—rather than all of them being adaptable—so their guests would be comfortable. She wondered if the room was always a "Human" room or if they reconfigured it for each guest. Either way, she'd been looking forward to trying out a bed that was built for multiple species.

"So we're here," Dai said as she sat in a chair. "Now what do we do?"

"Well, we need to figure out where the survivors of the Triple-Deuce went," Tak said. "Then we go there and I drop you both off. You'll be safer without me." Dai didn't like how he used the word "survivors."

As she looked at Tak, Dai couldn't help but hear Riya's voice in her ears. The woman had entreated her to leave Szan, and especially Tak, and come with her. She'd said Tak wasn't to be trusted and was a danger. When pressed, the woman wouldn't say *why* she thought that, just that he was hiding things and that Dai should get away as soon as possible. She had transferred her com-id to Dai's combrace, asking Dai to contact her if she needed anything.

Dai had thought about going with Riya—for more than a few secs. But Riya herself was clearly not someone to be trusted, either. Who had people they could call to sneak them through customs? What *did* her family do? From everything Dai had seen, Riya was just as shady and dangerous as Tak.

"Can't we just connect to the planet's infopool and find out?" Szan asked. "Seems like it would be public knowledge."

"Well, there's a problem." Tak rubbed his forehead and took a brief hit from his chempen. "I don't have a good way to get onto it."

"I thought all Centralers could access the infopool."

"Normally, yes," Tak said. "But since I'm a wanted man—for some reason—they'll have shut off my access. And if I even *try* to connect, they'll be able to know exactly where I am."

"You said you had a friend who'd help," Dai said. "Just talk to them."

"Yeah. That's the plan." Tak sighed. "But I need to get to Hkar'Trush to talk with them. I know someone who *may* be able to help with that here in Erd."

Dai was growing tired of Tak's vague answers. If he wouldn't trust her after everything they'd been through, then maybe she shouldn't trust *him*. Perhaps Riya was right.

They took a lift back to the lobby and grabbed an aircar from the queue waiting outside. When Tak noticed Szan and Dai's amazement at a *line* of aircars just waiting for passengers, he explained hotels were the only place they'd find a line of them like that. Otherwise, everyone just called them through their combrace.

They sped through the city, the elevated roadway swishing through the buildings. The aircar was almost completely glass, and Dai could see a lot more of the city than she had in Riya's luxury car. It was amazing. The towers seemed almost endless, their bottoms so far below them and their tops hidden in the clouds, which had grown more dense while they were in the hotel. Aircars hovered meters off the roadways, which twisted, rose, and fell between the buildings, sometimes rising to the clouds or dropping to the ground. The arteries of the city.

The trip made her realize how sheltered and constrained her childhood had been. She'd thought of herself as an adult, wise in the ways of the galaxy. But the scale of the cityscape around her drove home the realization she'd only ever known a minuscule portion of what there was.

"Is the entire planet like this?" Szan asked.

"No," Tak replied. "A lot of the planet is made of preserves and orchards. The Yoorkray have strict rules around it, from what I understand. Not sure why anyone would want to leave the cities anyways, though." Dai couldn't have disagreed more. She would have *loved* to see what it was like outside the cities.

The aircar glided down a ramp to street level, and the looming buildings blocked out the sun, making it appear dusk despite it being midday. Pedestrians of all species walked, crawled, slithered, and even rolled down the sidewalks on either side of the road. Bright animated signs covered every bit of the surrounding buildings, creating an overwhelming aura of chaotic light that irritated Dai's eyes.

The car came to a halt in front of a building with several storefronts and they stepped out. Dai got the impression that they were in a more run-down part of the town. There were fewer signs and pedestrians, and the ones that were around shuffled along with their faces downward.

"We've got a bit to walk," Tak said after the vehicle had left. "No way we're stopping right in front of their place."

He led them down the busy street, walking at a brisk pace. Szan and Dai struggled to keep up while also craning their heads to take in the sights and sounds around them. They headed down the broad avenue for several blocks before eventually turning down a side street and then doubling back. Tak turned again, heading away from where the aircar had dropped them off. The streets seemed identical to Dai, each with the same smattering of dour people, scattered lights, and derelict vehicles on the side of the street.

Tak abruptly ducked through a short doorway and held the door half open for Szan and Dai. Inside was a small, unremarkable lobby covered in marbled red stone. A balcony with a metal balustrade lined the four walls overhead. Black doors peppered the walls on both levels, their small sizes a clear indication that the building was not intended for Humans.

The lobby seemed so familiar but also foreign. The red and black reminded her of the stories of hell, not colors she would expect to see in an apartment building lobby. But the style was distinctly Human, albeit shrunk to a smaller size. As she followed Tak to the narrow staircase at the opposite end of the room, she pressed her hand against a column supporting the balcony and the smooth surface gave slightly under her touch.

Tak looked back at her. "It's a Yoorkray building. But they designed it to look Human. Why? I've got no idea. My friend's got a strange thing for Humans. It's a thing with some Yoorkray. A while ago, when this place was built, there was Human fever on Byrzyrk."

When they reached a door on the upper level, Tak knocked three times in quick succession, paused, then knocked twice more. The door remained closed. As they waited with nothing seeming to happen, Dai wondered if Tak's friend was there. She was about to say something when the pitch-black door silently swung open, revealing a black curtain.

They pushed through the curtain and into a Yoorkray-sized living room decorated in a style from early in Humanity's history. A lime-green sofa sat against one wall, with a padded easy chair next to it. Small holes had been carved into the sofa where the cushions met the back. When a Yoorkray walked into the room, its tail bobbing behind it, Dai realized what the modifications were for.

"Farg! I wish you hadn't come here..." It paused. "What name are you goin' by now?"

"Taksh."

"I wish you hadn't come here, Taksh."

"It's good to see you, too, Kritz." Tak flopped down on the sofa and pulled his chempen from his shirt pocket. "I wouldn't have come if I'd had any choice."

"That thing's gonna kill you," Kritz said with a wave of its feathery arm.

"It's gonna need to get in line."

"Who're they?" the Yoorkray asked, gesturing at Szan and Dai.

"Friends," Tak said. "Dai and Szan." They each gave a small nod as Tak said their name.

"If they were *really* friends, you'd get away from them as fast as possible."

"I tried." Tak took another hit. "But I can't yet."

"You got discovered," Kritz said as it sat down on the chair, leaned back, and put its clawed feet on the table. "I saw it on some of the security channels. I can't help you."

Dai knew Tak well enough to notice the small twitch around his eyes. That meant he was worried but didn't want to show it. "But you know as well as I that there's someone who might be able to," Tak said. "I need to know where the refugees from Station 222 are and a ride off-planet."

"You're not gonna be able to disappear again." Kritz grumbled to itself. "At least I can't help with that. *Maybe* Syn can."

"Right now, I need to get her"—he pointed at Dai—"to her mother. I'll worry about the rest later."

"You turnin' into a hero? The Human I knew wouldn't help a child unless there were credits involved." Kritz let out a loud cawing sound that Dai was pretty sure meant amusement. "Never thought I'd see the cycle where that'd happen."

"Can you help or not, Kritz?"

"Fine. Let's talk somewhere private."

"Wait here," Tak instructed Dai and Szan as he stood up. He followed Fritz out of the room, his head almost brushing the top of the doorframe. A few secs later, Dai heard a heavy metal door banging closed from the direction they'd left.

She stood up and inspected the room. It was strange to think that Humans used to live like this. The bright colors, the crude lines of the furniture, and the strange box-like screen in the corner. She wondered what it would have been like to have lived during this time. It couldn't have been too much fun. So much disease, ignorance, and violence.

She paused; violence was still around, and it wasn't confined to Humans. The Central Worlds claimed that they were civilized and peaceful, but even now there were politicians saying they should declare war against the Gyrdra, a species they'd fought to a standstill when the Central Worlds were formed. The Jackals continued to ravage stations and kill innocents. No, violence was *definitely* not gone.

"There's a lot more going on here than I thought." Szan sat back down on the couch and rubbed his temple. "What's happening with Tak? Which I guess isn't his real name." He looked at Dai. "Do you know why we're here?"

Dai paused for a sec. Tak had told her about his past in confidence. She hated breaking that. But Szan was a part of this and deserved to know what was happening.

"I know that Tak's on the run," she replied evasively. "That he's been on the run for a while. I don't know why. I don't think he does either." She took a deep breath and sat down next to her friend. "I think—I know—that he's trying to get us to safety."

"You're right. I'm sure you're right." Szan leaned against the back of the sofa and looked at the ceiling. "Still, it's a lot. I'd always dreamed of leaving Nashoba and Faltran, but I didn't think it was going to be like this. Still, no going back." He said the last part as if reminding himself.

"When we find my mother, she can help you," Dai said. "You were a facture, right? On a station, you'd be a builder. There's always a need for people who can make and fix things, wherever you want to be."

"I *guess* I'm a builder," Szan said, "though I never really thought about it. I did what the commune needed. Maybe I should be something else."

"I can relate. I was always supposed to be a mechanic, like my mom." She smiled conspiratorially. "Let's do something no one expects and become artists or mercenaries."

"What about musicians?" He sang in a mock falsetto, then erupted into a bout of laughter, and Dai joined in.

After they'd worn themselves out, singing and laughing, Szan turned to look at her. "You didn't get to decide either?"

"Well, I would've reclassed, I think."

"Reclassed?"

"On my station, the Triple-Deuce, we can try out for a different job family than what they originally place us in. Eventually."

Szan hummed thoughtfully for a moment. "I don't think it's *quite* the same. I don't think all that matters now, though. We're together on the same journey. Fringers in the Central Worlds. Aliens in a galaxy made up of aliens."

Dai decided not to mention that she wasn't *technically* a Fringer, that she was a citizen of the Central Worlds from her dad's side. It wasn't like it mattered. This was the first time she'd even been to the Central Worlds.

"We'll make it through together."

It felt strange comforting a man who was several rotations older than her. But Szan was clearly feeling the weight of everything that was happening to them. She remembered the same feeling on the emergency ship with Tak. It was a panic, a feeling like she was trapped with nowhere to run. If she could be there for him, then she would.

"My mom will—"

Metal plates slammed down from the ceiling, covering the apartment's front door and the window on the other side of the room. A sec later, the room shook as an explosion boomed on the other side of the front door. Dai heard a creak of bending metal as small bits of debris rained from the ceiling.

"Follow me!" Tak shouted as he ran into the room.

As Dai and Szan jumped up and scrambled to follow Tak, a steady pounding shook the room. Someone was about to break in.

Chapter Thirteen

Byrzyrk

I f he was being honest with himself, Tak had a hard time remembering how he knew Kritz. It was just an aspect of his memory, which seemed to be fractured since he'd found out his parents had died. He did know Kritz was a bit eccentric, but it had gone full-on 'noid since he'd last seen the Yookray. It'd installed a metal and poly-lined panic room in the back of its faux-Human apartment. Advanced computer systems lined the walls, with holo monitors above, the stream of Yoorkray symbols indecipherable to Tak.

"So, been a long time," Tak began as he stepped into the room.

"Stop it. You're putting me in a bind here, Rishi," Kritz complained as it closed the room's thick metal door with a clang. "Your family's done a lot for me and mine, but this is above and beyond. This isn't normally how we operate."

"I know," Tak replied. "I didn't have another place to go." He tried to think back and realized he couldn't remember how he knew Kritz or what their relationship had been before. Did they have some sort of drop location or encrypted network to communicate with? Was he not supposed to be there?

Kritz sat down at a terminal and began tapping at the input screen, then turned to face him. "Your name came down on some of the channels a few cycles ago. There are contracts out on you. Big contracts."

Tak's heart skipped a beat. He'd been so careful. He'd thought he might have finally escaped.

"Can you tell me where the survivors of Station 222 are?" he asked. "I know they landed somewhere in the Central Worlds." He pointed back to the living room. "I need to get that girl back to her mother."

"What happened?" Kritz asked. It turned back to his console, its talons flickering across the controls. "Where you been, Tak?"

Tak thought for a moment. How much should he say? How much *could* he say? The past few cycles had revealed enormous holes in his memory. He finally decided to just tell Kritz everything he knew, describing how the police notified him of his parents' deaths and how Syn had helped him create a new identity and disappear into the Fringe. He explained that he'd spent the past few rotations as a consulting geologist, traveling the Fringe from station to station, and finished with the Jackal attack and escaping the Triple-Deuce.

"Dai saved me," Tak finished. "A few times. I need to make sure she gets back to her mother and safety. She can't survive out here alone. She's an Orbiter that hadn't stepped onto a planet until a few days ago."

Kritz's expression changed into what Tak could only call one of suspicion. "So you're gonna help her out?" it asked skeptically.

"Yeah, I am."

"Interesting... Hero's not something you've done before."

"It's not being a hero. It's helping a friend."

"That's rich." Kritz trilled in laughter. "To think that a Chao would actually help someone else. Your family are scum. Maybe I should say *were* scum. You're the last one left."

The venom in Kritz's words shocked Tak. They were friends, or at least cordial. Weren't they? "I'm tryin' to start a new family tradition."

Kritz continued to tap at the screen while twisting the analog controls that jutted from the adjacent wall. "Found it," it called out in triumph. "The evac ships landed on Perridion."

"Perridion?" Tak asked. The name sounded familiar.

"Yeah, near the Fringe at the edge of the Central Worlds," Kritz said as it continued to work. "Seems like they've set up a camp."

"Great! Now how the hell can we get there?"

"Ah!" Kritz held up a single talon. "Now's when you pay me back for all the shrag you've put me through."

Tak calmed his breathing. What was he missing? Why did Kritz seem to hate—or at least strongly dislike—him? He couldn't remember ever having a cross word with the Yoorkray.

"I've got—"

A green light flickered on the ceiling. "Oh farg!" Kritz jumped from its chair and disengaged the large metal door to the room as the muffled thump of an explosion sounded from outside.

"They're in the building!" Kritz shouted.

One of the screens flickered to a live feed of the balcony outside the apartment. It was hard to see anything through a thick haze of smoke, but what Tak *could* see didn't look good. Shadowy figures—he couldn't tell what species—slunk through the darkness. They pushed a device against the wall between the apartment and the hallway. A piston slammed against the wall; their attackers were clearly trying to bash their way in.

"I knew it would come to this one cycle," Kritz said. "Just didn't think it'd be because of *you*."

It ran to the wall, opened a small panel, murmured something to itself, and went down the row of buttons inside with a claw, pressing them one at a time. A small hiss sounded from the equipment inside the room, and small sparks arced outward as they destroyed themselves.

"Please tell me you've got a way out of here," Tak said.

"Who do you think you're talking to?" Kritz pressed the last button and a small door opened in the floor. "Call your 'friends' in here and let's get the hell out."

Without saying another word, the Yoorkray jumped into the opening.

Tak ran back into the antique living room and called for Dai and Szan. They looked at him, their eyes wide with fear. He led them back to the safe room and pointed at the escape hatch in the floor.

"Jump in," Tak instructed.

"But—" Szan struggled to speak.

"No time to talk," Tak pulled the man into the room and pushed him toward the opening, almost causing him to fall in. "Get in there now!"

The two of them gaped at Tak for a moment. Then Dai nodded and jumped, feet-first, into the hole. Secs later, Szan did the same. Swearing to himself, Tak slammed the panic room door shut and hopped into the escape hatch. As he dropped through, he heard the crash of someone entering the apartment above.

Kritz's escape shaft dropped them several hundred meters into an underground tunnel. After landing unceremoniously on his butt, Tak picked himself up and rushed along the metal grate floor next to Kritz, while Dai and Szan followed closely behind. The dim halos of the utility lights above their heads cast bizarre shadows on the maze of conduits climbing the walls.

"What's this place?" Tak asked.

"It's a utility core," Kritz said. "All the water, specialized atmosphere, and links get pumped through here to the buildings above. I had to pay more than a few bribes to get an off-the-grid escape shaft built from my place to here."

"I really wanna call you paranoid," Tak huffed. "But considering what just happened..." Kritz seemed *under*prepared, if anything, based on recent events.

"Will they find us down here?" Dai asked apprehensively.

"Not for a bit," Kritz said. "The security protocols should have closed the entrance we came through. It'll take a bit for them to figure out where we went. We shouldn't hang around talking, though."

They came to a set of double doors and Kritz tapped on the small panel next to them.

"Things're getting worse," it said. The doors opened, revealing a small lift, and they stepped inside. "People are disappearing. You were one of the first. But there's been more. Whatever your family started is getting bigger."

For the life of him, Tak didn't know *what* his parents had started. He wished he did.

"You got a place to go?" he asked.

Kritz chirped, quick and high. "The old Rishi wouldn't have cared. You're getting all mushy." The door opened onto a small back alley, and they stepped out. "Yeah, I'm fine. I got resources. The question is, what are you gonna do next?"

"We need to get to Perridion." Tak looked at Dai. "That's where they took your mother."

"I don't know how you're going to get there," Kritz said. "You've got every mercenary in the galaxy looking for you." Its tongue darted out, moisturizing its eyes. A Yoorkray sign of uncertainty. "I've done what I can. More than I should. Now you're on your own."

"Wait," Dai said, her face turning red. "You're just leaving us here?"

"You brought whatever those things were to my apartment," Kritz said. Its multicolored feathers puffed out from its body. "Now I need to save my hide. That's the way these things work, kid."

"Thanks, Kritz," Tak said. He meant it. There was a certain code for people like them, the ones who treaded along the edge of the Central Worlds' underworld. Kritz hadn't had to save them; it could have just left them to fend for themselves.

"Any debt that you thought I might owe you is settled." Kritz walked away, stopped, and then turned to face Tak. "I'll say that I like this new version of you. Maybe not everyone in the Chao family are pieces of shrag." The Yoorkray turned and sprinted out of the alley, its birdlike legs carrying it faster than any Human.

"Farg!" Tak slammed his hand against a metal bin and immediately regretted it as the clang reverberated through the narrow passageway. *What the hell were they going to do?* "Let's go. Act natural. We've got to get out of here and then we can figure out what to do next."

They strode onto the busy street outside of the alley, trying to blend in with the throngs of creatures. It took every ounce of Tak's strength not to break into a sprint. He could feel eyes. Eyes everywhere, staring at him, studying him. He expected to hear a weapon firing or an explosion, but nothing came. By the time they stopped in a small park, his legs were aching and he felt like he'd run a marathon. Blues and grays of the flora native to Byrzyrk filled the area, creating an illusion of tranquility as long as he didn't look up at the immense structures around them. A shaft of sunlight darted through a pair of buildings, warming the small groups of aliens reclining on the ground in the center.

Tak led the other two to a small cleared area underneath a wide-leafed bush in the corner.

"So, should we call you Rishi, then?" Szan asked as they sat down. "That's your name?"

"I think it's pretty shraggin' obvious you shouldn't," Tak replied.

"We need to know what's going on," Dai said. "Whatever's happening, it involves us now." Her voice broke. "Who were those people? Why do they want you?"

They were good questions. Questions he wished he had answers to. Questions he *should* have answers to. "No idea." Tak held up a hand. "It seems insane. But I'll tell you what I know." He glanced around. "Have you heard of Chao Financial?"

"Yeah." Dai nodded. "They own like half the Central Worlds."

"Not half. But a lot." Tak's voice dropped to a whisper. "My real name's Rishi Chao. My family owns—owned—a controlling stake in the company. My great-grandfather started it over a hundred rotations ago."

"So, you're like Rat and the rest?" Szan asked. "Silly rich?"

"No. Not anymore."

"But you were?" Szan asked.

"Yeah. I was silly rich, as you say. My family had a planet we used for recreation. A small one near the Fringe. But that's all gone."

"I remember hearing something," Dai said as she wrinkled her nose in thought. "What happened? Why the hell are you sittin' under a bush in the middle of a park in Byrzyrk with two Fringers?"

"God, I wish I knew," Tak groaned. "It happened five rotations ago. I'd just returned to Hkar'Trush from university. When I'd spoken to my parents by relay, they'd told me they were throwing a party for me. Standard stuff. Planetary governor, heads of state, celebrities. The whole works." He remembered feeling annoyed. Another party that was more about the business than what they were actually supposed to be celebrating. "They wanted me to follow in my mother's footsteps in a few rotations and lead the company. It was the first step in cementing me as a candidate to take everything over with the board."

He took a deep breath and rubbed his eyes. The next part was tough for him to talk about, even now. The worst part of it was that he felt distant from it, as if remembering through a haze. His memories were not his own. It was as if they belonged to someone else and he'd watched them on a holo or read about them on an ocutab. It had all happened so fast. From the top of the galaxy to nothing in one night.

"There was a squad of security waiting for me when I got inside. They said my parents had died in an aircar accident."

"A squad?" Dai asked. "Isn't that overkill?"

"Well, looking back on it, yeah." Tak smiled thinly. "It didn't seem too strange to me at the time. I mean, I grew up with everyone's lips planted firmly on my family's backside." He chuckled. "Anyway, they told me my parents had been returning from a meeting when their aircar had malfunctioned and sent them right over the edge of a roadway. The emergency systems didn't activate, and, well... you can guess the rest."

Dai placed a hand on Tak's shoulder. "I'm sorry. Losing a parent's tough. I lost my dad when I was a kid and I still think about him."

Tak placed his hand over hers but didn't respond. He didn't want to tell her the truth. He felt nothing at the thought of his parents' deaths. "Well, it quickly turned into an interrogation. Somehow, the authorities learned that there were irregularities in the finances of the company. Money was missing. Lots of it. They asked me if I worked with my parents and questions about the company I couldn't answer."

"Couldn't or wouldn't?" Szan asked.

"What do you think?" Tak rolled his eyes. "I didn't know a thing. My only experience with the company was cushy internships. I spent most of my time in Hkar'Trush's Undercity, causing trouble, doing chems, or hanging out with other rich brats. They told me to stay on-planet, that they'd have more questions for me, and then left."

"Undercity?" Szan asked.

"It's a bunch of cities underneath the surface of Hkar'Trush. There are a lot of Grounders—that's what they call themselves—like Kritz, people who live on the edges of society. Many of them believe there's a lot more going on in the Central Worlds than it seems at first and see conspiracies in everything. I'd made friends with several of them. Used my family's money and connections to help them out. Maybe it was my way of rebelling." He honestly didn't know why he'd done it.

"Your parents were okay with you doing that?" Szan asked skeptically.

"I don't think they cared," Tak said with a shrug. The truth was, they had their own worlds and Tak had his. The two almost never intersected.

"So I went to a friend and told them what was going on," Tak continued. "He was even more freaked out than normal—and Grounders are *always* freaked out. He told me that there were groups in the Undercity that were after me. It looked like I was gonna be the next to die."

"So you ran," Dai concluded.

"Hell yeah I ran," Tak said emphatically. "If they were powerful enough to kill two of the richest people in the galaxy, some kid fresh from uni wouldn't stop 'em. I got off-planet, got my friend to help me create a new identity, Taksh Chan, and got out to the Fringe. Started taking independent consulting jobs and vowed not to return to the Central Worlds."

"Until the Jackals attacked," Dai added.

"Yup." Tak nodded. "I don't know why anyone would want me dead. I've had a while to think about it, and all I can come up with is that they think I know something. What that is, I have no idea."

"We need to figure out who's chasing you," Szan said. "And what your parents were doing."

"No." Tak shook his head. "I'm not taking them on by myself. I'm gonna disappear again. But first, I'm getting you both to Perridion. That's where they took the refugees from the Triple-Deuce. You've saved me enough times, and eventually, your luck will run out."

"What about you?" Dai asked. "Like you said, you need someone to help you."

"Not exactly what I said. But my friend can help me disappear again. Maybe this time I'll head out to the hinterlands of a planet in the Fringe or even head out to Gyrdra space."

"The Gyrdra aren't exactly friendly with Centralers," Dai said.

"Yeah," Tak agreed. But what else could he do? "I'll figure it out later. Right now, we need to get you back to your mother. You can both start a new life, one without people trying to kill or capture you."

"Question is, how do we get off Byrzyrk?" Szan asked.

"About that." Dai held up a finger. "I've got an idea. Any way we can contact a com-id without being traced?"

Chapter Fourteen

Byrzyrk

At first, Riya sounded happy when Dai messaged her. That happiness faded when she learned exactly *why* Dai was contacting her. They had no one else to turn to. Dai and Szan didn't have a credit to their names, and if Tak even *tried* to contact anyone, they'd probably all be killed.

"No way," Riya hissed through the line. "I gave you my com-id to get away from him. Not to *help* him."

"We're in trouble, Riya," Dai pleaded. "I can explain more if we can meet in person. I wouldn't ask if I had anywhere else to go and if I didn't trust Tak completely. Just meet with us and we can tell you everything."

"He's using you, Dai," Riya spat. "I won't let him use me, too."

"Just meet with us. I promise I can explain everything. We're screwed unless we get help. It's not just him who's in trouble. They're hunting all of us now."

"Fargin' Fringe," Riya cursed. "The one rule is, never bring back anything from the Fringe. I went ahead and broke it and now you can see where it got me." She sighed, her breath crackling over the line. "Fine."

Riya sent Dai an address for them to meet at. Thankfully, it was within walking distance from the park; Dai wasn't sure if they could have hailed a public aircar without alerting whoever was following them. She wasn't sure about a lot of things anymore. That someone had been hunting Tak—or Rishi—for the past five rotations was a shock. It was strangely comforting to realize he understood what she was going through. He'd also had his life torn apart, maybe even more completely than she had. At least she could go back to her old life on a new station. Tak would never go back to the life of privilege he'd had as a child. He'd never be able to have a normal life, period. Unless they could find out why he was being tracked. Who would want him so badly and be powerful enough to take down one of the richest and most powerful families in the Central Worlds?

"So, you own Chao Financial, huh?" Szan asked as they worked their way through the crowds.

"Quiet," Tak hissed. "Use that name and it'll get us all killed."

"I think it would bother me to go by a different name." Szan cocked his head, seeming to consider his own statement. "Yeah, I just *feel* like I'm a Szan."

"Well, I hate to break it to you, but you may have to think up a new one," Tak said. "You've been spotted with me. If they figure out who you are, then you won't be safe until you change it."

The Nashoban bit his lip, considering Tak's comment. "I doubt they can find out who I am. I mean, I doubt I'm on any of your Centraler databases or whatever they use."

Riya's address led them to a storage facility at the base of an enormous tower that looked identical to the others in the area, from what Dai could tell. She guessed the lower level of the building was a warehouse of some sort, based on its looks and the small skiffs that streamed in and out of squat cargo doors, carrying packages.

"Reso warehouse," Tak said, confirming her suspicion. "The bots carry things to people's homes in the nearby area."

Dai examined the tiny skiffs as they flew by. The sensor stalks at the front of the drones' rectangular bodies reminded her of a smiling face. "They're cute."

"Sure." Tak rolled his eyes. "Considering Riya had us come here, this place is almost certainly a front of some sort."

They opened a Yoorkray-sized door and stepped into a cavernous room filled with ribbons of conveyor belts and rows of storage shelves that stretched to the ceiling several floors above their heads. Despite the constant motion of the belts and skiffs around them, the room was relatively quiet.

"There you are. Come on in."

Dai couldn't see Riya, but her voice was coming from the other side of a relatively low set of storage shelves.

"Thanks for seeing us, Riya," Dai said loudly as they walked further into the room. "I'm not sure what we'd do without you. This entire thing is getting—" She stopped as she turned a corner and saw Riya, along with two Yoorkray. All of them had pistols pointed directly at her.

"You can stop there, Dai." Riya waved her gun at Tak. "I think it's time you told us exactly what's going on. Rishi."

Tak made a low sound, something between a groan and a whimper. "Seems like everyone's figuring out who I am all of a sudden."

"Well, Jackals attacking mining stations and mercenary kill squads tend to raise the ol' alarms," Riya said. "I knew there was something strange about you. I ran your biometrics using some samples from the *Nero*, and sure enough, a Rishi Chao showed up. He looks a lot like you, too. Features are slightly different, enough to fool most optical scans, but close enough."

"What does it say I did?"

"What *haven't* you done?" Riya asked. "Fraud, burglary, embezzlement, conspiracy, murder. The list is quite long."

Tak laughed, clearly forced. "Do you really think I've done all that? Really?"

"Riya, you can't believe it," Dai pleaded. "You should know him well enough to know it's all shrag. He's being set up."

"Why can't I?" Riya asked with a smirk. "I've done a lot of the same things myself. I know plenty of people who are as sweet as chay but can turn bitter as kaf when it suits them. A lot of them work for my parents, in fact."

"What about you?" Dai asked. "You're the one who has her gun pointed at me."

"Not at you," Tak corrected. "At me. Riya, what do I need to do to prove that I'm not a threat?"

"I thought you'd never ask." Riya's smile was feline, predatory. "I just so happen to have found a sweeper lying around. I figure we could go ahead and use it."

Dai'd never heard of a sweeper before, but what little color had been in Tak's face had drained away. "What's that?" she asked.

"It's like a stimpad, except used in interrogations," Tak replied dully, not taking his eyes away from Riya. "They're supposed to be illegal."

"Like I said, I found it lying around," Riya said. "Seems like a waste not to use it."

"Problem is, it messes you up real good," Tak continued. "I'll be out for standards."

"Look, Rishi," Riya said. "This is your *only* option if you want my help. I'll only make this offer once. Accept it or don't. I couldn't care less."

Tak looked at Dai and Szan. Dai wanted to tell him to say no, to tell Riya to go farg herself. But really, what choice did they have? Tak squared his shoulders. "Fine, let's do it."

Riya and one of her Yoorkray bodyguards escorted Tak to a small room at the edge of the warehouse while the other one watched Dai and Szan outside.

"This is not making me feel better about our situation," Szan said. He'd created a makeshift seat using a few of the boxes on the floor. Dai was too worried to sit still, so she paced back and forth in front of him. The bodyguard stood outside the room, its reptilian face impassive and its talon fixed on its pistol.

"It'll work out," Dai said. "Riya's helped us out before. She's just being careful." She said it to reassure him—and herself. How true was it really? She had no idea. Tak had warned her about Riya. But then again, Riya had warned her about Tak. The whole situation made her feel so frustrated. She'd stepped into an asteroid field without even realizing it.

"I dunno." Szan had opened a box and was pulling out the contents, a variety of brightly colored toys. "She seemed pretty crazy to me."

"It's a tactic. She's trying to intimidate us." *But why?* Dai thought. *What is Riya's angle in all of this?*

"Mission accomplished." Szan tossed a pink-colored tube into the air and caught it. "I am officially intimidated."

"How long do you think it'll take?"

"Beats me." Szan waved the tube in front of him, as if swinging a sword. "Do you think she *can* help us?"

"Yeah, I think so." She *hoped* so. "She clearly knows what she's doing."

The guard walked toward the front of the room, its pistol held close to its side. "Stay here." The words came through the small device still attached to Dai's ear. She could detect an inflection of worry in the translated speech.

Szan had let the toy drop and watched the guard as it stalked past the belts and skiffs. Whatever had happened, the creature was now on high alert. Dai felt a pang of fear as she watched it; something wasn't right.

"What's happening?" Szan whispered as the Yoorkray disappeared behind a row of shelves.

"Hell if I know," Dai said. "But I think we need to get ready to run." She thought she'd read somewhere that Yoorkray had much better hearing than Humans.

She walked to the door where Riya and Tak had disappeared and knocked. The sound of her fist hitting the metal reverberated through the room like a gong. For a moment, everything felt like it was balanced on the tip of a needle, ready to come crashing down. The reverberations died down, and all Dai could hear was her own breath, in and out.

She jumped back as the door opened with a metallic screech. Riya appeared in front of her, her tan face drained of color and her eyes wide. Dai wasn't sure what she'd expected, but to see the woman almost scared out of her wits was not it.

"We've got to get out of here," Riya hissed. The Yoorkray guard that had been in the room with her had Tak's unconscious body across its shoulder. If the weight bothered it, it didn't show. "Come on. I figured this might happen."

What might happen? Dai wondered.

Riya led them deeper into the warehouse. All of them remained silent, weaving through the belts as they methodically crossed the chamber, heading away from where they'd entered.

The enormous shelves seemed to close in on Dai, and every time they reached an intersection, she expected to see an assault team waiting for them, weapons raised.

She jumped as the staccato sounds of gunfire erupted behind them. They reverberated through the large chamber, making it sound like two armies going at each other.

"Sralt, go back and cover us," Riya instructed. "We'll drag him out."

The Yoorkray lowered Tak to the ground and then sprinted back toward the front of the room, unholstering its weapon as it ran.

"Grab hold," Riya said. "We don't have much further to go, but whoever's following us won't be held back for long."

Dai obligingly grabbed one of Tak's arms and pulled. She could feel small tinges of protest in her still-sore shoulder as they made their way. Tak's legs dragged behind them, and his head dropped back, almost touching the floor. An explosion sounded from across the room and sent shrapnel ricocheting into the walls and equipment with metallic pings.

"I can help," Szan said as he grabbed Tak's arms from Riya. "Just get us out of here." The gunfire had stopped behind them.

Not a good sign, Dai thought.

Riya rushed forward and pressed her hand against the lock on a small utility door at the end of the room. It swung open, revealing a sunlit backstreet. An aircar sat on the ground in front of them.

Riya jumped into the open door in the front of the aircar, while Szan and Dai climbed into the rear and stuffed Tak's body between the seats. Before the doors had closed, the car was already lifting off the ground.

"Hold on to something," Riya called from the front.

They launched forward and Dai fell into Szan. Then they both fell backward into the seat. She struggled to sit up but couldn't overcome the acceleration and sudden turns as they shot through the streets.

"Where're we going?" Dai asked.

"I've got to get you off Byrzyrk," Riya said. "But they're going to follow you wherever you go. Tak is a *very* wanted man."

"You're going to help us?" Szan asked. He'd managed to sit upright but had given up on trying to get off the floor.

"Yeah," Riya called back. "That guy's more important than he knows. This is a *lot* bigger than I expected."

The car turned onto an exit ramp and glided over the road as it soared off the ground and snaked through the buildings. They merged with a larger road filled with aircars, and soon, they were almost at a stop, hemmed in on all sides.

"Where are we going?" Szan asked.

"There's a private landing port near here. We're getting you on the first ship off-planet. We can figure out the next steps after that."

"You're not coming with us?" Dai asked. She thought of herself and Szan, alone on a strange ship with their friend still unconscious.

"Nope," Riya said. "I need to stay here. With what your buddy just told us, I can't leave. Besides—and I mean this in the nicest way possible—there's too much heat on you guys for me to stay around." She took a deep breath and turned around to look at them. "I know you've already been through a lot, but there's one other problem. You can't go to Perridion. At least not yet." She pointed at Tak. "That man needs to get to Hkar'Trush."

"Why?" Dai asked.

"He's got something inside his head," Riya said. "Something that's been imprinted into him, that even he doesn't realize."

"What kind of thing?" Szan asked.

"I can't say for sure," Riya said. "Whoever placed it in there also put safeguards in place. You try and hack someone's brain, you're gonna kill 'em. The only way to get access to the information is to find the person who put it there. Even he can't access it."

"What's that?" Szan leaned forward and pointed to a small aircraft that was flying toward them between the enormous towers. It was the first vehicle Dai'd seen that didn't hover over the road.

Riya squinted. "Airship. Security and responders use them. Helps 'em get around traffic. They're illegal for civilians to use inside the city since too many people end up crashing into buildings."

Dai eyed the vehicles around them nervously. They were trapped between the other aircars. They'd been found twice already and there was a good chance they'd be found again.

Riya continued squinting at the airship as it grew closer. "That's a *private* airship," she said quietly. "I'm pretty fargin' sure that they're looking for us."

"Can we get away?" Szan asked.

"How are we supposed to do that?" Dai asked.

"We can go over the side," Riya said skeptically. "But it's not exactly the most pleasant experience."

"Isn't that how Tak's parents died?" Dai eyed the metal railing next to them.

"Well, supposedly. But I think we all realize that's probably not what really happened." Riya pressed a button on the console, taking the aircar's AI offline, and gripped the wheel.

"What are you waiting for?" Dai asked, trying to keep her voice under control.

"We need to wait," Riya replied. "We don't know if that ship is looking for us or, if so, whether they'll be able to find us. I'm just hoping that it's someone who got lost. I *really* don't want to go over the side." From the tone of her voice, Dai didn't think she seemed too hopeful.

"Get him strapped in, now," Riya ordered, motioning toward Tak with her head.

He was still completely out. Dai and Szan fumbled with his body, grunting as they pushed and pulled him onto a seat. Finally, they were able to get him strapped down with a restraint.

Riya continued to gently move the aircar forward with traffic, keeping one hand firmly on the wheel and the other hovering over the main console. The airship drifted near them, facing the road while it slowly glided parallel to the traffic. It reminded Dai of an oversized aircar, except for the large nacelles on the top and the large thruster at the bottom.

"They're scanning traffic." Riya pressed a small button on the dash and the windows tinted around them. "Get ready. I think we're going to have to go to Plan B."

Dai pulled the shoulder straps from the back of her seat and buckled them into the small receptacle between her legs. Her hands were shaking so much that it took her several tries before she finally heard the click that meant it was secured.

"When will we know they've found us?" she whispered.

"When they start shooting," Riya whispered back, her eyes locked on the airship, which had stopped moving near their location. Its smooth, bare-metal hull glistened as it slowly pivoted in their direction.

"Damn damn damn damn damn," Riya whispered under her breath.

There were several flashes at the front of the airship, followed by the metallic pings of slugs hitting their aircar. With a final curse, Riya yanked the wheel to the side and slammed her hand down on the control console. As they launched over the barrier, Dai had a hard time processing what was happening. Her head snapped back and she could feel the car turning, end over end, as it fell through the air. Her vision fuzzed for a moment before snapping back into place as she heard the roar of thrusters.

Somehow, the car had righted itself and they were flying just off the ground, speeding away. Dai craned her head and looked behind them for the airship, but all she could see was the road they had just plummeted from and glass and metal buildings.

"We should be dead," Szan said with a sharp intake of breath.

"This car's got a few tricks up its sleeve," Riya said.

An explosion erupted on the road in front of them, close enough that there was no time to react. As they sped through the fireball, Dai could hear the clang of shrapnel bouncing off the vehicle's exterior.

"Change of plans," Riya announced. She yanked the wheel to the left, and the aircar pitched to the side, its bottom scraping against the road with a deep grating sound.

Dai looked behind them and saw the airship descending from the road and still in pursuit as Riya wove through the ground-level traffic. Small flashes came from the ship's nacelles as it poured fire at them. At each intersection, Riya waited until the last moment and then turned, seemingly at random.

"Listen," Riya said, eyes still focused ahead. "When I say go, you jump out of this vehicle and take Tak with you. You know the ship you arrived here in? The smuggler? You're getting off this planet in it. Drag him to it as fast as you can. Got it?"

"Got it," Dai responded.

"Hey, Muner, you got it?"

Szan jumped as if he'd been poked with a grounding rod. "Yes."

"Good." Riya spun the wheel and followed the road as it dipped into a small, vacant tunnel. Dai was pitched against her restraints as they slammed to a stop.

"Go! Go through that door." Riya pointed at a weathered door on their left.

Dai released her restraints and crouched in front of Tak, fumbling with his.

"Hurry! Hurry!" Riya scanned the tunnel around them.

Dai was finally able to get Tak free and he slid down in the seat. Szan had released his own restraints and grabbed him under a shoulder. Dai reached under the other one and they maneuvered his unconscious form out of the vehicle.

"Thanks," Dai said to Riya.

"No problem. Just get him out of here."

The aircar launched forward with a roar of the thrusters, the doors closing as it sped away. The metal door on the side of the tunnel suddenly slammed open, almost hitting Dai in the process.

"Give 'im here," Fix ordered. He rushed forward and grabbed Tak, picked him up, and hauled him across his broad shoulders. "Follow me."

Dai and Szan followed Fix through the doorway and onto the landing of a metal staircase. Fix rushed upward, taking the steps two at a time, with Dai and Szan following behind. Both of them struggled to keep up while the squat man seemed to almost effortlessly leap ahead. After several flights, the staircase ended at another landing and door. Fix barreled through it and into a small courtyard between mid-level buildings. The black smuggler ship sat in the middle, its engines already on.

Fix ran to the ship and dove inside, somehow managing not to hit Tak's head on the side. As Dai went to follow, she heard the small pops of projectiles burying themselves in the dirt around her. She looked in the air and saw that the airship had found them and was hovering over the buildings to their left. With a small prayer, Dai sprinted across the open ground and dove into the ship, running into Fix and Szan with an *umph*. Metallic pings sounded on the hull as the airship peppered them with fire.

"Get belted in," Fix ordered.

Dai crawled across the seats lining the floor of the ship, sat down, and furiously pulled a restraint across her body. Before she locked it into place, the smuggler shot straight into the air and then jumped forward. Tak was launched into the back hull with a thump, while Dai and Szan ended up caught in their restraints. Agony shot through her already injured shoulder, and she let out a gasp of pain.

"I said to get belted in," Fix taunted.

As Dai gingerly crawled onto a seat, she could see that they had already left the planet's atmosphere. Byrzyrk was spread below them. The rainbow-colored natural fauna marred with the splotches of gray of the cities. Dai tried to maneuver to where Tak was floating at the rear of the ship but was greeted with stabs of pain for her efforts.

"You okay?" Szan asked. He pulled himself along the seats to where Tak was. "I can get him strapped down. Just relax."

After he'd managed to fit Tak onto a seat and maneuver a belt around his waist, Szan returned to his seat and belted himself in. She could feel beads of sweat on her face from the effort.

With a sigh, Fix unbelted his restraints and turned to face them. "Okay, you can unbuckle yourselves now. We're probably going to be waiting here a bit."

"You sunnuva—" Dai reached out, trying to grab the man, but only managed to send herself floating off the seat and into the ceiling of the craft.

Chapter Fifteen

En Route to Hkar'Trush

After Dai had calmed down, Fix explained that the smuggler could not travel between planets so they'd need to wait until Riya could find another craft to take them. Dai wondered how long that would take. She couldn't imagine there was a plethora of ships just waiting to transport wanted persons between planets.

Tak slowly moaned as the effects of the sweeper began to wear off. Dai thought she heard a few words she recognized but couldn't understand anything he was saying. Small droplets of drool floated around his face, which was twisted in an expression of pain.

"Your friend's waking up," Fix observed. "He's gonna have a helluva headache for a while." He laughed. "Either Riya really likes you guys or she really wants something from you."

"He's got something stored in his head." Szan pointed at Tak. "Like data or something."

Fix looked at Tak as if he could peer inside his head and see what was in there. "Hmmm. I've heard of stuff like that. It's not cheap, though."

"Yeah, we kinda figured that," Szan replied.

Tak shook and then slowly looked around the cabin. "What happened? Did we get to Byrzyrk? Was... Did I dream it? What's going on?"

"You got swept, my friend," Fix said. "Glad to see your brain's not fried."

"Tak, do you remember meeting with Riya?" Dai asked. Tak considered the question for a moment, then slowly nodded. "Good. While you were under, whatever group's trailing you found us. We had to drag you out."

"Barely got away, too," Szan added. "If it wasn't for Riya and Fix, we'd be dead."

"Thanks." Tak looked at Fix. "What're we doin' now?"

"We're waitin' for our ride," Fix answered. "Didn't have time to line up a smooth departure so now we gotta hang in orbit until someone comes and gets us."

An alarm beeped in the front of the ship and Fix glided to the main console.

"Speaking of which." He pressed a button. "Hey, this is Fix. You gotta ride for us?"

"How's it goin', Fix?" Mujin's voice came from the speakers at the front of the cabin. "Seems like I got roped into this as well. Get ready. We're almost at your location."

"We're going back to the *Nero*?" Szan asked with surprise.

"I can think of worse ships to be on," Dai said. She just hoped that Rocious and Rat weren't on it anymore.

A few tics later, the *Nero* loomed in front of them, and Fix glided the small smuggler into one of its landing bays. After the doors had closed behind them and the atmosphere was pumped back into the chamber, they clambered out of the small ship. Dai winced as she scurried over the seats on the way out; her injured shoulder throbbed painfully under the artificial gravity of the *Nero*. She was thankful to know that the ship had a comprehensive aid station aboard. Tak stumbled as he exited the smuggler, clearly still feeling the effects of the sweep.

"Welcome back," Mujin said from the doorway. "I didn't think I'd be seeing you again so soon."

"Neither did we." Tak fumbled through his pockets and pulled out his chempen with a flourish, then took a deep hit. "We appreciate the ride to Perridion."

"We aren't going to Perridion." Mujin shook her head. "We're heading straight to Hkar'Trush."

"What?" Tak shouted. He placed a hand against the smuggler to steady himself. "I don't know if you understand what's going on, but that's basically a death sentence for me."

"I don't owe *you* a favor," Mujin said calmly. "I owe Riya one, and she said to take you to Hkar'Trush."

Tak took a deep breath. "Why?"

"I can explain," Dai said. "Riya told us that there's a message, or data, or something encoded in your brain. It must be why they're chasing after you."

"In my brain? There's nothing in there."

"I coulda told you that!" Fix bellowed with a laugh.

"You know what I mean." Tak shot the man an annoyed glance.

"What we're talkin' 'bout is called ECS, encrypted cerebral storage," Fix said. "I don't know much about it. But I do know that you can implant things into people's heads without them knowing. You can knock 'em unconscious or even do it while they're sleeping."

"So, if it's encrypted, we'll need a slicer to get it out," Tak concluded.

"And even then, it's unlikely they can do it," Fix added.

"So, you want me to go to Hkar'Trush to get the information out?" Tak asked.

"*We* don't give a crap," Mujin said. "Riya does."

"Well, I don't care what she wants," Tak said, clearly struggling to keep himself upright. "I'll go with you after you drop off Dai and Szan on Perridion."

"That ain't gonna happen," Fix said. "The boss told me to make sure you crack open that head of yours."

"Tak, you're going to need people with you," Dai said. "People who can help you."

"I've got friends on Hkar'Trush." Tak was now using the vehicle to support almost his full weight.

"That's not true," Szan said. "You told us before that you didn't have any friends."

"Fine. I've got someone who owes me. They'll help."

"Better than friends," Fix said with a small clap. "Either way, it doesn't matter. You're not going to Perridion."

"At least not now," Mujin said. "If you live, then we'll see."

Tak started to slide against the hull of the smuggler. Dai could see he wasn't going to give up, but she had no desire to see her friend fall face-first on the floor. She put his arm around her, wincing at the pain in her shoulder, and helped him right himself. "Let's talk about it later. You need to rest."

"We won't do anything until you recover," Mujin said. "She's right. You do need to rest."

"Fine, I'll lie down for a few tics." Tak started to hobble forward. "Then we'll figure this out."

After she'd helped Tak to his room, Dai went back to the ship's recreation room to find Mujin reclined in an alien chair, chempen in hand, staring out the large bank of windows. They were warping; the stars looked like small comets frozen in time, their tails stretching toward the front of the ship rather than behind.

"Such an odd view," Mujin said, somehow sensing Dai's presence. "The way the flex drive warps space around the ship is just so... unnatural."

"I thought we weren't going anywhere," Dai said. "You told Tak we would wait."

"Ah." She took a hit off the chempen. "I can't remember that far back."

"He's gonna be pissed."

"His *feelings* don't matter. Besides, he'll get over it. When we went out on our Binge, I knew we shouldn't have taken anything from the Fringe back with us, yet here we are." She motioned to the seat next to her. "You wanna seat?"

Dai lay down on the low-slung chair, wincing slightly as her shoulder throbbed.

"We'll get that looked at," Mujin said casually, noticing her wince. "You really should strap in when you're leaving a planet."

Dai felt a surge of anger but left the comment alone. She wasn't even going to humor the woman with a reply. "What about you? Why are you helping us?"

"I'm not. At least not intentionally. I'm helping Riya." She took another hit. "And I'm helping her because I owe her. Riya's family is generous, but they expect their favors to be returned."

"Then why is she helping us?"

Mujin chuckled and pushed a strand of green hair from her face. "Hell if I know. She hasn't told me, and I haven't asked. That's the way these things work, generally. What about you? You've had your chance to escape. Romance? Love? Lust?"

Dai shook her head. "No, nothing like that. Tak is a friend, that's all. And that's why I'm helping him."

Mujin turned in her chair to look at Dai. Her purple eyes seemed to shine in the dim light cast by the sconces in the wall.

"You *like* it." She smiled. "That's it, isn't it? You get a kick out of all this."

She's exactly right, Dai realized. She *did* enjoy it. In some strange way, she loved the excitement, the intrigue, the sense that something new was around each corner. It was all exciting to her, and for some reason, she felt more at home running from attackers than she had on the Triple-Deuce.

"Well, you hit the jackpot with Tak," Mujin continued. "From everything I've seen, he's got problems aplenty. We're going to take you to Hkar'Trush, but after that, it's up to you. Fix can help with some things, but he doesn't know the planet that well."

"Fix is coming with us?" Dai asked.

"Yeah, of course. Riya wants her own guy on the ground with you. To help and of course to report back. Fix may seem like a nice guy"—he seemed like anything but to Dai—"but never forget he works for Riya's family, not for you."

"Good advice."

"I give some, on occasion. But if you want one more piece, just remember. Have fun."

Dai chuckled, rolled her eyes, and waited for Mujin to laugh at her own joke. But she didn't, and her face remained as serious as ever.

"I'm not joking," Mujin added. "If you make it out of this alive, it'll be a helluva story. But since your chances are not the best, I'd say to at least have some fun."

The trip to Hkar'Trush was supposed to take a little under a cycle and Dai decided to get some sleep while she could. Mujin's advice might be misplaced, but there was an element that rang true. Dai should enjoy herself when she could, and getting rest was one of the top items on her priority list.

After waking up, she visited the med station, where one of the staff applied a concoction of chems and nanobots that greatly improved her shoulder. It wasn't fully healed, but she already felt a thousand times better than she had when she came onboard.

Then she decided to see how Tak was doing. When she got to his room, he was lounging in his bed, reading an ocutab. He looked a lot better compared to the last time she saw him. His skin was no longer sallow and waxy, he'd changed clothes, and from what Dai could smell, he had also taken a shower. When he saw her enter, he switched off the device and pushed himself up.

"You're looking better," Dai said as she flopped down on the chair at the end of the bed.

"Thanks." Tak rubbed his hand over his head sheepishly. "I didn't realize how bad that'd be. It was like every hangover I've ever had rolled into one."

"Well, at least it got Riya to trust you."

"I'm not sure if she trusts me. But she's certainly interested in what I've got in my head. But now I'm not sure we can trust her. I'm not sure exactly what she asked me when I was under, but I have a feeling it was pretty invasive."

"Do you know why she's helping us?" Dai asked. It was the question that kept nagging her over and over. Why would someone they'd met only cycles before be doing so much for them? Had Riya known they'd be on Faltran?

"No, but I think it's wrapped up in my parents. Somehow, she's connected to whatever happened to me." He grabbed his chempen from the bedside table and took a hit. "You ever get the feeling like you're a pawn, a puppet, but you don't know who's pulling the strings? That's me. I'm running away. I don't know who I'm running from, and I don't know why. I just know I *must* keep running."

Dai could understand that. She was caught up in whatever was happening to Tak but she could always leave. She'd already had several opportunities, but she hadn't taken them. For him, there was no option; he had to keep going or die. Dai thought it was somewhat ironic considering the level of privilege he'd grown up in.

"What are we running to?" Dai asked. "Is there really someone on Hkar'Trush who can help?"

"Maybe. I used to know a couple of people who could be helpful. But we'd barely arrived on Byrzyrk before whoever's chasing me found us. It'll be so much worse there."

"Maybe Fix can help us."

Tak groaned. "Is he really coming with us?"

"'Fraid so," Dai answered. "I think it's basically a condition of Riya's help. Do you know what's stored inside your head?"

"I have no idea what would be in there or who put it in." Tak let his head drop back against the bulkhead. "I was just a kid when this all started, maybe a little older than you." Dai let the comment go, but she certainly wasn't a kid. "I hadn't done anything, hadn't seen anything."

"So, what'll we do when we get there?" Dai asked.

"I've got a friend." He stopped and looked up for a moment. "Well, kinduva friend. He's helped me before. He's a lead at least."

"A lead?" Dai asked.

Tak nodded. "Yeah. I've been thinking about this. My plan was to disappear, right?" Dai nodded in understanding. "Well, that won't work. I gotta figure out who's following me and why. Otherwise, I'm just going to end up in the same place again."

Dai stood up and walked to the window, studying the luminescent streaks of the stars. Should she just leave? There was nothing keeping her with Tak. She could leave anytime. Tak wouldn't blame her; he'd tried to get her to leave already, in fact. But it just wasn't something she could do. It wasn't what she *wanted* to do.

"Well"—Dai turned around and smiled—"at least we've got a lead."

Dai couldn't resist visiting the *Nero*'s pool before they arrived at Hkar'Trush. If she was going to die, she'd get a swim in beforehand. She knew enough about ships and shipbuilding from her time on the Triple-Deuce to know that a pool was an incredible luxury. She'd never even heard of one being on a ship before seeing the *Nero*.

A screen displaying a bright sky and large, painfully bright sun covered the ceiling. Combined with the warm temperature of the room, Dai truly felt like she was at an outdoor pool on a sunny day. Of course, she'd never actually experienced that before, but it felt real enough to her.

She was surprised to see Szan already in the water, leaning back and watching the simulated sky.

"Guess great minds think alike," Dai said as she dropped her towel on a small lounge chair by the side of the pool and slid into the water. It felt like heaven. A combination of weightlessness and warmth that somehow washed away her worries—or at least moved them to the side.

"Yeah," Szan agreed. "We never were able to swim back at Nashoba." He smiled. "One time Rog and I snuck into the forest and swam in one of the ponds. It was freezing." He laughed. "That was my one and only time."

"This certainly isn't freezing," Dai said as she immersed her body, up to her neck, in the water.

"Yup," Szan agreed matter-of-factly.

Dai leaned her head against the edge of the pool and watched the clouds slowly float on the screen above her. For a moment, she imagined a life without fear or worry. Her mother would be with her, and her father would be miraculously alive. They would enjoy each other's company without worrying about Jackals, war, or people trying to hunt them down.

Dai pictured her father again. He'd died rotations ago. The pain of her loss was still there, always would be, but it was strange to be thinking of him now. Perhaps because he was a Centraler—which technically made her one, too. She knew he'd come to the Triple-Deuce from Hkar'Trush in search of a simpler life. Unfortunately, he'd died trying to return to the Central Worlds on a routine mineral shipment.

"What'll you do in the Central Worlds, Szan?" Dai asked languidly.

There was a pause. "I'm not sure. I have a dream of opening up my own shop one day. I figure I can sell gadgets and then repair them when they break. I don't know anything about running a store, though." A small chuckle. "We don't use money in Nashoba."

"Sounds like a good dream."

"I guess. It seems silly, but especially after what we've been through, it'd be nice to have a small shop somewhere and just build things for people. What about you?"

She'd never really thought about *living* in the Central Worlds. She'd always thought of herself as a Fringer and assumed she'd be like her mother and stay on the Triple-Deuce. But it was rapidly becoming clear that was not going to happen. How could she go back to living on a station for the rest of her life? Would she even be able to if she wanted?

"I don't know," she admitted. "I never thought I'd be living in the Central Worlds. All this wasn't supposed to happen."

"Wasn't it? How do you know what's *supposed* to happen?"

"I just mean it wasn't in my plan."

"From what you've told me, you didn't have a plan," Szan said. Dai could hear him moving toward the side of the pool. "I remember something one of my fathers told me. Often, the biggest obstacle to our dreams is ourselves."

Right then, living was Dai's biggest dream, but she knew that there was an unknown beyond that. If she survived, she'd have to see her mother and let her know she was okay. But Szan was right. Dai couldn't go back; she was irrevocably changed. Whether it was the Triple-Deuce or another station didn't matter. She couldn't go back to being an Orbiter.

"I don't think I'm ready to settle anywhere yet. There's still so much I haven't seen." The words tumbled out a bit, forming in Dai's brain and moving to her mouth before she had time to process them. "It's like an itch, you know? There's this itch that says I've got more to see, more to do. I've got to scratch it."

Szan hummed in acknowledgment.

"But I'll be the first customer at your store," Dai said warmly, turning to look at Szan.

"That'd be nice. Just remember you still gotta pay. I can't trust the credit of a drifter."

Dai laughed and splashed her friend.

Chapter Sixteen

Hkar'Trush

Byrzyrk was a large planet dominated by cities, but Hkar'Trush was a city that was an entire planet. From space, it was a metallic sphere, glistening in the light of the nearby star. When it had been discovered, there was no sentient life on the planet. The combined species of the Central Worlds had built large atmospheric generators and settled every bit of the planet's surface, even building over the oceans, until there was nothing that remained of the planet's natural habitats.

Tak had called the planet home for his entire childhood, but now, as he looked down at it for the first time in five rotations, it seemed foreign to him. It was just as unnatural, even more so, than a space station. A giant ball of lifeless metal floating in space. Having been to the Fringe and other planets in the Central Worlds, he'd begun to realize how strange his former home was.

He sat in one of the ship's observation lounges, chempen in hand, watching the planet grow closer through a large bank of windows. He had almost fully recovered from his sweep but still had a slight nagging headache.

Who put information in my head?

Tak couldn't fathom who would've had the access or means to embed something into his brain. It was a scary thought: that at some point, someone had messed with his mind without him knowing. His parents had operated in the highest circles of society, so almost anyone he had known had the means, but having access to him while he was at university would've been incredibly difficult. He also had the nagging question of the Jackal attack on the Triple-Deuce. Had it been directed at him? It still might have been a coincidence, though that was becoming harder to believe each time someone tried to kill him.

"What a pile of shrag," Fix commented, sitting in the chair next to Tak.

"It's got its good points."

"It's just a drain on the galaxy." Fix grabbed an olive from a silver tray next to him. "The Gaurz are right. This planet's become nothing but a temple to excess."

"Maybe," Tak admitted. "But it's still needed. You've had history before." Tak wasn't sure that was true; Fix didn't exactly exude academic excellence. "You know what it was like before the Central Worlds were formed. Hundreds of species warring against each other."

"Propaganda," Fix spat. "It's what bureaucrats say to justify their existence. You go out to any of the other Central Worlds." He popped another olive into his mouth. "Hell, go out to the

Fringe, and you'll see workers making things and producing value. These scum are there just to enrich themselves."

"This is coming from a smuggler and thief."

Fix laughed. "Smuggler, maybe. Thief, no. I ain't no Jackal. I provide services, valuable services, whether it's supplies, protection, or whatever else. I'm not a Jackal or like those people." He waved toward the window.

"You think you can get us into the Undercity?" Tak asked. "I've got to meet someone there."

"You were slummin' it, eh?" Fix chuckled.

"I made *some* friends down there and one of them *may* be able to help."

"Yeah, I can get you there." Fix grabbed a bite-sized piece of fruit from a nearby bowl and popped it into his mouth. "How easy it'll be depends on exactly where you need to go in the Undercity."

Tak had figured this would be the part where it got difficult. The area where they needed to go was almost completely inaccessible. It was to the Undercity as the Undercity was to the rest of the planet. Tak hadn't been there before; he'd only heard of it.

"Do you know the Cell?" Tak asked.

Fix's eyes narrowed. "The Cell? What do *you* know about it?"

"Not much, just that it's where we need to go."

The small man rubbed the thin layer of stubble on the top of his head. "Ah, that's a challenge. You can't just go walking down there. You got an invitation?"

"No." Tak wasn't even sure what Fix meant by an invitation. Was it a device? A code?

"Well, I'm gonna need to talk to some people in that case."

"I figured."

Fix spat a pit into the small bowl on the table between them and stared at Tak. "You might have gotten into some stuff on Hkar'Trush, but when we get down there, you do what I say. You aren't some rich heir anymore. I *might* be able to get you off this planet alive. It's my job, but I'm not dying for *you*."

"Got it," Tak said, struggling to meet the man's intense gaze. He wasn't sure what they'd find on Hkar'Trush, but he *was* sure that Fix meant every word he said.

After five cycles away from his home, Tak felt strange walking out into the main terminal of Hkar'Trush's Central Port. The planet had hundreds of ports, but Central was the oldest and largest. Ironically, it was also the best one for them to land in without attracting attention. They could hide in the crowds of aircars and travelers milling about the area. Every surface sparkled under the clinical white overhead lights. Holo-ads leapt from their frames, enticing passersby to various establishments. Tak had heard that Hkar'Trush's Central Port was the largest and most traveled in the galaxy, and he'd never had any reason to doubt that.

A skiff was already waiting for them at their landing pad's exit. Fix and Tak sat in the front, with Dai and Szan in the back. The vehicle glided through the busy passageways toward the port's main entrance. It was a ride Tak hadn't taken many times before. His family once had the resources and status to warrant traveling through the port's private hallways, away from the regular passengers and even the merely ultra-wealthy travelers.

Tak tried to appear calm as they glided through the large crowds. He reminded himself that no one would try and attack them in the port; there were too many eyes watching. Groups of every conceivable species walked around them, talking to each other in countless different languages. Thanks to his intellingua, Tak was able to make out a few scattered words as they zoomed past. The tiny devices were essential to living on a planet like Hkar'Trush.

"The dangerous part is coming up," Fix whispered to them. "When we leave the port, we'll be vulnerable until I can get us to a safe location. I've got no idea if anyone knows we're here, but we have to assume they do."

"So, what should we do?" Szan asked.

"Keep your head down, shut your mouth, and try to look inconspicuous."

As they sailed through the port's entrance, Tak obediently kept his head down and mouth shut, though he had no idea how to look inconspicuous. Instead, he looked down and tried to take in as much of the busy city beneath them as he could. Central Port was on the planet's Canopy, so most of the activity was below. Hkar'Trush was organized like a forest: the Canopy on top, with the Understory, Ground, and Undercity underneath. As they skimmed across a broad pedestrian bridge, he could see the mass of airships flying under them, traveling in almost uninterrupted lines. Underneath them, a mesh of tunnels wound between the buildings. Tak couldn't see the ground from where they were. All he could make out was a dark haze.

The elevated road led to a large lift that was filled with other vehicles and pedestrians. After a moment's pause, it descended, periodically stopping to let groups get on and off. The almost empty platform eventually came to a stop at the Ground, and their skiff sped out.

Tak knew that for those unaccustomed to it, Hkar'Trush's Ground could be ominous. Despite it being midday, dark shadows from the enormous buildings seeped across everything. When Tak looked up, he could faintly make out the light of the planet's sun peeking through the web of tunnels stretching between the buildings.

The Ground was the domain of the commoners, the class that made Hkar'Trush run. A light patina of grime covered its streets, and small pieces of refuse lay scattered on the road and sidewalks. Strands of light crisscrossed over the roads, casting everything in their pale glow. The pedestrians, each one seemingly a different species, scurried around them, their attitude one of sullen determination.

"Different than what I expected from Hkar'Trush," Szan said as he looked around.

"It's the part no one wants to see," Tak said. "The foundation of all the glitz and glamour that you hear about. All the people here are guest workers, allowed to stay on the planet for a few rotations before they have to return home. They get allocated quarters here in the Ground and save or send their credits back home."

"How often were *you* down here?" Dai asked.

"Probably never," Fix said.

"I didn't come down here much when I was in crèche," Tak admitted. "But in university, well, I made some friends and came down more often than you'd expect."

Fix looked back at him with a raised eyebrow.

"My friends lived down here." Tak rubbed his arms and shivered slightly. It was downright cold in the shadows. "They helped me learn how this place really works. It's the only reason I'm still alive."

"We're here," Fix announced.

They turned down a small tunnel that descended into the bowels of a building. The faint sheen of grime grew to a blanket that seemed to coat everything in the narrow passageway. Work lights jutted off the walls, casting faint halos of light around them.

The ramp twisted as it dove beneath the surface, sometimes seeming to loop in on itself. Tak had never been down it before and half expected them to end up going in circles.

"This is the way to the Undercity?" Dai asked.

"It's *one* way," Fix said. "There's tons of 'em."

The tunnel widened until it was almost a proper road again. Wire fences stretched from the litter-covered ground to the ceiling, blocking them from the doors and loading bays on either side.

"This is where all the supplies for these buildings used to come in," Tak explained. "These loading docks must have been decommissioned a long time ago. As Hkar'Trush grew, they built up the towers and these weren't enough to support them anymore."

The skiff turned, threading an opening in a fence that was so narrow the metal wires scraped against its sides with an earsplitting screech. Dai gave a slight start at the sound, hands clutching the small arms of her seat.

"You think we're safe?" she asked.

"Who knows?" Fix said breezily. "Best not to worry about it. Nothin' we can do about it now."

It was easier said than done. Tak wondered about their safety himself. If anyone attacked them here, they wouldn't stand a chance. Still, he felt he should say *something* to reassure his friends.

"I wouldn't worry too much," he said, trying to put as much confidence in his voice as possible. "There're almost no sensors in the area, and it'd be impossible for someone to monitor every entrance to the Undercity." Dai—and Szan—seemed less than reassured.

The dusty path they were on led to a hole that seemed torn into a small rockface. Metal panels were strewn around it, clearly having been removed to reveal the entrance.

"Hold on tight," Fix called back. "This can get bumpy."

Almost as soon as the words left his mouth, the skiff dropped, eliciting a small squeak of surprise from Szan. The road had turned into a rough path that wound through a cavern with a steep decline. Although it was hard to make out its walls in the small glow of the skiff's headlamp, Tak thought the cave looked to be natural, one of the only natural things on the planet.

They bumped along, continuing to delve deeper into the planet's crust until they turned a corner and an enormous cavern greeted them. A blanket of multicolored lights stretched below, making Tak feel as if they were in a ship descending onto a planet's surface. Avenues and small buildings became evident as they followed the path down the wall to the base of the enormous cavern.

"This is amazing," Dai gasped. "It's a whole other city."

"Yup." Tak remembered his amazement at seeing the Undercity for the first time. "Except there are thousands of these, all across the planet. The Undercity's not just one place, but many, an entire system."

"Who lives down here?" Szan asked.

"Freaks, mainly," Fix said flippantly. "Creatures that aren't able to fit in. They either leave the planet and go to places like the Fringe or head down here."

"Auggies, artists, dissidents," Tak added, exasperated. "Those that tend to think differently."

"Are there communes down here?" Szan asked.

"Yeah, there's a bunch," Tak replied. Szan gave a thoughtful hum.

"This particular area is called Tzoran," Fix said. "Named after some smuggler eons ago."

"This where you hung out?" Szan asked, looking at Tak.

Tak shook his head. "No, I've never been to Tzoran, but they're all similar, built in a large cave like this."

The skiff reached the cavern floor and they flew over one of the streets that wound its way through the squat buildings. There were no aircars or airships in the cavern; the largest vehicle that Tak could see was their own. The sidewalks were filled with a wide variety of creatures dressed in outfits that would be unthinkable in any other part of the city. The Grounders didn't want to fit in, and their clothing made that point clear.

Fix pulled into a small building that seemed to have been hastily constructed out of refuse and old scraps. Tak's first impression as they entered was that the building was abandoned. The rooms appeared to be completely empty except for the ancient furniture scattered around the dusty floor.

Fix hopped down from the skiff. "Follow me." He led them around a pile of broken chairs, knelt down, and pulled open a small hatch in the floor. A set of handholds allowed them to descend a shaft to a passageway that led to a small room that had been carved out of the rock—Tak could see the crude scrapes and gouges from the tools that must have been used.

"Fix!"

An enormous Anaryk appeared out of the shadows in a corner, one of its three tentacles extended. Fix grabbed the green appendage and gave it a quick shake. Tak had known a few Anaryk and he still found them odd. They reminded him of an undersea creature with their tentacles and rotund bodies.

"Eight," Fix said with a smile, "can't believe you're still oozing around here."

"I didn't think I'd see you again, flesh sack," the alien retorted with a small burble. It turned its cluster of eyes at the others. "Who are these?"

"Just some people I'm helping out," Fix replied. "I'd tell you names, but you'd forget them anyway."

Eight burbled with what Tak was pretty sure was laughter. "You all look the same. Skinny brown bags of bones."

"Right back at you, slug."

"What're you doin' here?" Eight asked. "Last time, you left in a bit of a hurry. I didn't think I'd see you back on Hkar'Trush."

"Gotta keep makin' those credits. You know how it is."

"Well, try and be a little less violent this time."

Fix shrugged. "Hey, is Boss in?"

"In the back." Eight pointed to the other side of the room with its tentacle. "They're not in a good mood."

"You know how charming I can be," Fix replied with a wink. "I'll catch up with you later."

Tak and the others followed Fix past the Anaryk and into a large room filled with cubicles occupied by workers sitting behind desks, furiously tapping at consoles. They filed through a small gap in the cubes until they came to a door with something scribbled on it in a language Tak wasn't familiar with.

"Boss!" Fix threw the door open, causing it to hit the wall with a clang. "Bet you thought you'd never see me again, you sunnuva bitch!"

Dai shrieked as a silvery form streaked from a desk on the opposite side of the room and jumped on top of Fix, knocking him to the ground. The creature picked him up and shoved him against the wall before Tak even had time to process what was happening.

The creature was humanoid, with a tall, slender frame that belied its very obvious strength. Its metallic skin appeared almost liquid as it glistened in the light.

Tak gasped when he realized what he was looking at. Boss was a Gyrdra. They were the stuff of legend, incredibly fast, intelligent, and ruthless. It was only through the formation of the Central Worlds, hundreds of rotations ago, that their plunder across the galaxy had been stopped. And now one of them was in front of him, holding Fix against the wall by his neck.

Chapter Seventeen

The Undercity, Hkar'Trush

"A little... too... slow," Fix gasped. His face was turning a bright shade of red, but he still wore the same smile. Tak realized the man had somehow pulled out his pistol and had the barrel firmly planted against Boss's side.

With a growl of disgust, Boss released Fix and glided back behind their desk. "Ugh, I hate Humans."

"What the hell?" Dai hissed in Tak's ear. "What's a Gyrdra doing here?"

Gyrdra were essentially banned from the Central Worlds. The long and brutal conflict that created the Central Worlds, called the War of Unification, had been long over, but the memories of scarred planets and wiped-out cities hadn't faded. Dai had seen them in holos, but seeing one in person was a completely different experience. She felt a shiver of fear as she looked at their almost featureless face; this was a thing from nightmares.

"Boss, you silly bastard," Fix said lightly. "You may be faster. But I'm quicker."

"That doesn't make sense. Like everything you say." Boss drummed their fingers on the desktop. "Why are you here annoying me?"

"I'm on the clock this time. Need some help. Not for me, but for my employer."

The only feature on the Gyrdra's smooth, silvery face was its mouth, making it very difficult to gauge their emotions. Boss's mouth curled upward in what a Human would call a smile. Whether it was good or bad, Dai had no idea. "Your employer has been an ally before. What do they need?"

"I knew you'd see the light." Fix sat down in the chair opposite Boss. "We need an invitation to the Cell."

"Of course you do." Boss emitted a series of chirps. "Need anything else? Perhaps a few billion credits?"

"Sure." Fix placed his feet on the desk. "That'd be helpful."

"If I had my way, you'd be killed," Boss said. "As slowly and as painfully as possible."

"Fortunately for me—and unfortunately for you and a bunch of other people—you can't have your way," Fix replied.

"It'll take a few standards to get an invitation." Boss tapped on an ocutab they had grabbed from the desk. "Walk around with your fellow meat sacks and come back."

"Well, there's one other thing." Fix took his feet from the desk. "Someone's tracking this one." He pointed at Tak. "And they're good. Very good. I bet they already know we're on-planet."

"Why the hell did you bring him here, then?" Boss stood up, their skin rippling.

Fix laughed. "Figured it would provide a little incentive for you to go quickly." His laughter stopped. "Seriously, though, whoever's tracking him is no joke."

Boss picked up their ocutab, which emitted a small click as it scanned Tak. The Gyrdra held up a finger and then let out a small sigh. Dai wondered what was going through the creature's mind. They were from a race that had almost destroyed the entire galaxy, and there they were, sitting in a small, dingy office beneath Hkar'Trush.

"Well, no wonder you're being followed. Your friend has a billion-credit bounty on her head."

"*His* head," Tak interjected. Dai knew the Gyrdra actually had three genders—he, she, and they—and could get confused by the binary designations of Humans, but she couldn't believe Fix felt *now* was the time to get all snippy about pronouns.

"Whatever. You all look the same to me. Odd angles and strange hair." Boss threw down the ocutab. "You've got every single mercenary in the Central Worlds on your ass. It's amazing you've made it this far."

"You got any screens?" Fix asked.

"I've got *one* viscreen," Boss replied. "Your friend can borrow it, but *she*"—Tak growled—"better make sure to take care of it. It's worth more than all your lives. I'll meet you at the usual spot in a few. Get the screen on your buddy over there and stay low."

Fix stood up. "Ya know, Boss, everyone says you're a pile of excrement, but I'd say they're only half right. You're a pile of *useful* excrement."

The silvery creature managed to jump over the desk and throw Fix out the open office door in the blink of an eye.

"I guess that's our signal to leave," Tak said.

"Ya think?" Dai asked.

It was strange seeing Tak with the viscreen on. After leaving Boss's office, Fix led them back to Eight, who'd provided the strange sack-like apparel. It looked like nothing special, just a black bag with a mesh of thin wires on the outside. But after a few adjustments and some quick taps on an ocutab by Eight, the sack constricted around Tak's head, and soon, another person was looking at Dai.

Tak looked at himself in an ocutab, humming slightly as he examined his new features. "Can you add a mustache? I've always wanted one. Last time I had some work done, I forgot to tell them to add facial follicles."

"Sure, one sec." Eight tapped at the tab's screen and an enormous black mustache appeared above Tak's smiling mouth.

"Can I?" Dai asked, her hand hovering by Tak's head. He nodded. She ran her hand along his cheek and could feel the rough texture of the viscreen. Her fingers left small black trails that rippled and disappeared after a sec.

"Feels different," Dai said, "but other than that, you can't tell the difference."

"Boss said you got some serious heat on you," Eight said, undulating two of its appendages.

"Yeah, apparently there's quite a bit of credits for whoever finds us," Fix replied.

"Better get out of here, then." Eight slapped Fix across the back. "We'll meet you at the normal place."

"You'd better believe it, slime trail," Fix said.

They walked out of the Anaryk's laboratory and into the main room of Boss's operation. As they headed back toward the ladder, Dai glanced around the room; the workers continued to methodically tap on their consoles. She wondered what they could be doing. Why would a clearly illicit underground operation need so many people working on consoles?

"We'll need to walk around a bit," Fix said after they'd returned to the streets of Tzoran. He winked at Dai. "Looks like you're getting a bit of a field trip today since we need to wait for Boss to get our invitation. The trick'll be moving around but not being noticed. Sucks we're all Human. That *will* attract a few eyes."

Dai had seen aliens countless times growing up; some of her best friends had been aliens. But the Triple-Deuce had been a Human station. Aliens were the exception. It was a jarring feeling to be on a planet where they were the minority—well, maybe not the minority, but definitely not the majority. Although most species coexisted, each station or planet usual-ly had one that was dominant. Since none were native to it, Hkar'Trush was a true melting pot of everything.

Her sense of discomfort was not helped by the dress of the aliens around them. Loud colors, strange pieces of garments missing, decorative spikes. It seemed like every single person had decided to dress in their own jarring way. It was a long way from the muted coveralls she was used to seeing growing up.

As they meandered through Tzoran, Dai couldn't help sneaking glances at Tak, looking to see if she could see any imperfections in the viscreen. There was nothing. She never would have known it was him if she hadn't seen the screen placed over his head herself.

She stopped in front of a small stage where a Tyraloo was standing. The bluish alien came up to her knees and had a face that she could only think of as adorable with its large eyes and small mouth fixed in an O. As a crowd of onlookers watched, the creature began to sing a low, soulful note, a sound that seemed to wipe away all the noise of the area. Another note came out, and another. The creature weaved them together, creating an auditory fabric the likes of which she'd never heard before. It was slow and deep, nothing like the rapid-fire music she normally listened to. Dai felt a sense of peace, as if nothing mattered but the moment she was in. She could tell everyone around her felt it, too, even Fix. They all stood, still as statues, watching with placid expressions.

"Beautiful," Szan gasped, his mouth open.

Dai nodded. She didn't think she could speak. She felt the emotions well within her. This was what she'd wanted. Adventure. Travel. She was seeing and experiencing things she'd never even heard of. Was the danger worth it? She realized that the danger was part of it. The excitement of knowing they could be caught at any time somehow made everything she was seeing even more exciting.

Fix shook his head, his trance broken by Szan's whisper. "Come on, we gotta go." He roughly pulled at their shirts. "Too many people here."

Dai reluctantly followed him and continued through the subterranean city. She tried to remain inconspicuous, but there was too much to see. She tried not to stare at aliens she'd only heard about before—and even some that she hadn't—as she walked past stalls filled with exotic foods and strange devices, the purposes of which she could only guess at. After several prompts from Szan, Fix let them stop at a small restaurant to grab some food. Dai continued to look around as they sat in the corner and ate their food, each one picking something from a different species. She chose a Grosk dish that Patroller Krishnal had always gone on about when they were waiting in line for food on the Triple-Deuce. She wasn't sure it was exactly to her taste—it was a bit too bland—but still was glad at the chance to finally try it.

As they finished their meals, a small tone sounded from Fix's combrace. "Finish up," he ordered. "We're gonna go meet Boss."

"How do you know we can trust them?" Tak asked.

"They're a good friend. Never let me down before."

"They attacked you twice," Dai said flatly.

Fix rolled his eyes. "They didn't attack me. If they'd done that, one of us would have been dead. We just have a love-hate relationship. They hate me and I love it that way."

"There's a huge bounty on my head," Tak said. "What's to say they won't turn us in?"

"Well, kid, I'm guessing you haven't met a lot of Gyrdra." Fix took the last bit of his sandwich and stuffed it into his mouth with a flourish. "They aren't like that. It's not their nature to lie or stab people in the back like that. Boss'll tell you straight up what they think about you. If they're gonna stab you, they'll do it to your face."

"That doesn't exactly fill me with warm feelings," Tak said.

Fix stood up. "Time to go. Trust me, if there's one thing you don't need to worry about, it's Boss betraying us."

As they walked, Fix explained that the normal meetup spot he had with Boss was the waste treatment facility for this part of the Undercity. It was perfect since no one, patrollers included, ever wanted to be there. "Great place to dispose of bodies," he confided to Dai.

The treatment facility's entrance was at the edge of Tzoran's large cavern. Dai never would have known what the opening led to; it was a featureless round hole drilled into the side of the cavern. Fix confidently strode through the opening, barely looking around as he entered.

"Boss betrayed us," he whispered as they walked through the metal-lined corridor. "Or *someone* did."

"What?" Tak asked. "Didn't you just say that they *couldn't* betray us?"

"It's not like it's a science." Fix grunted. "Other people have a way of surprising you. They're the big unknown. Give me a lovesynth any day."

"Gross," Dai said. She hadn't needed to hear that.

"How do you know that we've been betrayed?" Szan asked.

"Intuition," Fix spat. "Or how about I'm not gonna tell you? You're just gonna haveta trust me." He reached behind his back and pulled out a small pistol. "Just be ready to run. They'll have already posted people at the entrance, but there are other ways out."

Suddenly, Dai's joy and excitement from touring Tzoran were gone. She wondered how she could have ever thought this was fun. It seemed like everyone in the galaxy wanted to kill them. She couldn't live a life like this, where every meeting could be a trap.

"What can we do?" Tak asked. His synthetic face appeared calm and completely in control. She had to believe it was only the viscreen, though; she was terrified.

Dai felt her eyes water as the smell of sulfur and ammonia began to grow stronger. Szan and Tak obviously were affected as well; they began to sniff and Szan went so far as to hold his sleeve over his mouth.

"Ah, yes." Fix grinned, noticing their reaction. "Now you see why no one is ever here."

The tunnel led to a large chamber filled with several large metal vats of raw sewage. An elevated grated floor ran between the tops of the vats. Dai followed Fix onto the metal walkway and gagged as she saw lumps bobbing in the cloudy liquid filling the vats.

"Yup, not a single person," Fix said.

Boss appeared from the far corner of the room, their steps surprisingly quiet against the metal walkway. As they walked toward Fix, their skin morphed from matte black to the liquid chrome it had been back in their office.

"What's the story, Boss?" Fix had his sidearm trained on the Gyrdra.

Boss tilted their head. "What the hell are you talkin' about?"

"I know you've got people here," Fix said. "We're leaving this room."

"God, you are the biggest pain in my—"

The deafening report of a high-powered firearm ripped through the room and Boss fell back against a metal railing. Dai dropped to the floor, causing knives of pain to shoot up her arms as they hit the grating at her feet.

She looked back to where she'd heard the shot and saw Eight slither into the room.

"Eight?" Fix asked from the ground next to her.

The Anaryk pointed a large rifle at them with one of its tentacles. As it climbed the stairs onto the steel walkway, two other aliens trailed behind it, their weapons also trained on the four Humans.

"Hey, Fix," Eight said cheerily. "Sorry to be the bearer of bad news, but your friends are too valuable to let go."

Fix shook his head ruefully, then looked back at his former friend, his eyes narrowed to slits. "Eight? You turned us in?"

"Sorry, man. But you come in with these Humans that are worth a billion credits each. If you aren't gonna turn 'em in, then I will. It's just too easy."

"Ya know, you're a real piece of shrag," Fix spat.

"You and Boss are too soft. Boss with their Gyrdra morals and you with your loyalty. There's no right or wrong. There's only the powerful and weak. When I was a hatchling..." Eight waved its tentacles as it continued to drone on about its youth and the vagaries of the universe.

Fix swiveled his head to look at the other three Humans as Eight spoke, his eyes darting to the tanks below them. Dai's stomach lurched as she realized what he was trying to communicate.

Not in the tanks.

Fix jumped up and sprinted at a superhuman speed toward Boss's limp form while firing at Eight. He dove toward the unconscious Gyrdra and, in a single movement, grabbed them around the waist and rolled into one of the vats. At the same time, Tak and Szan rolled off the sides of the walkway and dropped into the vats on either side. As Dai watched her friends dropping off the metal grating, she held her breath and rolled. The three aliens started to fire, and slugs flew over her head as she felt herself drop from the elevated walkway.

Right into a vat of sewage.

Chapter Eighteen

Hkar'Trush

Tak's breath was forced from his body as he hit the frigid water. For a few secs, he was completely under the surface and could feel lumps brushing against him. Lumps he'd rather not think about.

He floated to the surface and tried to open his eyes before the stinging made him slam them shut. He felt something pulling at his legs and fought to stay afloat before several rounds hit the water near him, forcing him to dive. The force pulling him down grew stronger. At first, he tried to fight it. Then he realized that his only chance at freedom was at the bottom of the disgusting sewage-filled vat. The water must be getting sucked *somewhere*. He relaxed and let the water take him, hoping it would be somewhere he could breathe.

Tak was dragged along the bottom of the tank and ejected through an opening in the center. The current pulled him down a narrow pipe, battering him back and forth against its unyielding sides. As he bumped along the pipe, Tak's lungs started to burn. He felt a sense of primal panic as they called out for air.

He wondered how much time he had until his body's natural instincts gave in and he either passed out or involuntarily gulped down the sewage. It wouldn't be much longer; every fiber of his body wanted him to inhale.

Suddenly, he was flying, falling. He gasped as he sailed through the air, but the breath he'd taken was immediately knocked from his body as he landed on his side. The smell was overpowering. It was everywhere: around him, in his eyes, his mouth, his lungs. He couldn't open his eyes but he could hear the thunder of water crashing around him as he began to retch violently.

Tak's eyes stung as he slowly opened them. He was on all fours in a shallow stream of filth that coursed through a wide cavern. Several pipes jutted from the wall behind him, pouring raw sewage into the room. As he stood up, wiping the streamers of drool from his mouth, Tak heard a splash and groan as Szan was ejected from a pipe behind him.

The man lay prone on the ground and then tried to push himself up, vomiting as he did.

"Szan, it's Tak. You okay?"

"I... I think so." Szan rubbed his eyes against his shirt. "Where... are we?"

"I dunno."

Boss and Fix flew out from a different tube in a jumble of silver and brown limbs. Tak half expected to hear a clang of some sort when the Gyrdra landed, but they hit the stony ground with the same fleshy thump as Fix.

"Hey!" Fix shouted, his eyes closed, as he raised his hands to feel around him. "Anyone out there?"

"We're here," Tak said. He walked over, grabbed the man's hand, and pulled him up. Fix shook his head with a spray of squalid water and blinked his bloodshot eyes.

"Help me with them." Fix gestured at Boss. "Boss got hit. I've got no idea how badly, though. They're alive at least." He looked around. "We got everyone?"

Tak realized they were missing Dai. He'd thought he'd seen her start to roll, but it had been so chaotic that he wasn't positive what had happened. He started to panic. He couldn't bear to be responsible for her death.

"Dai's not here," he said frantically.

Fix cursed.

"She doesn't know how to swim," Szan shouted. "She's an Orbiter."

"You don't need to know how to swim to get sucked down a pipe," Fix said. "Grab Boss. If she's not here by the time we leave, then she didn't make it."

The man's words and clinical attitude pissed Tak off. He opened his mouth to tell Fix off but realized there was nothing to say. What could they do if Dai didn't appear soon? If nothing else, they'd have to leave where they were to look for her. He took a deep breath and resolved to find Dai if it was the last thing he did.

"You know a way out of here?"

"I know the general direction," Fix said. "Now help."

Tak bent down and grabbed one of Boss's arms. He expected their skin to be cool and as hard as metal, but it was soft, warm, and almost impossibly slippery. Szan reached down and grabbed the other arm, and together, they were able to pull the unconscious alien out of the shallow stream of filth.

As they set Boss down on the rocky ground, Dai catapulted out of one of the pipes and landed in the shallow stream underneath. She lay on her side in a motionless heap as Tak and Szan ran to her. They grabbed her arms and dragged her out of the water, setting her down next to the Gyrdra. Tak dropped down and placed his head against her chest. He couldn't hear any breathing, but then again, the water made it impossible to tell for sure. He grabbed her wrist and felt a pulse, then turned his head to see her chest faintly rising and falling. Dai suddenly shuddered, turned her head, and vomited onto the ground.

"You okay?" Tak asked quietly after she was done.

She looked at him groggily as if confused by the question.

"We don't have time," Fix said impatiently. "I don't know shrag about Gyrdras, but we need Boss alive. I'm not gonna leave them here. They have the info we need. I know some other places here in the Undercity where we can lay low. Places that slimy piece of trash Eight doesn't know about."

Fix ordered Tak and Szan to carry Boss's unconscious body and led the group along the winding stream of waste that coursed underground. The dimly lit tunnel narrowed, and the stream disappeared into a large hole in the middle, leaving a dry path beyond. They continued to walk forward, following the tunnel as it curved. Tak was pretty sure they were climbing. They reached a metal door embedded into the rock, and Fix tried forcing it open before giving up and blasting off the lock with his weapon.

The door opened to the edge of Tzoran and the city's lights rising like a small fire in front of them. Tak was glad they were far enough away that it was unlikely there were any witnesses as they emerged wounded and covered in shrag.

Fix kept his pistol at the ready as he led them around the perimeter of the subterranean city, his eyes darting around. Thankfully, Boss was much lighter than they looked, and Tak and Szan had no trouble carrying the creature. Dai clearly hadn't recovered from her experience in the vats and panted and sometimes had to bend over and clutch her chest for a few secs. Tak didn't know what exactly had been in the water, but he suspected she'd swallowed some of the vile liquid and it was affecting her.

Fix stopped and turned around to look at Tak and the others. "Listen, we got to go through the streets a bit to get where we need to be. The screen's still working so you should be okay. But we all smell like shrag and we're carrying an unconscious Gyrdra, so we're gonna stick out like a Jackal at a kid's birthday. Y'all do exactly what I say, when I say. Got it?"

They nodded in understanding.

"Okay, we're gonna have to be real quiet and careful."

They walked toward the city, trying their best to appear in-conspicuous while carrying a silver-hued alien that was forbidden on the planet. When they reached the edge of the city, Fix led the way, jumping between buildings, then motioning for them to either hide or follow him. Progress was slow, and Tak expected to see Eight and his goons at any time, but the only other people they saw seemed to want nothing to do with them, especially when they saw the unconscious Gyrdra.

As they reached a small domed building, Fix ran ahead and ushered them through the front door, leading them into what Tak guessed was a home. Several mismatched pieces of furniture were arranged around a threadbare rug that had probably once been considered luxurious.

"Okay, you can put them here." Fix pointed to a dingy couch at the edge of the room. "If we weren't followed, we should be safe for now."

"Is this someone's home?" Szan looked at the small holos lining the shelf next to him.

"Yes," Fix said. "And you'd better be on your best behavior, Muner. This isn't one of your homes, where you can take anything you want."

"That's really not how communes—"

Szan's protest was cut short by a small, delighted squeal. A small girl, perhaps ten cycles old, ran from the doorway on the far side of the room and wrapped herself around Fix's waist.

"Fix, you're back!" the girl shouted. "I missed you so much!"

Fix knelt down and hugged the girl back. "I missed you, too, kiyomi. Now, where's your mom?"

The little girl pointed at the doorway just as a young woman, no more than Tak's age, entered, brandishing a small knife in front of her. When she saw Fix, her mouth opened in astonishment, and she quickly tucked the knife into a flap in her sleeve.

"Fix, I thought you were dead!" She rushed forward. "Where have you been?"

Fix stood up, his hands turned up in an apologetic manner. "Jae, I'm sorry to rush in here like this, but I didn't know where else to turn."

"We're just glad you're alive," Jae said. "Myeong cried before going to bed for cycles when you left. We weren't sure you'd get off-planet alive."

Fix stood up and chuckled. "It'll take more than that to kill me." He patted the young girl's hair. "Isn't that right, my little kiyomi?"

The girl nodded, her jet-black ponytail bobbing up and down.

"Do you know anything about Gyrdra?" Fix asked, motioning toward Boss.

Jae gave a small start as if realizing there were other people in the room. Her eyes widened as she saw Boss's body, and she dropped to her knees next to the couch and started to examine the Gyrdra. "They've been shot. Hard to say how bad it is."

"Well, I know that," Fix said. Tak noted that his voice held none of the venom and sarcasm it normally did. "Can you help them?"

"Maybe. I'll need a few things, though."

"Okay, that's good enough for me." Fix motioned to the others. "These are my associates. I've been asked to make sure they don't die. Just tell me what you need and I'll get it."

Jae looked at the others skeptically. "You're keeping them alive? Really?"

Fix scowled. "What?"

"You don't exactly have the best track record."

Fix chuckled good-naturedly. "This time'll be different. You know what they say? If at first you don't succeed, try, try again."

For some reason, his words didn't inspire a lot of confidence in Tak.

After Jae gave him a list of medical supplies she needed, Fix left and she forcefully escorted the others to a small shower in the back to rinse off. Tak couldn't remember the last time he'd been so eager to get clean. Dai asked Tak and Szan to go ahead of her, saying that she wasn't feeling quite right. Jae set towels on the floor for the girl to lie on as Tak was entering the shower room. When he came back out, he found her sleeping with Jae kneeling over her, a small device in her hand.

"What happened to her?" she asked.

"We went through sewage vats," Tak said. "She can't swim. I think she inhaled some of the stuff."

Jae sucked in air through her teeth. "That's not good. Sewage is just a cocktail of toxins. Several species have waste that's poisonous to Humans. It explains what I'm seeing, though." She stood up. "Your friend's body is shutting down."

"What can we do?" Szan asked with a worried expression. He'd started to go into the shower room but turned back when they'd started talking.

"I've got some medicines that should be able to help," Jae said soothingly. "A toxin is a toxin, whether in sewage or in someone's drink. I should be able to stabilize her at least."

Jae firmly instructed Szan to take a shower and asked Tak to stay near Dai to help her if she needed anything while she got supplies from the other room. As Tak sat next to his friend, Myeong crept next to him and then plopped on the floor, cross-legged.

He decided to try and make conversation with the small girl. "Your mom a doctor?"

The girl shook her head, causing her straight black hair to cascade around her face like a curtain. "She used to be a doctor's aide. Then... something happened, and, well, Fix came and helped us. Brought us here to the Undercity to be safe."

"*What* happened?"

Myeong looked away. "I don't wanna talk about it."

Tak left it alone and they sat together quietly, the soft hiss of the shower in the other room filling the silence.

"What's out there like?" Myeong asked.

"Out where?"

"The Fringe. My mom said you're from the Fringe. Is it like they say? Do you carry guns all the time and ride strange animals?"

Tak laughed. "Well, I'm not a Fringer." Myeong looked disappointed. "But Szan and Dai are. It's not like the stories. There aren't gunfights all the time or anything like that. It's just emptier with more nature and less city."

"I'd like that." Myeong looked at Dai with renewed interest.

"Fix has been out to the Fringe. Didn't he tell you about it?"

"He just tells me to stay in the Central Worlds and to study hard in crèche so I don't 'become a burden on society.'"

"Good advice." He noticed the worried look on the girl's face and realized she must really care about the man. "So besides studying at crèche, what do you like to do?"

Myeong gleefully talked about her favorite holos, her art, and wandering around the Undercity with her friends. Tak made sure to continue to pepper the girl with questions, distracting her from the two unconscious people in her home and the fact that her friend was out scrounging for medicine to keep them alive. He tried to appear attentive while still watching Dai, looking to make sure her chest rose and keeping a finger on her wrist to feel her pulse.

Jae strode back in the room, a small cloth satchel in her hand. She knelt next to Dai, pulling out a chemsert and several opaque vials.

"These are wide-spectrum antidotes and antivenoms. Should at least stop the damage." She pressed the chemsert against Dai's neck and the device released a small hiss as it injected the drugs into her system. After putting it back in the bag, she pulled a band out and wrapped it around Dai's wrist. A small holo display appeared, showing—from what Tak could tell—her vitals. Based on Jae's reaction, the data wasn't good.

"She's worse than I thought. There's nothing to do now but wait. We'll know in a cycle if it's working." She turned to Tak and Szan—who'd returned from the shower. "I need to check both of you as well. Sounds like you didn't ingest the stuff, but you're probably still affected."

Sure enough, they both had mild poisoning symptoms. After a small injection each, Jae told them they shouldn't have any issues.

"What about Fix?" Szan asked. "He was in there as well."

"Fix's an auggie," Jae replied. "And Boss shouldn't have an issue either since they're a Gyrdra."

"Auggie?" Szan asked.

"Means he's augmented," Tak explained. He hadn't really considered it, but Fix being an auggie made a lot of sense. "Auggie's have biological and mechanical augmentations. Run faster, lift more. That sort of stuff."

"Really? I didn't notice anything different about him."

"Considering his line of work, I'm not surprised," Tak said. "He wouldn't want to be too obvious about it."

"Not obvious?" Jae asked incredulously. "The man has metal circuits on his skin."

Tak flushed. "I thought they were just tattoos."

"Fix is the most augmented person I've ever met," Jae said. "I don't know how many he's got, but it's enough that he can do things you and I couldn't even dream of."

"Myeong told me that he helped you out," Tak said, trying to change the subject to something less embarrassing.

"Yeah." Jae nodded. "I was in the wrong place at the wrong time, and he got me out of it. We wouldn't be here if it wasn't for him."

"What did—"

The door launched open, and Fix barged into the room, his face red from exertion. He held out the large bag he had strung over his shoulder. "Here ya go. There're people in the area snooping around. I'm pretty sure it's some of Eight's friends."

"They know about me?" Jae asked with alarm.

"No way," Fix said. "Someone must have caught sight of us on the way here. That one"—he pointed at Boss—"don't exactly blend in."

Jae grabbed the bag and knelt by the couch, laying the contents neatly on the floor, looking over each piece carefully. She gave a satisfied hum, walked out of the room, and returned with an ocutab.

"Okay, let's see what we got," she mumbled to herself as she read from the device. "Gyrdras are a bit strange in that they don't heal. They're harder to injure than a Human but also a helluva lot harder to fix."

She placed a round device topped with a screen on Boss's abdomen and slowly pushed it across the alien's silver skin.

After a few tics, she let out a triumphant shout. "Found it! The slug's still inside their body."

Jae consulted the ocutab, then grabbed a small rod and gently inserted it into the entry wound in Boss's side. She carefully maneuvered it deeper into the Gyrdra's body and then pulled it out with a small yelp of triumph; the slug was attached to the end. She grabbed a different device that looked like a cube, suspended inside another wireframe cube, and placed it over the wound. Once it had attached itself, Jae used the chemsert to inject the contents of one of the vials into the Gyrdra.

"This should be the easy part," she said. "The machine'll stimulate their regrowth process. If it goes correctly, Boss'll be good as new."

"And if it doesn't?" Dai asked weakly.

Tak turned to look at his friend. She was still lying on the floor but had turned her head to watch Jae work.

"Glad you're up." Jae shrugged. "If it doesn't work... I have no idea."

Tak reached down and grabbed Dai's hand. It felt unnaturally cool and clammy. "Welcome back," he said. She smiled back at him and gave a small nod.

The machine on Boss emitted a low hum. Nothing happened for a few secs, but then the silver flesh around the wound began to constrict and close. Soon, the skin had completely knit itself shut, leaving no trace that a wound had ever been there.

"So, they're supposed to wake up now, right?" Szan asked.

"Yeah, they're *supposed* to." Jae gently prodded at the area where the wound had been.

Boss's hand suddenly flew up and grabbed Jae's wrist. In a single smooth motion, the Gyrdra sprang from the couch, flipping the woman onto her back.

"Mom!" Myeong cried.

"What the farg is going on?" Boss asked. Their head swiveled around quickly. They spotted Fix—though Tak had no idea how Gyrdra "saw" things without eyes—and rushed at him.

"Hold on," Fix shouted with his hands extended to ward off Boss. "Eight betrayed us."

Boss stopped in their tracks, hand already grabbing the man's shirt. "Eight? Really?" Boss let their hand drop. "That slimy Anaryk. I'm going to kill it."

"Not if I do it first." Fix cracked his knuckles. "We need to get out of here first, though. What did you find out? You got us an invitation to the Cell?"

"Of course." Boss tapped at their combrace. "You've got less than a cycle to get there, though. There'll be a skiff waiting for you at the coordinates I just sent."

"What about you?" Tak asked.

"I'm going to take care of our friend, Eight. It's been a while since anyone's been stupid enough to betray me." Their mouth curved into a smile, revealing rows of jagged, pointed teeth. "This'll be fun."

Chapter Nineteen

Hkar'Trush

Fix led them through the backstreets of Tzoran toward the edge of the large cavern that encircled the city. Dai still felt unsteady. Jae had given her a chempen filled with a medicine she said would help recovery but had warned it would take rotations for her to be fully healed.

A skiff was waiting for them exactly where Boss had promised at the edge of the city. They jumped aboard and were off, heading down one of the tunnels that wound its way further into the planet's crust. The air grew warmer as they descended a shaft flooded with light from a wide strip of lights overhead.

The tunnel abruptly ended in a smooth wall of metal that appeared to be embedded in stone. As they came to a stop, Dai noticed a small panel against the wall.

Fix hopped down and placed his combrace against it, and the metal wall slid upward, revealing a tunnel identical to the one they had just traveled down. He wordlessly jumped back on the skiff and they continued down.

The heat started to become stifling, and small beads of sweat trailed their way down Dai's body. How far below the surface were they? The tunnel leveled off and opened into a small chamber with another wall of smooth metal. Small eye-level portholes were at either side of a central door, wide enough to let almost any species through.

"Everyone get out," Fix ordered. "We walk from here."

They hopped off the skiff and it immediately turned around and zoomed back up the tunnel toward Tzoran. As they approached the wall, a voice emanated from the ceiling. Dai couldn't place the language, but her earpiece instantly translated.

"State your intention."

The entire scene reminded Dai of a holo she'd seen once, where the heroine had been trying to find a relic in the temple of an ancient civilization. As Dai recalled, the temple had turned out to be a trap and the heroine barely escaped. She tried to sneak a peek through the portholes, hoping they'd have a better result, but they appeared to be one-way glass and she only saw her own reflection.

"We've got an invitation," Fix said, holding his combrace against a panel on the wall.

"Wait."

As they stood in a line in front of the door, Dai looked at the others. Were they as nervous as her? Fix rolled his eyes impatiently while the others craned their heads, looking around the chamber uneasily.

"Enter," the voice ordered as the central door clicked open.

They walked through the door into a small metal-lined chamber. As soon as they were inside, the door slammed shut and a fog sprayed from the ceiling and walls.

"Decontamination," Tak whispered, noticing Dai's alarm. "The only life that's native to the planet's down here. Also, the Cell is home to some of the biggest recluses and hypochondriacs in the galaxy." After their brush with Eight, Fix had changed Tak's face again. She had a hard time reconciling his voice with the elderly man she saw before her.

A piece of the far wall suddenly retracted and then slid open, revealing a Yoorkray, feathers died black, standing on the other side with a small pistol in its talon.

"Let's go, skin bags," the creature said.

They entered *another* featureless room, this one slightly larger than the previous one. The bright light emanating from the ceiling and bouncing off the pristine white walls was almost blinding.

"Two of you are new," the Yoorkray stated. "So, real quick, here are the rules: no violence. The penalty for a violation is death." He pressed a button on a wall panel and another door opened. "Enjoy."

Fix gave a nod of acknowledgment and then strode through the door. After a moment's hesitation, the rest followed. A long white hallway, bathed in bright light, stretched before them, seeming to go on forever.

"They really like light," Szan observed.

"Makes it much more difficult to sneak in or bring in contraband," Tak said.

Fix turned to Tak. "Okay, I got us in. Now take us to wherever the hell we're going." He raised his arm, gesturing for him to go in front.

Tak took the lead and led the group down the hallway, stopping at each intersection to examine the plates embedded into the wall. Dai looked over one of them. It was a small map filled with symbols she didn't recognize. The hallways were silent, except for the soft thuds of their boots against the floor.

"Where's everyone?" Dai whispered to Fix. For some reason, speaking felt like it would be akin to shouting.

"Like he said, place is full of hermits. The Cell is where people who are crazy and rich enough go to get away from everyone else. These people have enough clout to make sure the authorities don't bother them, and they remain holed up in their little compounds here. They don't step outside often."

"So, it's like a hideout for rich people?" Dai asked.

"Yeah, really rich eccentrics or really, really good criminals," Fix whispered back. "I'm guessing we're going to see one of the latter."

They ended up outside a door. It was white, like everything else, and Tak pressed a button on the wall next to it. He turned and gave a weak smile to the rest of the group.

"Wrong door!" came a shout from the speaker next to the door.

"It's Rishi," Tak said. "I'm just wearing a viscreen."

"Take off the screen and all of you stand still."

With some help from Fix, Tak took off the viscreen. As they waited outside the door, Fix began to tap his foot against the floor impatiently.

"We're being scanned," Tak said to Dai. "He won't let us in until he's sure we don't have trackers or listening devices."

Finally, the door opened with a small click. Tak hesitantly walked in and Dai followed with the others. The interior was completely pitch black, but there was the glow of countless screens scattered throughout the area. The room was clearly large, though it was impossible for Dai to tell its exact size in the darkness.

"What's going on, Rishi? I see you got my message." Dai couldn't tell where the voice was coming from.

"It's Tak now. And yeah, I got it."

"Ah, Tak's your name now." The voice held a tone of amusement. "Who are the others?"

"They're friends. You can turn on the lights already. I'm not being held against my will or whatever you're worried about."

Several dim overhead lights came on, illuminating a large room filled with consoles and equipment. Dai guessed they were in a control center of some sort. As she noticed the machine parts and scientific equipment strewn about, she revised her opinion; it was a workshop, a very messy workshop. A balcony filled with more junk and equipment encircled the room.

A humanoid bot stood in the center of the room. It was not like any bot that Dai had ever seen. Its body was a smooth metal, like a Gyrdra's, except it had blocky devices—Dai could think of no better word—attached to it around the abdomen and limbs. A screen, with a holo of a man's face, occupied the center of its head.

"Listen up, carbons, you tell anyone you saw me and..." The bot crushed a metal rod in one of its tri-tipped claws.

"I don't know what the farg you are," Fix shot back.

"I'm Human, like you," the bot said.

"Well, that's kind of a stretch, Syn," Tak said diplomatically.

"I forgot how annoying you are," Syn said peevishly. "Just because I'm not biological like you doesn't mean I'm not still Human."

"Syn's a unique lifeform," Tak said. "He used to be Human, but at some point, he moved his consciousness into this body."

"Took a helluva lotta work, too," Syn added with a look of pride on his digital face. Dai reexamined Syn with a new appreciation. What he'd done shouldn't have been possible. "It was a while ago and the technology was not even close to today's. Now, I assume you're here because someone tried to kill you."

"Several times actually," Tak replied.

Syn whistled—or emitted a whistling sound from a speaker in his head. "Ah, they're on your trail again for sure." He motioned for them to follow him to one of the consoles. "I've been looking into this since I last saw you. Truly fascinating enemies you have. I haven't seen anyone cover their tracks like this in ages. All those politicians and bigwigs on Hkar'Trush couldn't do it half as well as whoever these people are."

The Bot-Human placed one of his digits into a receptacle on the top of the console and a large screen on the wall flickered to life.

"Any idea why?" Tak asked.

Syn glanced at him sharply, then shrugged. "Somewhat. As expected, the kill order came from your family's company, Chao Financial. Took a bit to trace through the various shell companies, but in the end, they all lead back there."

"As expected?" Tak asked, confused.

Syn stared at Tak for a moment with a neutral expression on his synthetic face. "Yes. As expected. How much do you—" Syn paused. "Chao Financial is the only organization that has the means and motive to hunt you down, as far as I know."

"It must have something to do with the ECS in my head," Tak said. "Too many odd things for it not to be related."

"You've got an ECS?" Syn asked with a flicker of surprise. "That's new info. Did you know?"

Tak shook his head.

Syn tapped a finger against his thigh. "That is *very* interesting. Considering your previous status and wealth, implanting it without your knowledge would be difficult." He ran across the room. "Come here."

Syn motioned for Tak to sit in a chair and attached small nodes along his hairline. He picked up an ocutab and then shoved one of his digits into a small port on the side and studied the screen for several tics without saying a word.

Finally, the bot let out a small sigh. "There it is. Shrag!"

"What?" Tak asked.

"That is the highest-grade ECS I've ever seen. This is some top-level shrag. There's no way I can even begin to crack this thing."

"Even you?" Tak asked. "I thought you were the best."

"I am. That should tell you something. This is a one-of-a-kind ECS." He drummed his fingers against the side of his metal head.

"Which might help us out," Fix said. "If it's one of a kind, then we should be able to trace it somehow."

Syn pointed at Fix. "Exactly. There's only one place I know of in the Central Worlds that could produce something like this, and lucky for you, it's here on Hkar'Trush. The Central Worlds Institute of Applied Neuroscience builds cutting-edge rigs like this. The CWIAN"—he pronounced it like the name Quan—"is not an easy place to get into. Luckily, I've helped them out with some items."

"We're being hunted," Dai said. "How can we get inside?"

"There's more than one way to get where you need to go. The Cell has exit tunnels that go all over the planet." Syn strode to a container with a half-open lid and pulled out several viscreens. "Also, I have resources you can use."

The CWIAN occupied several levels of an enormous tower that was identical to every single other one on Hkar'Trush. Before they left, Syn uploaded directions from the Cell and the exact location for the lab to Tak's combrace, saying cryptically that he'd meet them there.

True to the bot's word, a small tunnel snaked its way from the Cell directly to the planet's surface, ending in a utility room in the basement of one of the enormous towers. Dai had a hard time reconciling the Hkar'Trush of the Undercity and the Cell with the glittering towers on the surface. They were almost two planets in one—four, really, if she included the Canopy and the Understory. On the Triple-Deuce, she'd only ever heard about the glamour and power of the politicians, but it was becoming apparent that there was much more to Hkar'Trush—and the Central Worlds—than she'd realized.

Dai was surprised how easily she'd become accustomed to the viscreen that covered her head. She only really noticed that she had it on whenever she absentmindedly reached up to touch her face and felt the rough fabric. To the people walking past them, she appeared to be an elderly Human woman with short gray hair and a smattering of piercings across her face. It was a look she'd chosen herself. "I'll be lucky if I look this good when I'm older," she'd told Tak as he programmed her screen.

As they reached the base of the CWIAN's tower, Dai felt a moment of nervousness. They were about to infiltrate a high-security lab. It was the sort of adventure she'd dreamed about when she was bored in crèche, so why did she want to run away?

There was no sign of Syn. She figured the bot would have a disguise of some sort, but she couldn't see anything as she studied the aliens around them, all of them walking past without giving the four Humans a second thought. If the bot wasn't nearby, they couldn't just wait around for him. It would be too conspicuous.

"Hey, meat sticks!"

Dai looked around for the source of the high-pitched voice.

"Down here, biowastes."

A small animal, no larger than Dai's fist, crouched by Tak's foot. He was brown and furry, with a small pointed nose, a thin tail, and two beady eyes. The creature scrambled up Tak's body and perched on his shoulder with his hind legs.

"You can head in," Syn said.

"What are you?" Szan asked.

"You haven't seen a mouse before?" Syn asked. They all shook their heads. "Have any of you even *been* to Earth?" They all shook their heads again.

Syn let out an exasperated groan. "Ugh, Humans nowadays. Let's just get going."

"You sure this'll work?" Szan asked doubtfully.

"Are you sure this'll work?" Syn mimicked. "Yes, I'm sure it'll work. Or at least reasonably sure. Now get inside."

The entire ground floor of the building was a single multi-story atrium filled with planters and vendors selling food and wares out of stalls. A large desk topped with screens, angled toward the door, was in front of them. At the center of the room, a bank of glass lifts rose through the ceiling.

"Punch in 'Dr. Shri'tar,'" Syn instructed.

Tak walked to one of the screens and tapped on it. A moment later, a small bell rang, and a door in the bank of lifts behind the desk lit up and opened.

"So, Rishi, you remember how to act like an entitled prick?" Syn asked.

Tak took a deep breath. "I can act like that, yes."

"Great, I knew you still had it in you. The only civilians who come to the CWIAN are people like that. Rich stuffed shirts looking to check in on their investments. As far as they're concerned, your name is Derk Richards." Syn's tiny avatar scurried from Tak's shoulder and burrowed into one of the pockets of his pants.

The door of the lift opened, revealing a sumptuous wood-lined waiting area. A Zzyr behind a large semicircular desk looked up as the door opened. Tak sauntered out of the elevator and turned to Dai.

"So, like I was saying, my family's got quite a few little investments like this. Just a few hundred million, but it could be a big deal if it pays off. I think Dr. Shri'tar will help us connect some of the dots."

Tak strode past the desk as if the attendant wasn't there.

The Zzyr gave a small buzz of annoyance. "Hold on, sir. Who are you here to see?"

Tak regarded the creature as if it were something he'd scraped off the bottom of his boot.

"It's Mr. Richards to you. I'm here to see Dr. Shri'tar," he replied, condescendence dripping from each word. "I've never seen you before. Who are *you*?"

"Dr. Shri'tar?" The Zzyr looked down at the screen embedded on the desk's surface. Its single enormous eye widened slightly in what Dai thought was surprise. "She's waiting for you. Please go ahead. Just follow the red line."

Tak led the group through the grid of corridors that made up the lab, following the incandescent red line that appeared on the wall. Dai peeked into the open doors as they passed. Most of the rooms were labs, filled with technicians busy at their workstations or patients—she guessed—unconscious on medical beds. The entire place gave her an uneasy feeling. Experiments and operations on the brain seemed unnatural to her.

"So, you're Syn's friends," a mechanical voice said as they walked into a large lab. A bank of windows lined one wall, while workstations and equipment covered the others.

The voice came from an enormous aerosphere that contained a purplish black Sworomo. The creature herself was an amorphous blob about the size of Dai's head, but her suit towered above them. It was humanoid in shape, with a large glass enclosure at the top, where the Sworomo sat on a small platform within a fine mist of pink gas. Sworomo were one of the few non-oxygen-respiring life-forms in the Central

Worlds and needed the suits to survive outside of their native methane-dominant atmosphere.

"What's up, gas bag?" Syn asked, scurrying from Tak's pocket and back onto his shoulder.

"Ah, Syn. Your new avatar is impressive. It didn't even set off our alarms."

"Yeah, I'm sure that you'll be upgrading those systems, though. So I'll need to rework this form a bit."

The Sworomo's large black eyes peered out at them from within her glass enclosure. "So, what do you need my help with? I'll admit that my interest is piqued. You never come to me in person—or mouse, as it were—for help, so whatever it is must be a doozy."

"See," Syn shouted triumphantly. "Even a Sworomo knows what a mouse is."

"I've got an ECS embedded in my brain," Tak said. "But I've got no idea how it got there and even Syn can't crack it."

"It's high-grade stuff," Syn added. "Like top-of-the-line hardware that could only come from here."

"Interesting..." The Sworomo propped herself up inside the tiny tank in its suit, pressing her eyes against the glass. "You're probably right. Something like that could only come from here, but this shouldn't happen. We follow the Cerebro Code of Ethics. No one should have anything implanted into them without their consent."

"So, can you take a look at it or are you just gonna stand there?" Syn asked, raising his tiny paws in the air.

Dr. Shri'tar sighed and then motioned to a table. "Lie down."

Tak lay down on the table, and the scientist pulled a large machine from a corner and rolled it over his head, completely covering Tak above his shoulders. Shri'tar walked to a nearby console and plugged a small cord from her suit into a port. She tapped at a small display inside her enclosure in the suit while the machine hummed softly.

Dai walked to the side to get a better view of what the Sworomo was studying. An image of the inside of Tak's head was on the screen in front of her. His brain was a soft gray, surrounded by the bright white of his skull. Small tendrils made from a rainbow of colors spread from the base of his skull, weaving through the entire brain.

The scientist turned in her enclosure to look at Dai. "People think an ECS is a box or some device that's surgically implanted into people. They never realize how complex and extensive they really are. But this is the most advanced one I've ever seen."

"So you've never seen this before?" Syn asked.

"This one specifically, no. I would remember seeing it if I had. But it's clearly a custom, one-of-a-kind device. You're right. It must have been made here." Shri'tar rotated the three-dimensional image of Tak's brain on the screen. "Yes, it was clearly designed for a Human brain, and it's secure, almost invisible to normal scans. The interface on this is amazing. It's wired to practically every single receptor in his brain."

"Can you get it out of him?" Dai asked hopefully.

"Nope. No one can. It's basically a part of him at this point. It's more than just an ECS. How much more, I can't tell." Shri'tar ran a tendril across her eyes. "I could spend rotations just trying to reverse-engineer this, but I am guessing you don't have that kind of time. What I can tell you is that there are at least a couple things here that I recognize. Experimental technologies that were devised in this lab. I may be able to track anyone who looked up the research."

"Look for someone connected to Chao Financial," Tak said, his voice muffled from the apparatus. Dai jumped slightly; she'd thought he was unconscious for some reason.

"Anyone as big as Chao is not going to use their real name," Fix said with a scoff.

"There're only a few pieces on this rig that I can actually trace," Shri'tar said as she tapped on the small computer inside her suit. "They're all coming up as 'missing.' No trail to follow in the system." She made a strangled noise. "Strange. This tech is old. Over twenty rotations old, in fact. The experiments were closed out by the researcher as unsuccessful."

"What do you mean 'old experiments'?" Tak asked. "I thought you said this was all cutting-edge stuff."

"We're a research facility. That's part of research. Sometimes, things don't work out. We often make things that just plain don't work. Most of the time, whatever's produced is broken down and the materials are reused. Your ECS has several components that are tagged as part of a failed experiment from a long time ago. Seems like the head scientist on the project had asked for the pieces to be broken down, but his supervisor ordered it stored with a note that they may be useful in the future."

"Can you cross-reference *when* the pieces went missing and the visitor logs?" Syn asked. "You *do* have access logs."

"That's what I was going to do." Shri'tar continued to focus on the screen inside her small gas-filled container. "Yes! We've got a match. Seems like they were all discovered missing after we had a visit from a... Rishi Chao."

Dai heard a thump as Tak tried to sit up and hit his head against the scanner. "That's me!"

Shri'tar pulled the device off Tak and walked to another screen. After a few swipes and taps on her suit's internal computer, the screen flickered to life, showing a high-resolution video feed.

"This is from the last time you were supposedly here."

The feed was from a camera above the desk at reception. Visitors and employees scurried in and out, their motions rushed and jerky from the high-speed playback. Dai studied the faces as they sped past but didn't see anyone that looked like Tak. To be honest, she couldn't believe she would. Someone must've used a fake credential to gain access.

"I don't recognize anyone," Tak said. "It could be any—"

"Stop the feed," Fix called out. He stood up and tapped the screen, looking back at them grimly. Tak's face was clearly visible and staring directly at the camera.

Chapter Twenty

Hkar'Trush

After downloading the video feeds and logs from the CWIAN, Syn strongly suggested they head to one of his safe houses in Hkar'Trush's Canopy. He said he needed to do some "digging," as he called it, and they needed to be off the streets while he did.

As they headed to the safe house, Tak tried to remember how he knew Syn. He believed it had something to do with a project his parents had been working on. They'd asked Tak to make contact with the being since he was already familiar with the Undercity.

Wait, that wasn't quite right. What happened again?

Tak did remember working with Syn. He was unique, one of a kind, a man who'd been so brilliant—and some would say insane—when living that he'd been able to fully transfer his consciousness into a bot. Tak didn't know exactly how old he was, only that he was the oldest being he'd ever met.

As they walked, Tak thought about the video feed. How had someone been able to fake his appearance and credentials and get into the CWIAN to build an ECS? The mystery of his parents' deaths and everything that had happened since continued to grow more complex.

Syn's safe house was at the top of one of the most exclusive buildings on the planet. His three-story penthouse was like a museum, filled with priceless antiquities from Humanity's past. Tak had been around opulence his entire life but had never seen a place filled with so many rare and exotic items.

He studied a painting that hung over the mantle. Five dogs, dressed as Humans, sat around a table, playing poker. Tak was no artist, but the skill and attention to detail were breathtaking.

"Like it?" asked a small version of the 'real' Syn as he walked into the two-story foyer.

Tak nodded.

"I spent about fifty rotations gathering everything you see here," the bot said. "It's all one-of-a-kind stuff in this place. Relics from an Earth that apparently has been forgotten."

"It's all... amazing," Szan said as he slowly turned to take in every detail of the room.

"Yeah, this place was a nice little pet project," Syn said. "Unfortunately, no one really gets to see it."

"Why do you need a safe house?" Dai asked. "I thought you stayed in the Cell."

"I do. But sometimes, associates—like you—need a place to hide out."

"Nicest safe house I've been in," Fix said. "Safest too."

"Ah, you *can* see some of my protocols, then," Syn said as if confirming a suspicion.

"This place is wired tighter than a Trebularian—" Fix stopped and glanced at Dai. "It's got a lot of security."

"It's a dangerous galaxy out there," Syn said. "And getting more dangerous every day. With all the activity and scheming around the Council, things are on a razor's edge."

Tak thought back to the conversation he'd overheard on Faltran. He really should have tried to keep up with current events while trying to avoid being killed.

"So, now we're safe. Level with us." Fix turned to stare at Tak. "What's going on? What did we just see on that screen at the CWIAN?"

"I have no idea," Tak said. Fix kept an even gaze on him, his mouth in a twisted, hard line. "Honestly, no idea."

Fix grabbed Tak's shirt. "I'm back on Hkar'Trush—a planet I hate and one where there's a warrant out on me—trying to help *you* out, and every time it seems like we're getting somewhere, everything just gets worse."

"I do not know what's happening or who actually picked up the ECS," Tak protested. He tried to brush off Fix's arm, but his grip held firm. Tak grabbed his chempen from his pocket, took a hit, and blew a stream of vapor into the man's face. Fix let go and pushed Tak back.

"Well, we need to figure out *something*," Szan said.

"Don't tell Shri'tar, but I downloaded a few extra files while we were there," Syn said.

"Which files?" Dai asked.

"All of them." Syn walked to one of the walls and it flickered, turning into a large screen with indecipherable characters across it. "I took the liberty of cross-referencing some of the donation files at the CWIAN with known associates and employees of the Chao family." The screen flickered to a list of names. "Any of these names look familiar?"

Tak studied the five names on the wall and softly said them to himself, seeing if any of them jogged his memory. None did.

"What about these?" Syn asked. The screen turned into the headshots of five different people of different species.

Tak studied each one, trying to imagine them as if they were standing in front of him. There was one, a Human woman with blond hair past her shoulders and deep blue eyes. "She looks familiar. I must've seen her around my parents," he said, pointing at her photo.

"That's Vera Trask. Chao Financial's finance head," Syn said. "You probably saw her at parties, but we should probably still pay her a visit."

"Easier said than done," Fix grunted. "People like that have security out the wazoo. We can't just take a lift to her living quarters."

"Give me a cycle," Syn said confidently. "I'll figure something out."

Despite its opulence, there was very little to do in Syn's safe house. The bot had a firewall around his systems and a signal blocker, preventing communication in and out. The only contact with the outside world was via a holoscreen that Tak had found on his second tour through the apartment.

Tak turned it on and began searching through the various feeds. Syn had set the device to prioritize Human-generated content so there was a mélange of soaps, comedies, and flash-reality shows. Growing up on Hkar'Trush, Tak was used to a variety of different species' programs and felt the Human-centric ones were boring at best and offensive at worst.

"You found a holoscreen," Dai said as she sat next to him.

Tak stopped flipping through the channels and took a hit from his chempen. "Yeah, at least there's something to do here."

"So you don't remember them implanting the ECS?" Dai asked. "I mean, we saw you walk into the CWIAN. You must have some memory of it."

"No." Tak shook his head frustratedly. He could see the look of doubt in her eyes and understood it completely. "I don't remember it. That wasn't me. I just don't understand how it could have happened."

"We'll figure it out," Dai said. "There's got to be a reason for all of this."

"I'm sorry you got caught up in it."

She smiled. "It's not a problem. Like you said, I could have always left if I'd wanted to."

"Still, it bothers me. Why would Riya tell you we have to go here?"

"I don't know. I don't think she knew exactly what was happening either. She was clear that we needed to go and sent Fix here with us."

"We wouldn't have gotten anywhere without him," Tak admitted. "But as soon as our interests don't align with his, that'll be the end of it."

Dai glanced at the holo and gave a start. "Isn't that the woman we were just talking about?"

Tak paused the feed. It was a newsfeed and a static image of Vera Trask was hovering on the screen. He pressed play. "—was found in the Undercity. Security patrols are still investigating how the woman ended up there, though they did say that her death is being classified as suspicious."

"What. The. Hell?" Tak wanted to punch something. Instead, he took a deep, deep hit from his chempen.

"Do you think it's connected to you? To us?" The feed had already moved on to another story, but Dai still stared at the screen, biting her lip. "What does it mean?"

"Nothing good," Tak said. "That's for sure."

It took another few cycles before Syn called them back. "Guessing you all heard what happened?"

"Yeah. Our one lead is dead," Fix snapped.

"It wasn't the best news, but remember, a lead is just something that's leading you somewhere. It's not the destination." Syn gestured to the screen behind him. "I still was able to get access to Vera's—I don't think she'll mind me calling her that since she's dead and all—living quarters. I think her death only confirms our suspicions that someone at Chao Financial is behind all of this."

"The security patrols will be all over it," Fix scoffed. "No way we can get close."

Syn laughed. "Do you think someone like her would let her *real* home be listed anywhere? The police are all over her *official* residence. I found where she actually lived and I have cameras on it now."

"Well, let's go, then," Dai said. "What are we waiting for?"

Less than a cycle later, they stood outside Vera Trask's front door, halfway up a mid-level housing unit in a mid-range tower. It was the kind of neighborhood where average—at least for Hkar'Trush—workers lived. Two- and three-bedroom units. Not the kind of place Tak would expect the finance head of one of the largest companies—if not the largest company—in the Central Worlds to live.

Once Fix overrode Vera's security and they stepped through the door, Tak realized that her quarters were anything but average. An enormous staircase, made from a silver-veined white stone and lined with intricate stone figures, led from the entrance. Their footsteps echoed through the domed room as they climbed the stairs and entered a large common room, filled with a mixture of Human and alien art and furniture, at the top. Despite its size and obvious cost, the room looked lived in. A few stray ocutabs lay about on tables, along with bowls and plates.

"She must've bought the units around here and converted it into one enormous apartment," Fix said. "Perfect way to stay incognito."

"What're we looking for?" Dai asked. "This place seems pretty enormous."

Syn had joined them in his small furry mammal form and was perched on Tak's shoulder. "Look for any sort of work terminal. Someone like Vera would always be working. She'd want a secure way to access her office computer from home."

They split up and searched through the quarters. Although large and well-furnished, the apartment felt empty and cold. Tak wasn't sure if it was just an extravagant safe house like Syn's or if Vera was like his parents and never spent time at home. He remembered his parents spending most of their time traveling to meet clients, attending events, or inspecting investments. In the past cycle, as some memories had been jogged free, he realized he'd been more involved in that world than he'd originally thought. But always on the sidelines.

There were several bedrooms in the place. Each in a different style, and each seemingly untouched. There were no trinkets or knickknacks, no signs of a life well-lived.

"This woman didn't seem to have much other than work," Tak observed.

"For some people, work is their lives," Syn said. "No judgment here. It's mine too."

"What do you do for work?" Tak asked. He realized with a shock he had no idea. And he thought they were business associates. "As far as I can tell, you just like to cause trouble."

"Exactly," the furry avatar said. "And it takes a lot of time."

"Hey, come in here!" Dai shouted from another room.

Tak rushed over to find her in what must be the master bedroom. It was enormous, easily large enough to fit a small ship or aircar. An intricate mural of an ancient battle adorned the recessed ceiling, and a terminal sat on a white desk with gilded carvings in the corner of the room.

"Bingo." Syn scurried down from Tak's shoulder and climbed up the desk.

"Someone like this has to have the best security protocols in the galaxy," Tak said. "We're not going to be able to crack it."

"Well, fifty-fifty we already tripped a silent alarm—"

"What the farg!" Fix grabbed the tiny creature. "I thought you could get us by the security in this place."

"No need to get emotional," Syn said. Fix's grip tightened, the color draining from his knuckles.

"I wouldn't squeeze any harder." Syn's voice had the same even tone. "I'm the one thing keeping you alive. You need me to get access to that system and to get you past the security patrols that are very likely making their way here."

Fix snarled and dropped Syn back onto the desk.

"What's next?" Tak asked. He should've remembered that Syn wasn't someone who could be trusted—he was always playing his own game.

"Someone like Verna will have all her information stored in a central database and encrypted using a physical key on this terminal. We need to get the key from the device as well as a few other items, and then I can work on getting us access somewhere there isn't a team of highly trained patrollers bearing down on us."

Syn proceeded to bark out instructions on how to dismantle the terminal and retrieve the necessary parts. After secs of watching Tak fumbling at the machine, Dai pushed him out of the way and pulled out a small unitool from her pants. In no time at all, she had the machine open and was pulling out the key and other items, stuffing them into a small sack she'd pulled from her pants' cargo pocket.

"Nice work," Fix said after she'd pulled out everything from the console. Dai smiled slightly at the praise. "Let's get the farg out of here."

"Hold on," Syn said. "I've been able to access the building's security feeds. The lifts are shut down and there're at least two squads on their way here now. You go out the front door and you're gonna be dead. Even with your augmentations."

"Is there another way out of here?" Tak asked.

"I didn't find anything on the planet's zoning database," Syn said.

"I thought you were gonna get us past the security patrols," Fix growled.

"I'll *help* you," the small rodent said. "I can't do everything for you, though. I can't make an exit appear out of thin air."

Fix growled in annoyance, glaring at Syn. "I haven't known you very long, but you're a giant shraggin' pain already."

"Wait," Szan said. "You said that she must have bought the places around hers and combined them into a single unit, right? Maybe the old doors are still there, or at least maybe we can break them somehow."

"Finally, someone says something useful," Fix said. "Start looking." He ran along the walls of the room, studying them while lightly rapping on them with his knuckles. "Nothing." He turned and looked at the others. "Don't just stand there like a bunch of slack-jawed morons. Start looking for a way out. Go to the other rooms and tap the walls. Listen for a change in pitch."

Dai, Tak, and Szan rushed out of the room. Tak ran to one of the adjoining bedrooms and started tapping on the walls. He wasn't sure what he would hear if there was a door—or former door—there. He hoped he'd notice a different tone. He could hear the frantic sound of tapping from the nearby rooms as the others followed suit.

"Found something," Fix shouted from another room. Tak ran back to find him in a glass-topped art gallery. Even rows of sculpture-topped pedestals stood in the center of the room, surrounded by large paintings on the walls. Tak wasn't into art, but he guessed they were all *very* expensive. Fix was staring at a large painting easily as tall as himself.

"There's something behind this painting." Fix pulled out a short blade and cut through the picture, revealing the white wall behind. "Trust me. There's something here."

Dai raised an eyebrow and shot Tak a look. "Augmentation," he mouthed back. It was becoming clear that there was a lot more to Fix than met the eye.

"Question is, how do we—"

Fix stepped back and slammed his foot into the wall, creating an enormous dent. He punched the area around the dent, creating small craters and a healthy cloud of dust. Fix pulled at the dented and damaged wall and threw the pieces across the room, revealing a metal door.

Tak felt a surge of triumph as he saw the dust-coated metal. They might actually get out of there.

Fix slammed his foot into the door with a hollow clang. Grunting, he did it again to no effect.

"Even augmented, you can't kick through a security door," Syn chided. "We need to use our brains, not our muscles."

"Do you see anything through the wall?" Dai asked. "Like wires, a metal box, anything like that?"

"Yeah, there's something right here." Fix tapped at a point to the bottom-left of the door with his knife.

"Stab around it with your knife," Dai ordered. "If the construction crew that closed up the door had been a bit lazy, they might not have disabled the existing door before covering it up."

Tak was impressed.

Fix took his knife and began to stab a square shape through the wall. After he'd cut out the perimeter, he used the knife to wedge the cut-out piece from the wall, revealing a metal box about the size of Tak's hand.

"Give me the knife," Dai said. She held out her hand and Fix handed it over. As she bent down and pried open the metal box, the deafening sound of an explosion came from the front of the apartment. Tak felt the shock wave reverberate through the floor and up his feet.

"We need to hold them off," Syn said as he scurried next to Dai.

How are we gonna do that? Tak wondered. He had no illusions about his fighting prowess.

"Stay here," Fix ordered as he strode to the doorway, pistol in hand, and stalked out of the room in a low crouch.

From Tak's perspective, watching over Dai's shoulder, the inside of the box was an indecipherable mass of wires and electrodes. Dai seemed to know what she was looking at, though. She looked back at the rest of them. "I can open it, but I need a power source."

"Use me," Syn said. He scurried into Dai's hand. His head swung disturbingly far upward, and two tendrils slid out from his body.

A staccato burst of gunfire sounded from the front of the apartment. A few secs later, another explosion followed, then more gunfire. Tak worried about Fix. It was a concern rooted more in self-interest than any particular concern about the man's health. They definitely needed him if they were going to get out of the apartment alive and find some answers.

"Ugh." Dai delicately picked up the two wires protruding from Syn's body and carefully inserted them into the box and wall and then attached a small wire from her combrace into the box. A few secs later, the door slid open, revealing a hallway.

"Fix, get back here," Szan shouted.

A black-clad Kyrillian patroller appeared in the doorway, its weapon raised. As it stepped into the threshold of the room, the three Humans dove to the ground, trying to avoid getting shot.

As the Kyrillian swung its rifle toward Szan, Fix appeared in the doorway and swung around, kicking the patroller in the head hard enough to knock it halfway across the room, its helmeted skull bouncing against the tiled floor as it landed.

"Just in time," Dai said with a note of gratitude.

They rushed into the hallway and Tak looked for an obvious way out. Rows and rows of doors stretched in either direction without any sign of an exit.

"I see a way out on the video feeds." Syn scrambled up to perch on Tak's shoulder. "There's a bridge leading out just that way." He pointed to their left with his nose.

They rushed down the hallway and reached an elevated tunnel that connected the buildings at the city's Understory level. As they ran through the passageway, Tak glanced out the windows on either side of them. They were suspended above the Ground and under the Canopy. Above them, the tops of buildings were lost in the clouds while shadows hid everything underneath.

He sprinted forward when he heard explosions behind them. Whoever was following either was close enough to see or hear them or was just trigger-happy. Either way, it wasn't time to sightsee.

With Syn's help, they made their way through several intersections, eventually ending up in a small shopping area filled with a mélange of species. Fix slowed down to a trot, not even winded by their escape. Tak, meanwhile, felt like his lungs were going to explode.

"Well, that was fun," Fix said. "Now, let's see what Vera has."

Chapter
Twenty-One

Hkar'Trush

A lift took them back to the Ground and Syn called out instructions from Tak's shoulder. As they made their way through a maze of backstreets, tunnels, and security doors, Dai clasped and unclasped her hands, her gaze darting around, waiting for an airship to appear. Thankfully, nothing happened and they reached the Cell several cycles later without incident.

As her adrenaline subsided, Dai thought about their narrow escape. If Fix hadn't returned—as if out of nowhere—to take the Kyrillian patroller out—she'd be dead. His strength and speed had truly been superhuman. How much work had the man had done? What were the limits of his abilities?

The bot Dai thought of as the "true" Syn was waiting for them as they entered his quarters in the Cell. He grabbed the pieces of the computer they'd been able to gather and walked over to one of his workstations.

"Great job back there," Tak said as he pulled off his viscreen and shuffled next to her and Szan.

Dai blushed. "You can thank seventeen rotations of station maintenance."

"*You* actually helped," Tak said. "Shrag, you saved us all." He looked at the ground.

"He's right. You did good." Fix gave her a considering look. "You don't have strength or training, but you got smarts, and more importantly, you got the instincts."

"Thanks?" Dai wasn't sure what to say. What the farg were "the instincts"?

"If you don't die, give me a call in a few rotations," Fix said. "I'll have some work for you."

"She's going back to her mother," Tak said.

Fix let out a hearty guffaw. "Sure."

Dai wandered around the large chamber, idly examining the machines and parts while Syn continued to work on decrypting Vera's private data. "Don't leave the room," Syn warned, noticing her meanderings. "My security system will vaporize you, guest or not."

Dai grew more and more excited as she looked through the area. It wasn't filled with junk; it was filled with some of the rarest and most expensive parts in the galaxy. Syn clearly didn't seem to care about the price of things or have any sort of system of organization. He had tied a stack of parts together using a several million-credit neuroimpulse cable. Piles of ship parts were mixed with cooking utensils while sensitive medical devices were stacked on top of agricultural parts. From what she'd seen of Syn, Dai guessed there was a method to the madness of how the room was arranged, but she didn't have a clue what it was. It was impossible to tell his age, but the bot seemed to be several hundred rotations old, and a genius to boot. He'd either gone slightly batty or was operating at a level beyond her comprehension.

"Okay, I'm in," Syn announced. "Rishi, your old company does a pretty good job with security."

"Not good enough, apparently," Tak replied dryly.

Syn chuckled. "No one can keep me out forever. Let's just take a look around, shall we?"

Dai walked back across the room to the console the bot was standing in front of. Cables connected the pieces of Vera's computer and Syn's metallic body to the workstation in front of him.

"Where's the data?" Dai asked, looking at the blank screen in front of Syn.

"It's all up here." The bot tapped his metal head. "I'm well beyond a screen. Besides, at the rate I'm processing the files, it would just be a blur to you anyways. Hold up. Found something."

A screen on the wall flickered to life and a man's angular face appeared. His cheeks jutted out from his face, thinning into a narrow chin with a small, puckered mouth. Dai thought he looked like someone who had never seen joy or happiness in anything, the kind of person who saw anything outside his own work as frivolity.

"I know him," Tak said. "He's—" He stopped abruptly and ran a hand across his scalp, clearly trying to remember. "He's someone important."

"Interesting you should say that," Syn said, disconnecting from the machine. "His name's Dergod Mallic, and according to everything I can find, he's most decidedly *not* important. Which makes it all the more interesting that he seems to be at the nexus of everything."

"What do you mean *everything*?" Dai asked.

Syn whistled, and his holo face lit up in glee. "I mean the whole kit and caboodle. He was involved with the credits that disappeared from Chao Financial. He's also been transferring credits to unknown parties outside the Central Worlds for rotations now. In the last couple cycles, some of those credits have been siphoned off to known mercenary organizations, coinciding almost exactly with when you showed back up on the radar. This guy seems like someone who's at the heart of everything that's happened to you."

"Why the hell can't I remember him, then?" Tak asked. "Someone like this must have been close to my parents. I must have seen him at least a few times. There weren't many people in Chao Financial who could do this kind of thing."

"Perhaps that's because he didn't want you to notice him," Szan said. "Or maybe your parents kept you away from him."

"It's the ECS," Dai said. "Dergod installed that in your brain and wanted you to forget everything." She studied the face on the screen. To think this man could be responsible for so much pain. "He's obviously the person behind it all. We capture him and we can end this."

"He must have decided he wanted to control Chao Financial," Tak said, anger tinging his voice. "So he took out my parents, and now he's trying to take out me. Then he can sit in the shadows, pulling the strings."

Dai nodded, but she still felt like there was something missing. Something they weren't seeing. "We'll find him and then the running can finally stop. You can have a life."

"When we find that piece of shrag..." Tak picked up a small piece of metal and chucked it across the room.

"Can you pick that up?" Syn asked. "It's a high-explosive charge. Best not to be throwing it around."

Who leaves a HE lying around? Dai wondered.

"Sorry." Tak walked toward where the explosive had landed and bent down, feeling for it with his hands. "So what do we do now?"

"We get the bastard," Fix said. "That's why we're all here, isn't it?" He looked around the room. "Fine, I know that's why Syn and I are here."

"Syn's here to get to the bottom of this," Tak said. "He's been duped, just like my parents and me."

"Listen, kid"—Tak bristled at the word—"there ain't no way some super-intelligent ageless biomechanical life-form is going to help you for vengeance or for idle curiosity." Fix eyed Syn. "He's got his own reasons for helpin' you, same as me. I'm just more honest about it."

Tak looked at Syn questioningly and the bot shrugged. Dai felt a small pang of sympathy for Tak. He was several rotations older than her, yet in that moment, she felt like the older sister. Tak's previous life had been ripped—or at least partially torn—from his memory. Taken away in such a manner that he clearly didn't know what was real and what was fake. Now that he was putting together the pieces, he was beginning to see the enormous gaps he was still missing.

"Why *are* you helping us?" Tak pulled his arm back to throw the explosive again and then seemed to think better of it. "I just can't remember. What are we? Friends. Business associates? Enemies?"

"Now, now." Syn held up his arms calmingly. "Let's not become overdramatic here. You did help me in a fashion, and I'm most certainly helping you now—in case you've forgotten. Let's just say our interests happen to align. You want to be free from whatever your parents were involved in, and I want to get to the bottom of a puzzle I've been working on for some time, longer than you've been alive. Let's agree that we can be friends—or coworkers at least—and resolve it together."

"See?" Fix flung his arm out. "At least I don't talk like that. You got a few screws loose and want to live. I've been paid to help you stay alive until I get the information I need. We work together and then we part ways." He slapped his hands together. "Simple."

"And what information is that, Fix?" Szan asked with a sneer.

"I can't tell you," Fix said.

"So you're not exactly as up front as you claim to be," the Nashoban spat back. "You're here until you get what you need—and you won't tell us what it is—and then you leave us high and dry. You're like a ticking time bomb, and when you go off, the three of us"—he flung his arms toward Dai and Tak—"will have to pick up the pieces."

"This entire conversation is shragged," Tak said sullenly as he slumped to the ground, his hands on his head. "I can't process this."

"Look, we got enough info to go on without you," Fix said. "I'll give you the opportunity to join us, but now I got a name and you'd better believe I'm gonna talk to 'im. I can make sure he doesn't bother you again. As a courtesy."

"What about the rest of us?" Szan asked. "What do we do?"

"Well, that *is* hard to say," Syn said. "Ideally, you could just walk away. I certainly won't stop you."

"I am *so* sorry," Tak said to Szan and Dai, still running his hands over his head. "I didn't know that you'd get caught up in this."

"We don't have that much time to lose," Syn said. "Dergod is going to be looking out for us now that he knows we were at Trask's quarters."

"Can we get, like, five tics?" Dai asked. What Fix and Syn were asking was a lot. She could tell her friend was reeling. Tak hadn't had a chance to process everything, and he was being asked to make a huge decision.

"We?" Tak asked, looking up at her. "It's not a 'we' question. You and Szan should get the hell outta here. No question."

Dai wanted to kick the man. After all she'd done for him, he wanted to try and act like she wasn't a part of it and could just walk away. "Yes, us. You heard them. We're part of all this now, too. You'd better believe we get a say."

Tak met her eyes for a moment, then looked down. "You're right." He grabbed a workstation and pulled himself up. "You two wanna walk for a sec?"

"You know I can hear you wherever you go?" Syn asked.

"Yeah, I know, you rusty ol' tin can," Tak shot back. "I wanna *feel* like we can't be heard."

"Then by all means, go ahead."

Szan and Dai followed Tak to the far end of the room and walked behind a large cylindrical machine that Dai was pretty sure was an advanced engine prototype.

"You guys heard what they said. You sure you wanna be a part of this?" Tak asked in a whisper.

"They're going to do it either way," Szan said. "I don't think we can change that."

"We don't have to be with them when they do, though." Tak scanned both their faces. "You've put yourselves at risk for me so many times already. You should stay out of danger now that you have the chance."

Dai knew he was right. Their presence didn't make it any more likely that this Dergod would be captured, killed, or whatever Fix and Syn had in mind. The smart move was to stay away and out of sight. Wait for everything to blow over.

"You're right," Dai began, "but I can't help but feel that if we don't go, everything will be..." She searched for the right word.

"Incomplete," Szan finished. "I don't trust Fix and Syn one bit. I kinda like 'em—or at least I did up until the last few tics. But I don't trust 'em. There's a mystery here, one that's touched all three of us. I want answers. I want to know what's going on."

"Szan's right." Dai nodded. "This won't be finished for me unless I'm there to finish it."

Tak sighed. "Okay, I guess we're gonna do this."

"Good decision," Syn called from across the room. "Wait, sorry. I meant to say, what's your decision?"

"We'll go," Tak shouted back.

"Good decision."

Chapter Twenty-Two

Hkar'Trush

S yn spent the next few standards conducting a full background check and surveilling Dergod Mallic. Tak spent that time searching through his fragmented memories, hoping to find anything he might remember of the man. Unfortunately, there wasn't much for him to find. Just single images of Dergod that weren't tethered to any location or event. Tak knew he'd met and perhaps even talked with the man, but he had no idea of when or the context.

"What're you thinkin'?" Dai asked, sitting next to him on the metal floor.

"Just trying to remember." Tak was frustrated by his inability to understand what had happened to him. What annoyed him even more was that he hadn't realized the full extent of the enormous holes in his memory until recently. How had he gone for rotations without realizing something had been done to his head? Damn ECS.

Dai must have read his thoughts on his face. "I know it's tough, but you'll get it back." She rested a hand on his shoulder.

"Whatever happens, you'll at least have some peace. You'll at least know what happened."

Tak hoped she was right, but he saw so many ways it all could go wrong. They'd been following a trail ever since they'd met. It finally looked like they were about to find where that trail led. However, they had no idea what would be at the end. He hoped he would find out what had happened to his parents and why he had a fargin' ECS in his head. But maybe Dergod wouldn't talk or wouldn't be able to help Tak put together the fragmented pieces of his past.

"What about your mother?" Tak asked. "You haven't talked about her."

Dai blushed slightly. "I haven't thought about her. I know she's safe. Don't ask me how. I just know. She's safe and you need my help, and frankly, I want to know *why* the Triple-Deuce was attacked—was it a random Jackal attack or was this Dergod responsible? I need answers, too."

"What about Szan?" Tak looked over to the Nashoban, who was quietly pacing through the room, idly picking up pieces of equipment, looking them over for a few secs, and setting them back down.

"What about him?"

"You think he needs answers?" Tak asked.

"Szan's the kind of person who doesn't let others down," Dai said. "He's here because of us."

Tak wondered if that were true. But why else would the man be with them? The thought of him being some sort of sleeper agent or somehow having an ulterior motive was farfetched at best.

"Okay," Fix shouted, "we're ready." He'd been standing next to Syn, whispering to him in hushed tones as the bot did his work.

The group congregated around Syn's screen, which was filled with images and information about Dergod Mallic. He clearly was someone who had a lot to hide, but there was almost no evidence of his existence other than what they'd found in Vera Trask's files. Syn had been able to locate several feeds of him entering and leaving the same building, and Syn and Fix agreed that it would be the best spot to get him. What they meant by "get," Tak wasn't sure. They'd pulled the building's schematics and found there were several floors that were suspiciously missing from the public records.

"I've been monitoring the area and there's no obvious security from the outside," Syn said.

"Obvious being the key word," Fix said. "It'd be great to get more time to be sure what we're up against. But if we wait, the bastard'll run."

"I didn't think you liked to wait," Tak said.

"I don't. But I've been doing this long enough to know that sometimes you need to take a moment to see what you're aiming at before you pull the trigger, so to speak." Fix cracked his knuckles. "Especially when you're going up against someone like this."

"The fact that even *I* can't find out anything is a bad sign," Syn added.

Dai smiled. "When's the last time we had a good one?"

———⋈———

All the buildings in Hkar'Trush were starting to seem the same to Dai: never-ending towers of metal and glass. The only thing that seemed to be different about Dergod Mallic's suspected residence was the building's slightly rounded corners.

The floors that were missing from the public record were in the middle section of the tower, same as Verna's apartment. Syn had explained that it was the ideal height; it was high enough that an airship could park there while at the same time not having the added scrutiny of being near the Canopy. The plan that Fix and Syn had laid out was simple; they'd enter separately, wearing their viscreens. Each of them would have a small chip that Syn had fabricated in their combraces; it should allow them to bypass security and gain access to the maintenance area at the very core of the building. From there, they'd regroup and make their way up together.

Although the plan *was* simple, even Fix had admitted that a lot could go wrong. The fact that Dergod seemed to be a ghost didn't help Dai's twisting stomach. She walked through the glass doors at the bottom of the building and tried to appear nonchalant as she strode across the veined stone floors. She breezed past the central welcoming station and its screens and suite of sensors that recorded everyone going in and out of the building. Syn had made them each repeat the bottom-level floor plan from memory, and Dai had thought she'd had it down cold, but now she was struggling to remember which way to go. Looking down at her combrace for directions was not an option; it would have been a dead giveaway that she was not where she was supposed to be.

The large main atrium led into a grand hallway, its ceiling at least three floors tall. Although it wasn't crowded, there were still several groups walking past as she made her way, including a Tyraloo that nodded at her with its cherubic blue face.

Syn had warned them that the utility doors were meant to blend in, and they had to search carefully for them. Dai kept her eyes on the walls as she walked, looking for a telltale seam or discoloration that would let her know where the service door was. Finally, she saw the razor-thin line of a small door outlined in the wall and placed her hand on the side. Syn's chip worked, and the door swung open, revealing a light gray utility corridor running parallel to the hallway she'd just been in.

"Hey," said an elderly man standing by the door.

"Hey," Dai replied. She still had a hard time believing she was looking at Tak. The viscreens were amazing. She'd never heard or seen anything like them back on the Triple-Deuce.

"I figured I'd wait before heading down to meet the others." He raised a gloved hand. "We started this adventure together, so I figure we should end it together."

"'Think this is the end?" Dai wasn't sure why she asked that. Of course this was the end. Dergod *was* the man who'd been paying off all these people. He would have the answers they were looking for.

Tak shrugged. "I've gotta hope. Either way, we're getting close."

They followed the well-lit passageway until it ended at a set of silver lift doors with a short, bookish man standing in front of them. Fix. Dai was pretty sure that Syn had decided to make him look as silly as possible just to mess with him. His broad, pitted face and patchy facial hair reminded her of a few of the miners she'd known back on the Triple-Deuce.

"Glad you two could make it," Fix said. "The bug over here said there hasn't been anyone matching Dergod's height and body shape coming in or out."

"Your Muner pal should be here shortly," Syn chirped. His avatar was a dark brown nine-legged bug that was perched on top of Fix's head.

"Can you get off my fargin' head?" Fix asked. "Like, go anywhere else?"

"Oh, so sorry, but I need your height to be able to see what's going on." Dai definitely detected a hint of glee in the bot's voice.

Szan arrived shortly after, appearing as a distinguished-looking middle-aged man with a brush mustache and eyebrows that sprang wildly from above his eyes, giving the impression he'd sustained a significant—though not fatal—electric shock.

"Okay, we're all here," Fix said. He rotated the satchel strapped to his back and pulled out several weapons, handing one to each of them.

Dai wanted to give hers back; it felt heavy and wrong in her hands.

"Don't worry," Fix said, looking at Dai. "Like I told you back at the Cell, these are shorters. They aren't deadly. They only *stun* biological life forms. I wouldn't trust any of you three with a *real* weapon."

"Still don't like it."

"Still don't care. If you need to, use it." Fix looked at the other two. "What about you two? Ready?"

Tak shifted nervously. "Guess so."

"Good," Syn said. "Because I just overrode the lift controls. It's on its way to us now. I've tried to avoid tripping any alarms, but you never can be a hundred percent sure."

"We're on the clock, then," Fix said grimly. "Remember, do what I say."

All three of them nodded. Dai gulped and flashed a nervous smile at Szan and Tak, who returned it with smiles of their own.

The chrome doors opened and the four of them stepped into the utilitarian metal-lined chamber. Dai was half surprised the others weren't looking at her, considering how loud her heart was beating. It sounded like a drumbeat in her head.

"Going up," Fix cackled as the lift doors closed.

———◄▷◄———

In most public places, lifts were either made of glass or had screens on the walls so the passengers were entertained as they were taken where they needed to go. Even the Triple-Deuce's lifts had small panels to show where the car was going on the station. Service lifts like the one they were in only had a small screen above the door. On this particular one, Dai couldn't even read it since it was in an alien language.

Absent anything else to attract their attention, the four passengers glanced around the car without speaking and looking anywhere but at each other. Even Fix, who appeared as calm as always, said nothing until the doors in front of them opened with a small ping.

"Okay, weapons ready," he ordered.

"We don't know the exact layout of this floor," Syn said, still perched on Fix's head. "But the utility areas should be the same as the other floors. Head down this hallway and take the first right. There should be an entrance into the public area of the floor."

The hallway looked identical to the one they'd entered the lift from except for a small band of red near the ceiling. Fix took lead, followed by Tak, Dai, and then Szan in the rear. Dai tried to steady herself, keeping the shorter down and close to her side like Fix had instructed earlier.

"Okay, we're at the door," Fix said. "Can you open it?"

"Hold on," Syn said. "I'm checking the security system. We don't want any nasty surprises."

Fix motioned for the others to stand away from the door. "If there's something on the other side, you don't wanna be standing right in front of the door."

"Okay," Syn said after a few tics. "Opening now. I can't see any alarms. Can't see anything on the other side at all, actually."

Dai didn't like the sound of that.

The door gave a small click, and Fix slowly pushed it open, with his weapon—which Dai noticed was *not* a shorter—pointed at the crack. He leaned forward, gave a small chuckle, and then opened it wider, motioning them to follow.

Dai had seen the building's plans, and most of its floors had several apartments with a corridor connecting them. This one appeared to be a single large apartment that was decorated in a style that she could only describe as "beach party." Screens displaying hyper-realistic, warm-looking blue waters gently lapping against yellow sand beaches hung on the walls. The ceiling, which was a single giant screen, was a crystal-clear blue sky with a bright yellow sun shining almost directly overhead. Several straw-sided cabanas furnished with wicker furniture filled the floor. Little bits of kitsch were scattered around the area. A chipped metal sign that read *I'd rather be fishing* hung next to another that read *My other ship is a dingy*. Old-fashioned fishing rods lay stacked against the side of one of the cabanas next to tackle boxes.

Dai couldn't process what she was seeing. This was not what she'd expected. "What the—"

"Hell," Tak finished.

"Are we in the right place?" Szan asked, idly picking up a small shell from a tile-topped wicker table.

"Beats the hell out of me," Fix said. "But there's only one way to find out." He made his way through the cabanas, weapon still out and by his side.

The other three followed him. The screens and eccentric furniture made it difficult for Dai to picture how the floor was laid out in her head. When she looked back, she couldn't even tell where the door they'd entered through was.

"This is the home of the criminal mastermind who's trying to kill me?" Tak asked disbelievingly.

"Maybe," Fix said questioningly. "We don't know it's his place for sure. But he's gotta be the guy paying out the people trying to kill you. You can't get much higher in Chao Financial than this guy."

They came to a large hut made of bamboo. Dai hastily corrected herself. It *looked* like a hut. In reality, it was just another room that looked like a building through the screens on the ceiling and the straw coverings on the wall.

Fix carefully opened the wooden door, peeked through, and then waved them in. It appeared to be a living quarters of some sort. A large, single room with a small kitchen area, dining area, and a bed against one wall.

"Look around," Fix said, "and tell me if you see anything. Syn, are you able to scan for any systems in the area?"

Dai walked toward the wicker bed in the corner. There was a small holo frame propped up on the table next to it.

"Syn?" Fix asked.

A smile caught Dai's eye. It was familiar yet somehow strangely alien. It was Tak. He stood with his arm around Dergod, beaming at the camera. This version of Tak—Rishi—had a different smile. More cunning and cynical. They were standing in one of the cabanas in this very apartment, drinks in their hands.

"Tak!" Dai looked back toward her friend. He was directly behind her. On his face was a look of pure terror.

"I don't remember this," Tak whispered.

"We've gotta get out of here," Fix said. "Syn's offline. We're compromised."

Szan dropped to the floor, his shorter hitting the ground with a clunk. Fix turned to look and then dropped unconscious as well, hitting one of the dining chairs on his way down.

"What's going on?" Dai pleaded, looking at Tak. How was he friends with Dergod?

"I don't know." Tak looked as terrified as she felt.

Dai felt a sudden wave of nausea and everything went black.

Chapter Twenty-Three

Hkar'Trush

Tak opened his eyes. He was lying on a plush sofa and the beach scenery was gone, replaced by the hard edges and chrome frames of typical office furniture. He pushed his torso up and looked around, blinking. Whatever had knocked him out didn't seem to have any lingering effects; aside from a small throbbing in his head, he felt fine.

Dergod jumped up from a chair on the other side of the room with a smile on his face.

"Rishi, I can't believe it's you!"

Tak touched his face and realized he wasn't wearing the vis-creen any longer. He turned and placed his feet on the floor. Dergod must have carried him onto the small sofa. Fix, Szan, and Dai lay on the ground next to him, their hands bound behind their backs.

"I wasn't sure what to do with them," Dergod said. "I didn't know if they were with you or they'd somehow captured you."

He clapped his hands together. "I just can't believe you're back! I thought you were dead. We *all* thought you were dead."

The man in front of Tak was a far cry from the severe-looking man they'd seen on the screen in Syn's quarters. His face practically radiated happiness. He wore a loose-fitting bright-colored shirt that seemed to go along with the beach of the other part of the apartment. Despite his obvious pleasure at seeing Tak, Tak couldn't remember anything about him.

"Thanks. They're friends."

"Oh, good." Dergod held out a small glass of water. "When I realized my intruder was you, I called off the security patrollers. You can imagine my confusion when I saw you here with her." He pointed at Dai. "After you vanished, we didn't know what to do. First your parents die. Then you disappear without a trace. It was just too close together to be a coincidence."

"Yeah," Tak muttered. He wanted to remember so badly. How did he know this man? What was he talking about? "I've had some... holes in my memory."

Dergod shook his head. "They warned us that might happen. But you went ahead with it. You can't keep a Chao down, right?"

"Er, right."

"Well, looks like you did it, though!"

"Did what?"

"You got to Station 222."

"The Triple-Deuce?" Tak asked incredulously. He'd felt something pulling him to accept the assignment on the Triple-Deuce. Now he knew what it was.

"Obviously." Dergod chuckled. "I mean, you've got his daughter with you. I verified her genetics. Actually, all of your genetics." He looked at Fix. "That one's barely even Human anymore."

Tak regarded Fix's unconscious form. How many augmentations did that man have?

Dergod tilted his head and studied Tak for a moment, the smile fading from his face. "So did you find Stromsky's location?"

Tak cleared his throat, trying to buy some time. What should he say? Who was Dergod Mallic really?

"You have his daughter, so you must have found his data," Dergod said expectantly. When Tak didn't say anything, the man continued. "We have a team that's headed to Perridion for the wife. She actually—"

"What?" Tak asked with alarm.

Dergod was studying him intently, his good humor gone. "What happened to you out there, Rishi?"

"I..." What could Tak say? "I don't know. I don't know anything. Who I am. Who you are. What happened. None of it."

"The doctor said this might happen." Dergod flopped back into the chair. "Tell me what you *do* remember."

"I'm Rishi Chao, son of Sandra and Altan Chao and primary owner of Chao Financial."

"*Former* primary owner of Chao Financial," Dergod corrected. "You were forced to give up ownership after the scandal broke."

"Right." Tak remembered—kind of. "So, after the scandal, I had to go into hiding. Someone was after me, and they still are."

"Well," Dergod said, "they're not looking anymore. Haven't been for a long time. Do you remember why they were looking for you?"

Tak felt himself at a loss for words as it dawned on him. The hit squads. The mercenaries. No one was chasing after him; they were chasing after Dai. He'd been chasing after Dai when he'd gone to the Triple-Deuce; he just hadn't realized it at the time. *I thought it was you*, he wanted to say. Instead, he shrugged. "I'm not sure."

"That ECS did a number on you, didn't it?" Dergod asked, his mouth twisted into a frown.

"Look, we're obviously friends," Tak said. "Help me out here."

"You aren't friends."

Tak looked down to see Fix staring up at him intently. "You aren't friends," Fix repeated. "He's an employee."

"*Was* an employee." Dergod sneered, his friendly mask dropping. "Not any longer. I don't see any need to keep this facade up any longer. I just needed to make sure."

Tak moved before he had time to think, bounding from the couch and tackling the man back into his chair. Dergod had already started to bring up a pistol that he'd been holding out of sight, but Tak was able to knock it to the side as it fired, and the round whizzed past his head. The chair fell backward, and Dergod's pistol flew from his hand, clattering against the floor.

"Rich puke," Dergod grunted.

Tak focused only on the task at hand. He wasn't a fighter; in fact, this was the first one he could ever remember being in. Luckily, it didn't appear Dergod was either. They rolled on the floor in a bundle of arms, elbows, and legs until Dergod pressed his hand against Tak's face, knocking his head against a table. Tak felt a sharp pain and saw stars, temporarily paralyzing him and allowing Dergod to wriggle free from under him.

"You fargin' Chaos. I've worked for your parents for almost thirty rotations, and you all treated me like shrag." Dergod pulled himself up, wiping a small trail of drool and blood from his chin. "After all that planning, this is where you end up. I told you messing with that ECS was too risky. You told me to shove it. Well, guess I was right."

"Screw you," Tak said.

Dergod laughed. "Ah, Rishi Chao, always so eloquent. You thought you could control the Central Worlds, that you were so rich the galaxy would bend to your will. Now look at you. Lying on my floor, bleeding."

Tak turned around and tried to push himself up, but Dergod stomped on his back, sending him crashing back to the stone floor.

"Now, time to finish this. Guess I'm the new majority owner of Chao Financial after all."

Tak looked around, trying to find anything he could use. A large metal fish with enormous eyes and a dopey grin lay just out of reach. If he could just get to it, he might have a chance.

"You know, Rishi, there's so much I want to say to you, but I'm gonna keep this short and sweet. A single slug to the back of the head and then the same for your three friends—actually, not for the girl. I'll need her and her mother to find her father. That's a thread that still needs to be pulled."

"My father?" Dai asked. Tak could detect a sharp edge of pain in her voice.

"Ah yes, your father," Dergod said. "We'll find him together. Rishi here didn't finish the job, but no worries, I can."

Tak pulled himself forward, grabbed the metal fish, and turned, swinging his arm around with everything he had. The statuette hit Dergod on the forehead with a clang, knocking him to the ground instantly and causing him to drop the pistol that had been pointed at Tak's head.

Tak scrambled to his feet and snatched the weapon from the ground. Dergod lay on his side, a small trickle of blood trailing down his face.

"Let's get out of here," Tak said, turning to face the others.

"Hurry," Szan called out. "Dai's been shot."

Tak felt a wave of fear grip him as he saw his friend grimacing with a pool of blood underneath her.

———⬩✕⬩———

Tak searched through Dergod's office and finally found a knife to cut through Szan's and Dai's restraints. Fix's were a different story; made from a weave of metal cables, they were impossible to cut through with the knife. After another tic of searching, Tak realized that Dergod must have had some way to release the restraints. Sure enough, a small key in his pocket instantly released the bands around Fix's arms and legs.

"We need to get Dergod tied up," Fix said, rubbing his wrists. "You two find something and I'll take care of the girl."

Tak shuffled through the built-in drawers on one of the walls in the room. The restraints hadn't come from thin air. There had to be more. Finally, he pulled open a drawer to find a small bundle of them and pulled one out. *What sort of person keeps a stash of restraints in their home?*

Just as Tak pulled one tight around Dergod's wrists, the man woke up with a groan.

"I've got her stabilized. Let me do the talking." Fix stood over Dergod and delivered a sharp kick to the man's ribs. "We need answers," he said with an icy calm. "I'm gonna ask questions. You're going to answer them. I don't like your answer, then I hurt you. We're in a bit of a hurry so I won't be gentle."

Dergod stared back at Fix, blinking as blood and sweat trickled into his eyes.

"Who is your contact in the Jackals?"

"Wait, Fix, that's—" Tak stopped talking as Fix pointed his pistol at his head. "What's going on?"

"Told you, Tak—or Rishi, or whatever the hell you wanna be called—I'm here for my own reasons. This is it." He motioned to the sofa. "Now sit down. I like you, but I gotta job to do."

Tak backed up and sat down on the sofa, clenching his hands. The bastard had used him.

"Again. Who's the contact?"

"That's what you want to know?" Dergod smiled. "What a simple—" He groaned as Fix delivered a kick to his side.

"Like I said, I don't like your answers, I hurt you."

"Fine." Dergod coughed. "They're on Janissary. I don't know the name. I don't make contact myself. There's a drop at the Red Feranaught."

"Who's funding all of this?" Fix asked. "I know this isn't just Chao, so who's pulling the strings?"

"You'd have to ask him." Dergod tilted his head at Tak. "Damn Chaos didn't tell me that sort of thing. It was just do this, do that."

"Well, why did I want a damned ECS in my head, then?" Tak asked.

Fix looked back at him. "Like I said, I'll ask the questions." He turned back to Dergod. "What is the ECS for? How does that fit in?"

"It's the key to it all," Dergod said. "That's why the idiot risked his own brain to have it implanted and why he had me clean up his mess afterwards. With that and the information her father—"

An explosion sounded below them, rattling the windows that looked out onto Hkar'Trush and sending items clattering from the shelves on the walls.

"What the hell was that?" Szan asked.

"You bastard," Fix said. "You called them after all, didn't you?"

Dergod smiled cruelly. "You come into my home and think I'm not prepared? You're gonna have every single patroller in the sector on you."

"We've gotta go," Tak said. "Forget him. Let's get out of here."

"One last thing," Fix said as he turned to Dergod, raising his pistol at the man's head.

Tak wasn't sure what possessed him. Perhaps it was seeing enough violence for the day. Perhaps it was realizing what kind of person he'd really been. Either way, he couldn't let Fix kill a helpless man. No matter how evil he might be. Tak jumped off the couch and tried to tackle Fix. Unfortunately, he was ready for him and stepped back, raising a foot and sending Tak sprawling forward, his arms windmilling wildly. As Tak hit the ground, he heard shots ring out and turned to see Fix firing at something behind him.

"Dammit, Tak," Fix said, his hand on a small patch of blood growing on his shirt. "You got me fargin' shot." An armor-clad body lay on the ground in the doorway.

Tak was surprised by how calmly the man was taking his injury. "Let's get out of here," he said as he stood up. "I'll owe you."

Fix raised his weapon at Tak's head and fired. Tak could hear the slug flying past him and turned to see another black-clad patroller drop to the ground next to the first.

"You owe me two. Now, grab her," Fix ordered, pointing at Dai. "We'll have to find another way out."

Szan and Tak dutifully grabbed Dai's arms and legs and began to drag her out of the room. Tak winced as he thought of what they were doing to her already painful injury. Unfortunately, leaving her there was tantamount to leaving her to certain death.

They followed Fix through the quarters. The cabanas and beach scenery were nowhere to be found. Around them were the light woods and silver inlays of typical—albeit luxurious—office space. Tak had no idea how to get out. Since Fix was scrambling and searching in front of them, apparently neither did he.

"This place is a maze," Szan said. "They've got to have every exit blocked."

"Hold on." Tak lowered Dai's upper body gently to the ground. "Give me a sec. I must've been here before." He knew he had been, in fact. It was at the edge of his mind, just beyond the haze. He'd been in this apartment many times before. In fact, he knew it actually belonged to Chao Financial, not Dergod.

If only he could remember.

"You'd better think of something pretty damn quick, buddy," Fix said, hunching slightly and holding his wound. "When they get to Dergod, they can activate the security protocols and we're done."

Tak banged his fist against his head, willing the memories to come back. "Shut up and let me think."

A small photo frame caught his eye. The picture was his parents flanking Dergod, all three of them smiling. They were in one of the cabanas in the apartment. Tak remembered. He remembered that day. They'd just been at an event and had come back to Dergod's quarters to talk business. At the time, Tak was slowly becoming a part of the family business. His parents wanted him to stay out of the spotlight, play the part of a rich kid coasting on family funds and partying. In reality, he was a critical part of their plan, the only person they trusted who could operate without constant scrutiny. If some rich kid went slumming into the Undercity, who cared?

Tak remembered. Not all of it, but enough.

"There's no easy way out of the apartment," he said. "It was designed so intruders can't escape."

"Then how do we do it?" Fix asked. There was a small note of alarm in his voice, which would be akin to a complete frenzy in anyone else.

"We need to reach Syn somehow," Tak said. "You still have his avatar?"

Fix felt around in his pocket and pulled out Syn's lifeless avatar.

"Great." Tak felt along the wall in the small kitchen area of the room they were in. Like many rooms on this level, it was meant for entertaining. He patted the undersides of the shelves and then he felt it, a small biosensor. Tak pressed the button, hoping that Dergod hadn't removed him from the protocols.

A panel in the wall opened, revealing a large security console. Tak tapped on it, remembering when Dergod had shown him how to use it. The man had been laughing as he explained how to disable the security protocols, saying there would never be a time they'd need to do it.

Wrong again, Dergod, Tak thought as he disabled the scrambler that prevented Syn's consciousness from reaching the avatar.

The small insect immediately popped back to life. "Glad to be back," Syn said.

"Welcome back," Tak said. "How fast can you get an airship up here?"

"I've been positioning assets around the building ever since I got locked out," the insect said. "It can be here in a tic."

"Then do it." Tak pointed to the windows. "Fix, can you shoot those out?"

In a single motion, Fix raised his weapon and shot out the windows one by one. By the time the last shard of glass had fallen to the ground, his weapon was already back in its holster.

An aircar careened through the opening, landing with a skid in front of the four Humans.

"Not my best landing," Syn quipped, "but it'll do."

Chapter
Twenty-Four

Hkar'Trush

Tak and Szan carefully lifted Dai into the back seat of the aircar. Her tunic was stained a bright red and she groaned as they set her down. Szan slid into the seat next to her and fastened the restraints around her body.

"Get in," Fix said as he jumped into the passenger side of the vehicle. Tak noticed the mercenary twitch and groan as he entered; the wound was more serious than Fix wanted to let on.

As Tak ran to the front of the vehicle, one of the doors to the room exploded inward and four Kyrillian patrollers stormed in, firing as they entered. Tak jumped into the driver's side and heard metal slugs ricochet against the floor behind him.

"Hold on," Syn said as the aircar lifted from the floor and flew out of the tower.

Tak fumbled as he put on his restraints. As soon as they were on, the aircar dropped from the sky like a stone. Tak's stomach seemed to catapult into his throat as they fell. He could see their aircar in the glass facades of the towers around them. Just as he was sure they'd crash, the aircar slammed to a halt meters from the ground, sending his stomach back down to his feet.

"Thanks for that," Tak said sarcastically as they sped away from the tower.

"Don't thank me yet," Syn warned. "We've got three aircars and at least two airships on us."

Tak cursed and looked around, scanning the skies for the airships. The car made a hard right turn, catching him by surprise and slamming Dai against the side of the cabin.

"Can't you be more careful?" Tak asked.

"No, not really. Not if you want to live."

Tak looked to the back seat and saw Szan trying to pull Dai's limp form into a more secure position. Her eyes were fluttering slightly, and a blossom of red was growing in the center of the hastily prepared bandage Fix had put around her. Meanwhile, Fix wasn't doing much better; he had both hands over the wound in his chest and his skin had gone pale.

"So, what did you find out?" Syn asked.

"Can we talk about this later?" Tak asked. "Like when people are not trying to kill us?"

"I can drive and talk," Syn said. "I need you to tell me exactly what you learned."

"Later," Tak said.

"I need... to get out," Fix said. "My augmentations are overloaded. They're not hunting me. I need to get to someone who can... fix this." He waved his hand over the wound in his chest.

"We'll get you help," Tak said.

"You can't," Fix said angrily. "Auggies can't be treated by just anyone. Let me out—now. I know people."

The aircar screeched to a halt. Fix's door swung open, and the man staggered out.

"Don't worry about me," he said with a wink and a weak smile. "I'll find you later. Syn, can you get me a ride?"

"Yes," the insect avatar said from Fix's shoulder. "Get outta here."

Fix ran into a dark passageway without looking back.

Tak tried to apply the accelerator but the aircar wouldn't move. He pounded at the console in frustration.

"Rishi, I need to tell you what you found out," came Syn's voice from the vehicle's console. "I'll go when you start talking."

"Fine," Tak spat. "Raz, Syn. How do I even know you?"

The car took off. "I thought you knew that already. Business associates, right?"

"You know that's not true." Tak hated realizing how few friends he really had.

"You came to me for help on behalf of Chao Financial," Syn said. "You needed information."

"What kind of information?"

"Tell me what happened first." The aircar slowed.

Tak glanced back. Now he could see the airships. Two glittering spheres soaring toward them. The traffic had been a trickle when they'd first gotten into the car, but it had grown significantly, and they were weaving through cars as they made their way across the city.

"Apparently, I wasn't the clueless rich kid I thought I'd been," Tak said.

"No, you weren't." The aircar sped up again.

"Fix asked most of the questions. He wanted to find out who was the Chao contact with the Jackals."

"And who is it?"

"Dergod didn't know. He just said there's a drop at the Red Feranaught on Janissary."

The aircar next to them exploded in a ball of flame, causing them to swerve and smash into the car on the other side. Tak turned back to see the two airships practically on top of them. One of them zoomed ahead and pivoted in the air to face them. A gout of flame erupted from the front of the ship and a symphony of pings rang through the cabin. These people were not messing around.

"Can you do anything about them?" Szan asked.

"I'm working on it," Syn said. "I've got help on the way."

They continued to weave through the traffic as the road climbed off the ground and meandered through buildings in the Understory. Despite being a planned planet, Hkar'Trush was a maze in many respects, most likely the byproduct of having so many different species take part in its construction. The road's circuitous path gave them some breathing room since the airships were forced to back off and dodge around the towers.

"What about the ECS?" Syn asked.

"He didn't say. It's important for some reason."

"Uh, yeah, I could've guessed that," Syn said condescendingly. "That rig is the most advanced technology I think I've ever seen—and I'm including myself. What else?"

"There wasn't much else." Tak wavered. What else could he say? He couldn't tell the bot about Dai. It would just put another target on her back. Tak had no clue how Syn would use the information.

"There *was* something else," Syn said suspiciously. The aircar slowed again. "Why is Dergod doing all of this?"

"Fine," Tak said, trying to figure out a believable lie. Syn was advanced enough he probably had ways to sense if Tak was lying. "There was someone on the Triple-Deuce. Apparently, that was why I'd gone there, even if I didn't know it at the time."

"Who? Why were you looking for them?"

"A man named..." Tak trailed off. He couldn't let Syn know that Dai was the person he'd been looking for and was sure the bot would instantly cross-reference any name he gave him with the station's employment records.

"Who!" They were going so slowly that other cars were passing them on either side.

"Rigel Dorrick," Dai interrupted weakly. "He loaded and offloaded ships."

Tak looked over. She didn't acknowledge his glance but gave his hand a small squeeze.

"Perfect," Syn said.

Their aircar picked up speed just as the road was straightening and the two airships swept back toward them from either side, taking positions at their front and rear. A small delivery drone shot out from behind one of the towers flanking the road and slammed into the bottom thruster of the airship in front of them. It hovered for a moment, seemingly undamaged, then began to slowly drop from the sky in a controlled descent. A moment later, it dropped from view, blocked by the clouds beneath.

The airship to their rear picked up speed and fired at them as it zoomed past. As the bullets began striking cars, they swerved back and forth, out of control, crashing into the clear barriers on the side of the road.

"Where are we going?" Tak asked.

"It's time to get you off-planet. Past time, actually. I've arranged to have a private ship set up for you at one of the less lawful ports on the planet."

The airship turned and headed toward them for another run. Its cannons fired, and a burst of gunfire strafed through the front of the aircar. Sparks flew from the central console, and shattered glass flew through the cabin.

"Dammit... hit... coordinates... on combrace..." Syn's voice elongated and deepened, fading away to nothing.

"I think we're on our own." Tak grabbed the wheel that had popped from the dash.

"Can you drive this?" Szan asked.

"Maybe," Tak said as they bounced off another aircar. "Guess I'll learn as I go."

A fork appeared in the road ahead. Most of the vehicles were peeling off to the right.

"Check your combrace," Tak shouted to the back seat. "Where do we go?"

Szan tapped furiously at his wrist. "Take a left."

Tak swung the aircar to the left, bouncing off the wall in the process, and shot down a ramp that descended toward the ground. Fire from the airship hit the aircar in front of them, causing it to swerve and launch over the barrier and off the road. Secs later, another explosion blossomed behind them, close enough that Tak felt the car jolted forward by the shock wave.

"Tell me we're close," Tak said.

"We're close," Szan replied. "Actually, I have no idea. I *think* we are, though."

As the words left Szan's mouth, a roar filled the cabin and the aircar turned sideways and flipped them over the glass barrier. For a sec, Tak had a hard time understanding what was happening; he saw clouds and then the shadow-covered ground beneath them.

The aircar crashed, roof-first, into a small pond. Water immediately poured through the shattered windows and filled the cabin, sending a shock through Tak's body. Szan fumbled at Dai's arms, pulling her back toward him. She'd become wedged between the front and back seats. Tak turned and tried to help dislodge her. Together, they got her free, and Szan was able to pull her out through the vehicle's rear door.

The pond wasn't deep. When Tak and Szan stood, the water reached just below their shoulders. They were at the center of a small ornamental garden. Small gravel-strewn paths crisscrossed through ornamental shrubs, with intricate pedestrian bridges crisscrossing the network of canals that wound through the area. It looked to be empty.

Perhaps, Tak thought, *having an aircar crashing into the pond made people decide to eat their lunch elsewhere.*

They quickly ran underneath one of the bridges, dragging a groaning Dai by the arms.

"We're close," Szan said, looking at his combrace. "Actually, we're here. It should be *right* here."

The two men scoured the area under the bridge, looking for anything unusual: a panel or screen perhaps. There wasn't anything to see, though, just a concrete walkway on either side of a narrow waterway.

"There's got to be some way to get to the ship," Szan said.

The whine of engines grew closer as the airship that had been firing on them circled overhead, then touched down on a small clearing on the other side of the ornate pond. They had only secs before the patrollers dismounted and continued their attack.

Tak scanned across the pond, examining the underside of the other bridges—they all looked the same. Syn wouldn't have sent them there if the ship wasn't nearby. It wouldn't make sense. There had to be a passageway or—

He dropped his head under the water. A small panel was on the side of the concrete walkway directly below them. He placed his open palm on the black square and waited for movement or a light of some sort. After a couple of secs, he felt an insistent tap on his back and pulled his head out.

The sound of metal slugs hitting the ground and walls near them echoed underneath the small bridge as Tak lifted his head from the water. A small door, reaching to his shoulder, had opened up on the abutment next to them. Szan had already picked up Dai's hands and was pulling her toward the opening. Tak ran ahead to find a spiral staircase curving downward. He rushed back and picked up Dai's legs.

Several mercenaries wearing tactical armor rushed from the airship towards them, firing their weapons. As he heard the pings of slugs hitting the concrete, Tak cursed and picked up Dai's legs, pushing her through the doorway and taking Szan with them. They fell through the opening and landed in a pile inside.

Szan picked himself up, then stumbled backward with an oath, managing to somehow prop himself against the stairs' railing. Tak jumped up and slammed his hand against a yellow button on the wall and the door slid up, sealing them in the stairwell.

"Let's see what we got," he said after taking a moment to catch his breath.

They struggled down several flights of stairs before ending up in a large hangar. Lights traced the perimeter of the ceiling, illuminating the subterranean cavern. A matte-gray ship sat in the center; its low profile and sleek lines seemed to disappear against the dark gray of the walls.

As they ran toward the ship, a door on the hull swung open, and they stepped inside, holding Dai by the shoulders. The ship had much of the appearance of the smuggler they used to get onto Hkar'Trush. But it was larger, with a plusher furnishing, more headroom, a large console at the front, and even some beds and storage lockers in the back. It was an interstellar ship.

"Lay her down," Tak said. "I'm gonna figure out how to get us out of here."

"No need." Syn's voice rang through the cabin. "Just get strapped in and I'll get us out of here."

"I'm guessing we're under the pond," Tak said.

"Yup," Syn said gleefully. "I had this built a long time ago. Glad to finally use it. Our friends up there are about to get a surprise. Now get strapped in. They can't reach us down here but they're bringing a helluva lot more ships into the area. The sooner we leave, the better."

Szan and Tak strapped Dai down onto one of the beds in the back. Her eyes fluttered as the restraints tightened around her chest and legs.

"Wha—" She looked at Tak with a confused expression.

"We're getting out of here," Tak said. "Fix bailed on us."

"Where're we goin'?"

"We're heading to Perridion. You're gonna get to your mom."

Dai's eyes widened, and she strained against the bands securing her to the table. "He sent a team to capture my mother."

Tak nodded. "This ship is fast"—he wasn't sure about that, but it *looked* fast—"and we'll get to her before they do."

"There's some medical supplies in this crate," Szan said. "I can at least stabilize her before we take off." Tak was no expert, but he at least knew a medpatch when he saw one. He didn't know exactly how the devices worked, but he knew that, when placed over a wound, they could work miracles. Szan unwrapped the bandages from Dai's wound and placed a patch on it. Almost immediately, the small box on the center of the patch started to hum.

The two men scrambled into the seats at the front of the craft. The door had already shut, and the cavern was almost pitch black in the window in front of them. As the ship lifted from the ground, a small trickle of water splashed off the front windscreen. The trickle quickly transformed into a deluge as the contents of the pond above their heads poured down onto the small ship. They rocked back and forth, hovering meters off the ground as the water poured down.

"What's hap—"

Szan's question was cut off as they shot straight up, through the hole where the pond had been and past the enormous towers. The ship soared above the Canopy, reorienting itself as they climbed, until the only thing they could see outside was stars.

Chapter Twenty-Five

En Route to Perridion

Dai felt sore. The medpatch had helped to numb most of the pain and get her up again, but every time she twisted in the ship's zero-g cabin, she felt a lance of pain stabbing through her side. Their escape was still something of a blur. She remembered pieces of it—getting placed in an aircar, traveling over the roads, and the shock of being submerged in icy water—but they didn't completely fit together in her head. She could sympathize with Tak. For her, it was just a cycle in time. For him, his entire life was a faded memory.

After they'd escaped the planet, Syn wanted to head for Janissary but relented after Tak and Dai insisted on taking her back to her mother. By unspoken agreement, they didn't say the real reason—that her mother was in danger. There was no way they could trust the bot.

As they warped toward Perridion and her mother, Dai began to think back to what Dergod had said. Her father was still alive. Despite her fond memories of the man, his life and his death were a mystery to her. What had happened on the Triple-Deuce was not an accident, not a case of wrong place at the wrong time. She was the target, not Tak. His presence on the Triple-Deuce had not been a coincidence either.

Dai glanced at Tak. She knew she could trust him; he'd done too much to make her doubt him now. But Rishi was a different story.

"What?" Tak asked, noticing her look.

"Just thinkin'."

"Yeah?"

Dai took a deep breath. Syn was listening. She couldn't say the things she really wanted to. Syn's motives and reasoning were unabashedly his own. He was a formidable opponent, and the fact that he didn't know Dai's father was mixed up in all of this was a good thing.

"What's it like realizing that you used to be..."

"A fargin' piece of shrag?" Tak asked ruefully.

"Well, yeah."

"Not the best feeling." Tak bit his lip. "I don't think I've fully accepted it yet."

"It doesn't matter," Szan said. "You can't change the past."

"Maybe, but I'm still guilty of some pretty bad things, from what I can tell."

"Are you, though?" Szan asked. "I mean, are *you* guilty of them? Or is it the person you used to be? I don't think Rishi would have done half the things you have."

"Well, I *did* them."

"Rishi did them, not you."

Dai had thought about that as well. Were Tak and Rishi two different people? She wanted it to be true. She didn't dare speak her worst fear, that somehow Rishi would come back.

———◇———

Perridion was one of the more recent additions to the Central Worlds and lay at the very edge of its space. The trip took more than a cycle, and by the end of it, they were ready to get off the ship. The medpatch continued to work its magic and Dai could almost *feel* her body somehow putting itself back together. It was amazing to experience the patch's healing powers firsthand.

As they drew close to the planet, she thought more and more of her mother. What had she been through? Was she injured? Dai knew that she was alive. Just knew it. But she didn't know much else. She just hoped they could reach her before Dergod's mercenaries did.

"We're approaching Perridion," Syn said. "Strap in 'cause I'm goin' in fast."

From space, Perridion's three continents appeared to be a uniform shade of beige. As they came closer to the planet, Dai spotted a few features on the surface. Small patches of shrubs. Ice-capped mountains. Trickling streams and a few lakes. Occasionally, she'd see a road, mine, or some other sign of civilization. Overall, it looked like Faltran or any other Fringe planet, desolate and wild. It was hard to believe they were still in the Central Worlds.

"Why is *this* planet in the Central Worlds?" Szan asked. "This is even worse than Faltran. At least back on my planet our buildings were actually taken care of."

"Minerals," Syn said. "This planet is essentially one big mine. Too valuable for the Central Worlds not to stake their claim on it. The Gyrdra were sniffing around here for a while so the Centralers decided to annex it."

"So they get all the advantages of citizenship?" Szan asked. It was the first time Dai could remember seeing him so incensed.

"As we used to say, 'Them's the breaks,'" Syn said.

Dai could understand the man's anger. He'd spent his life in the Fringe, caught between Jackals and people who hated him. Seeing another planet with the wealth and resources of the Central Worlds all because of some rocks would be infuriating.

"The refugees from the Triple-Deuce were sent to a camp outside of the capital," Syn said. The town was nestled at the base of several foothills, surrounded by inhospitable slopes on three sides. It reminded Dai of Capital, on Faltran, a border town made from prefabricated buildings and left-over materials. Before Dai had left the Triple-Deuce, it would have seemed like a metropolitan city to her. Now she could barely think of it as a town. It probably had a few hundred thousand inhabitants at best.

"Over there," Dai shouted excitedly, pointing to a cluster of tents on a plateau near the town. Tak changed their heading and landed in a level area on the perimeter the tents that was already littered with ships. There was no port control on Perridion—no port at all—and each ship simply set down wherever there was space. As Dai felt the gentle thump of their ship landing, a small shiver went through her body. It was as if a circle had been completed; she'd been cast from her mother and her friends and now she'd get to see them again.

A small insect scampered from a small hole on top of the console and crawled onto Tak's shoulder. "Let's go," Syn said from his new avatar.

"How are you able to even be here?" Tak asked, looking askance at the small bot. "There's no way you're communicating from Hkar'Trush and I doubt you uploaded yourself into the ship."

"Haven't you realized yet?" Syn asked. "There's no single me. I, Syn, am a collective of multiple versions of one consciousness, existing in many places at once, with each version communicating and overwriting the others continuously."

"You're a self-replicating collective?" Szan asked.

"Sure, in a way," Syn said lightly. "But that sounds dark and I'm super nice and friendly." Dai doubted that.

As they headed toward the tent city, Dai had to control herself to avoid running ahead. As they got closer, she started to make out familiar faces—miners, shopkeepers, and technicians that she'd seen her whole life. They looked familiar, but her time away had changed her perception of them, making them appear duller.

"Daiyu!"

Dai smiled as she recognized the broad smile and sandy-blond hair of the man running toward her. She gave a small yelp as he picked her up in a giant embrace.

"You made it."

"Of course I did," Dai said happily, trying to ignore the stab of pain on her still-healing wound. It felt good to see someone she could trust.

Max let her back down.

"You think I can't handle myself?" Dai asked as she punched him playfully on the shoulder.

Max's face contorted for a sec and he pulled her back in, nestling his head in her shoulder. She could hear the small sniffles of her friend in her ear and realized that he'd thought she'd died.

"It's okay. It's okay. I'm fine," Dai said reassuringly. "I'm totally fine."

"Have you seen your mother?" Max asked.

"No, we just got here," Dai said. "But I need to find her, right away."

Max looked past her at Szan and Tak. "Who are your friends?"

"Just her fan club," Tak said smoothly.

Max's expression hardened. "I guess you'll be off soon, then, huh?"

Tak shrugged. "As soon as we can." He held up a hand. "Honest."

Dai kept walking and pulled at Max's sleeve so he'd walk with her. Tak and Szan naturally stepped in line behind them. Dai hated the thought of Tak and Max not getting along, but she wasn't surprised. They were like oil and water.

"So where is she?" Dai asked. "Where's my mom?"

"She's over there." Max pointed to the far edge of the formation of tents. "She said she knew you were still alive." He turned to look at her with his typical earnest expression. "I'm ashamed to say I doubted her."

"Well, doubt no more, my friend." Dai wrapped an arm around his shoulder and gave him a quick embrace. "I'll talk to you later."

She felt like a celebrity as they crossed through the small tent city. Person after person called her name or rushed up to give her a hug. The settlement had the same vibrancy and sense of community she remembered growing up. Although the station was destroyed, the Triple-Deuce was still very much alive.

Dai pushed open the flap to her mother's tent. Tejal was sitting at a small makeshift table, working on an air purifier with her sleeves rolled up and tools strewn out in front of her. She turned and dropped the part in her hand with a look of surprise on her face as she saw her daughter. A split sec later, she jumped up, sprinted across the room to Dai, and wrapped her arms around her.

No words were said. None were needed. Instead, they held on to each other, tears streaming down their faces and falling onto each other's shoulders. Dai could feel small shudders running through her mother's body and hear her own choked breath as she held on tight. After what was not enough time, they pulled apart, still resting their hands on each other's shoulders.

"I knew you'd survived," her mother said.

"I knew you knew." Dai smiled.

"Now..." Tejal looked guardedly at Tak and Szan, who had remained respectfully waiting at the tent's front flap. "You need to tell me *everything.*"

"I will," Dai promised, "but first, we need to get out of here. There're people coming to take you and we don't have much time."

Dai quickly told her mother what had happened since they'd said goodbye at their quarters on the Triple-Deuce. She left out some parts, like why Tak had come to the Triple-Deuce, but otherwise, she told her mother everything, ending with the revelation that her father was still alive and a team of mercenaries was on their way to Perridion.

By the time Dai finished, her mother was sitting on the sofa, the happy expression replaced by one of concern.

"So, we've got people coming here," Tejal said, her voice surprisingly calm. "Because they think I can lead them to you or your father?"

"Pretty much," Dai said.

Tejal bit her lip and thoughtfully stared off into space. "Szan and Rishi—"

"Tak," Dai corrected.

Tejal smiled. "Of course—Tak. Could you both give me and my daughter a moment? Why don't you check out the camp for a moment? There's a central pavilion where you can get something to eat."

"We don't have time for this, Mom," Dai said. Why was the woman being so fargin' calm about all this?

"I just need a moment, please."

Tak and Szan nodded and disappeared from the tent. As soon as they left, Tejal wandered to one of the cabinets and rummaged around inside, finally pulling out a small kettle.

"They could be here anytime," Dai pleaded.

Tejal slowly meandered to another cabinet. "I'm not going to rush off anywhere," she said in a firm voice, "until we've talked some more. You haven't even been here a cycle and you want to leave."

Dai felt like hitting something as her mother painstakingly prepared a pot of kaf and poured two cups. As she worked, she idly talked about the survivors and how she'd already found another job on Station 125.

"There's a position open for you there, too," Tejal said pleasantly, handing a cup to Dai and sitting back across from her. "You'd have to finish your training, of course, but I already had management promise to keep it open."

Dai wanted to throw the cup across the tent. Instead, she took a small sip. Farg, it was good. "Mom," Dai asked. "What's there to think about? We need to go. *You* need to go."

Tejal took a deep breath and sighed, her pleasant expression hardening. "Sweet, I'm not going anywhere, and neither are you. Have you ever thought that Rishi is just using you? He claims to have lost his memory but he somehow managed to end up on the Triple-Deuce when the Jackals attacked and now he's here, right as we're about to be attacked again."

Dai couldn't believe it. Some sort of kill team was on its way and her mom wanted to stay. She wanted to strangle the woman—well, hug her again, and then strangle her.

"Haven't you heard what I said?" Dai asked disbelievingly. "They're coming to get you."

"No, honey, they're coming to get Rishi," Tejal said calmly.

Dai felt a moment of shock. "What are you talking about?"

"Some officials came here a couple of cycles after we landed, asking about you. They told me you'd been sighted with a known fugitive from the law. When they told me everything your friend had done"—Tejal whistled—"I couldn't believe it. I was so worried for you." She placed a reassuring hand on Dai's arm.

"Mom, they're not—" Dai paused, realizing something. "Wait, you haven't said a word about Dad. Did you know he was still alive?"

"I've had my suspicions," Tejal said calmly. "Your father was the most brilliant person I ever met." She chuckled. "Well, at least in some respects." She turned serious again. "I suspected that when he suddenly disappeared in an accident after leaving that"—she pointed to Dai's pendant necklace—"with you, he might still be alive. I always knew he was running from *something*."

"You never told me," Dai said, trying not to let her hurt show. She took a sip of her kaf and tried to process what her mother was saying.

Tejal rested her hand on her daughter's leg. "I wasn't sure, and giving hope to a young girl seemed cruel. But I think he knew people, bad people like Rishi, were going to look for him and decided to run."

Dai looked at the crystal pendant around her neck. Why had *that* made her mother think her father hadn't died? "Why did he know people were going to look for him? What's special about this?" She held up the thumb-sized crystal.

Tejal opened her mouth but was interrupted by shouts from outside the tent. She dropped her cup and it shattered on the rough wood floor as shots rang out.

Chapter Twenty-Six

Perridion

The small refugee camp was an odd place for someone who'd grown up in Hkar'Trush high society. Besides being mostly Humans, the people actually seemed to enjoy each other's company. They sat between the tents playing games, eating, or casually talking with each other. As Tak walked through the camp with Szan, he couldn't help but feel a bit of jealousy.

They found the pavilion in the center of the encampment, set off from the camp around it by meters of sand. The structure was the size of several tents and looked to have been built using found wood, with open sides and a crude roof dotted with holes, revealing patches of the darkening sky. Several fires and lights draped from the ceiling cast flickering shadows across the area. Tak was happy to see several portable tables covered with food, surrounded by small groups of refugees, underneath the lights.

"Not bad," Szan said as they stepped into the pavilion.

Tak looked around at the smiling faces. The man was right, but they *really* didn't have time for this. He wasn't going to stop Dai and her mother from talking, though. Tejal's tone had brooked no argument, and they needed her to come with them willingly.

"Seems like everyone's here," Szan observed, scanning the crowd that filled the pavilion. The wind had picked up significantly since they'd landed, and the flames arched from the pits, their tendrils seeming to grasp at the attendees.

"You're not much for parties, huh?" Szan asked.

"Right now? No." Tak wasn't sure what Rishi would have done. He had a feeling *he* would have been comfortable in a situation like this.

Screams erupted from the other side of the pavilion, followed by short staccato bursts of gunfire. Tak dove to the ground and heard someone shouting in an alien language. He wasn't close enough to hear the translation. But he didn't need to be. It was the buzzing sound of Zzyr, and he would have bet everything he had they were looking for them.

Tak motioned for Szan to follow him and low-crawled out of the pavilion and onto the sandy ground. He turned his head to the side as he crawled, trying to escape the fine grains of sand that were whipped up by the rising wind. Tak half expected to feel a hand on his arm or a slug ripping into his back.

Need to get to Dai.

He remained focused as he crawled forward. When he reached the edge of the tents surrounding the pavilion, he pushed himself up and jumped into the nearest open flap, with Szan right behind. Outside, he could hear more gunfire and screams coming from the pavilion. It didn't sound like the Zzyr were firing just to get attention anymore; Tak suspected the Orbiters from the Triple-Deuce weren't the type to give up in a fight.

"What the hell?" Szan panted.

"Syn, any idea... who that is?" Tak asked, coughing from the sand. "How... many of them... there are or... what they've... got?"

The small avatar peeked out from his pocket. "No idea. I'm disconnected out here, but from what *this* version knows, it's impossible to tell."

"We've... gotta get to... Dai," Tak said.

"Then what?" Szan asked, gesturing toward the closed tent flap. "Whoever the hell... is chasing... us doesn't... seem to be giving up."

"We'll have to figure it out... after," Tak said with determination. "One step at a time."

They found small cloths in the tent and wrapped them around their mouths, then scurried out. Tak took the lead, trying to head toward Tejal's tent by going around the periphery of the camp and using the tents as cover from the mercenaries that still seemed to be combing through the crowd in the pavilion.

The screams in the pavilion had died down, but the sound of people walking, and the panicked murmurs of the crowd, remained. What was going on there?

Szan grabbed Tak from behind and dragged him into an adjacent tent, eliciting a small yip of surprise. They landed on the packed dirt floor in a small cloud of dust.

"What—"

Szan put his hand over Tak's mouth, cutting off his whispered protest.

That was when Tak heard them. Footsteps. Right outside the flap they had just ducked through. There had to be two or even three of them on the other side. Their steps sounded light, clearly not Human.

"Find him?" a voice asked. It was a Zzyr.

"Not yet. We've cordoned off the area and are converging. We'll find him soon enough."

"The girl?"

"We've got both her and her parent. They're uncooperative."

They had Dai. How the hell were he and Szan going to free her? How were they going to even *find* her?

A small clack that Tak interpreted to be a laugh. "We'll fix that. Let's get the male first. One more thing, Seeker wants this to be quiet. It's already gotten too big. Contract says no witnesses."

"Got it. We'll liquidate the inhabitants once we find him."

Another laugh and the two footsteps went off in different directions.

Seeker. Where had he heard the name before? He felt that itch in the back of his head. An itch that had become more familiar lately, which meant he was starting to remember more. He'd found trying to force himself to remember never did any good. It was better to just let it lie, and the memories would eventually come.

After waiting for the area to clear, Tak and Szan crawled back out of the tent. They started to head in the same direction they'd been going.

"No, this way," Szan hissed. He pointed toward their right, in the same direction one of the creatures had walked off.

Tak looked at him quizzically.

"That was their boss, or leader, or whatever. He's probably going to where Dai and her mother are."

Tak nodded and motioned for Szan to take the lead. He had experience avoiding the Jackals on Faltran. The only tactical experience Tak could remember having was sneaking past his parents to go out as a kid.

Szan gracefully ran from tent to tent, each time kneeling and looking around before proceeding forward. Tak couldn't see anyone in front of them. The storm was continuing to pick up, and it was impossible for him to hear anything except the wind and the snaps of the waving flaps on the tents around them. The sand stung his face and eyes, making it difficult to keep them open for any extended period of time.

As they crept through the camp, Szan pushed Tak into a tent a few times. Each time, Tak wondered if his friend was hearing things. But sure enough, the quick-paced footsteps of a Zzyr mercenary would pass by moments later. The entire process was slow going.

When they were near the edge of the camp—Tak couldn't tell how close—Szan pulled him down by his arm and crouched behind a tent.

"They're up ahead," Szan hissed. "I'm gonna check it out."

"You sure?" Tak asked fearfully.

"Farg yeah I'm sure." Szan smiled at him manically. It was an expression Tak hadn't seen before.

Szan leapt forward and disappeared into the howling wind. As Tak waited, he felt more alone than he ever had. It was one thing to go through life without friends. It was another to have them and then suddenly be alone.

The time stretched on and Szan didn't return. Tak heard someone coming toward him over the howling of the wind. His momentary joy turned to fear as he realized the footsteps were the quick-fire steps of a Zzyr. He froze for a moment, then dove into the tent.

Too late.

"I heard you," the Zzyr merc said condescendingly. "Come on out."

Tak looked around; there had to be something, anything, that he could use. The only things in the tent were a small cot against one side, a dresser opposite it, and a table and chairs in the center. There wasn't even a chest or anything lying around he could use as a weapon.

"Just come on out." Now there was a trace of annoyance in the Zzyr's tone.

"No!" Tak blurted out defiantly.

He grabbed the chair next to him and picked it up. It had clearly been made in a hurry out of whatever plastic, wood, and metal the Orbiters could find, and it shifted and groaned slightly as he pulled it behind his back, ready to swing.

The Zzyr stepped through the flap with its rifle raised. It jumped to one side of the flap, expecting Tak to be hiding at the side of the door. Tak rushed forward and swung the chair, connecting with the merc's torso. The chair seemed to burst on contact, sending pieces flying across the room and leaving Tak with just a single piece of heavily weathered wood in his hand.

The Zzyr ducked down and turned, extending its wings and slashing Tak across the face. He dropped the piece of wood and fell backward. His hands came up to his head and he felt the warmth of blood trickling down his fingers.

"What the raz, Human?" It flicked its tail into Tak's midsection, causing him to gasp and roll onto his side. Tak continued rolling away from the mercenary. There, he had it. He could feel a piece of the chair—one of the metal legs—directly beneath him, pressing into his side.

"What's your name?" the Zzyr asked, its weapon pointed in Tak's face.

Tak needed to buy time. He motioned to his ear: the universal sign that his translator wasn't working. The Zzyr sighed and turned on the small box on its chest. Meanwhile, Tak tried to slowly move himself off the metal bar.

"I said, what's your name?"

"Taksh." Wriggling a little bit more, he moved his left arm back and felt the cold metal leg.

"Ah, good." The creature flipped a switch on its weapon. "Need to know whether I'm killing or stunning. See you in a bit."

Tak jumped up, swinging the chair leg as he rose, but knew he wasn't going to get there in time. He heard the click of the weapon's trigger stud being pressed, and then the gun exploded in the Zzyr's hands, knocking them both onto the ground.

Tak's head felt like it was practically splitting open. What had happened? Guns didn't just blow up like that, did they?

The Zzyr lay motionless on the ground, the mangled wreckage of its weapon still smoking next to it. Tak crawled on his hands and knees toward it. He could hear the small whistle of breath coming from the creature's beak. At least it was alive. A clear viscous fluid was leaking onto the wooden floor from several gashes in the creature's large compound eye.

Tak shook his head, then suddenly felt his body let go and heaved on the floor. The entire scene was too grotesque for him to deal with. He staggered up and dove out of the tent, his head still throbbing. He had to save his friends and time was running out. Zzyr didn't have the best hearing, but even they would have heard the explosion.

Chapter
Twenty-Seven

Perridion

D ai peeked through the flap of her mother's tent but couldn't see anything in the sand-filled air other than the surrounding tents. She could hear the sounds of weapons over the whistling of the wind and the rattling of tent fabric.

"What did you do, Mom?" Dai turned back into the tent, securing the flap behind her.

"Nothing." Tejal shifted nervously in her chair. "They're just going to find your friend and bring him to justice."

"These are mercenaries," Dai seethed. "They're going to kill him—and us!"

They both jumped back as a silvery Gyrdra slid through the front flap of the tent and stood between them, its movements graceful and deadly.

"Ms. Stromsky," the Gyrdra said with a smile. "We received your call."

"Seeker, glad to see you," Tejal said uncertainly. "I heard gun-shots outside."

"Yes," Seeker replied. "Our quarry is not being cooperative. But we'll bring him in, one way or another. I'd like to take you and your daughter to my ship for your safety."

"I'm not going anywhere," Dai spat. "I'll wait right here."

"It's too dangerous. You must come with us." Seeker held out a metallic hand.

"Maybe we should stay here," Tejal said uncertainly.

"I insist." Seeker swept forward, grabbed them both by the arms, and pulled them out of the tent. A small circle of Zzyr mercenaries was waiting outside.

They escorted Dai and her mother through the encampment. The sandstorm made it impossible for Dai to tell exactly where they were going. Ahead of her, she could see that the tents ended, and a dark shape loomed in front of them. As they got closer, she realized it was an assault ship, used by militaries and paramilitary organizations the galaxy over. Its angular black surface was pitted and scarred from rotations of flying. Seeker roughly shoved them inside the ship's dimly lit interior and sealed the door behind them.

"What did you do?" Dai asked, slumping against the hull.

"Look, these are representatives of the Central World's Congress," Tejal said. "Your friend Rishi"—she spat out the name—"is an outlaw. He's behind the attacks on the Triple-Deuce and other stations."

"These people are responsible—or at least the people who sent them." Dai couldn't believe her mother could be so naïve.

"These are officials from the Central Worlds," Tejal repeated, as if trying to convince herself. "They're trying to stop your friend before he kills more people."

"What are you talking about?" Dai asked.

"Chao Financial has been behind the attacks," Tejal said. "They're using them to boost their bottom line."

"Mom, these people are using you." Dai slammed a hand against the smooth bulkhead and was rewarded with a twinge from her still-healing side and a bolt of pain in her hand. "They *work* for Chao Financial. They aren't the good guys here."

"Dai, wake up," Tejal almost shouted. "There aren't any good guys or bad guys."

"Well, considering they've been chasing me across the galaxy, I would consider them pretty bad." She lifted her shirt, revealing her still-healing wound. "I mean, they're the ones who did this, after all."

Tejal's face blanched. "What happened?"

"The same group of people—or at least ones working for the same person—shot me," Dai said. "When we were escaping from Hkar'Trush."

"You didn't tell me." Tejal held a trembling hand near her daughter's wound. "Why didn't you tell me this?"

"I didn't want you to worry."

"Raz, Dai. How did you get mixed up in this?" Tejal's face darkened. "It's that Rishi, isn't it? Centralers can't do anything without getting everyone around them mixed up in it."

"*I'm* a Centraler, Mom," Dai reminded her gently.

"Yup." Tejal scowled. "Don't remind me. Your dad knew his past would come back..."

"What aren't you telling me?" Dai asked.

"What do you remember about your father?"

"Honestly, not much. He was happy a lot." She remembered looking up at the mountain of a man, his bushy beard and wide smile.

"Well, that was because he was with you." Tejal smiled affectionately at her daughter. "You were his sun and his stars. But he was a man who had his demons. He hadn't always been a mechanic. He'd worked at some lab in the Central Worlds—"

"The CWIAN?" Dai asked hopefully.

Tejal screwed up her mouth. "Maybe. But either way, he'd made *something*. Wouldn't tell me what it was, just that it was bigger than he'd realized. Much bigger. People had started to realize what he was doing, and he got scared. He came to the Triple-Deuce to get away, and, well, that's when he met me"—Tejal smiled wistfully—"and decided to stay."

"Why haven't you told me about this before?"

Her mother sighed. "I dunno. Lots of reasons. Not my story to tell, for one. Your dad only told me about this once. When he'd had too much." She shook her head. "Never touched a drop after that night. I always got the impression he felt it was dangerous for people to know. At least that's what I tell myself when I think about how he left."

"Where is he?" Dai asked, grabbing her mother's hand. "They're after me—after us—because of him. Dad knows something or has something that these people want."

"Do you know what that is?" Tejal pointed to the crystal pendant around Dai's neck.

"No, what?"

"It's not just a pendant." Dai's mother pulled the crystal from her chest and gently turned it in her hands. "Your father had a great many inventions. The same night he told me that he'd run from the Central Worlds, he told me about some of the things he'd invented. I'm pretty sure that crystal is one of them. It's a device that can be used to store a whole bunch of information and can be locked to only a single biological signature. I think there's something from your father in there."

"How do I read it?"

Tejal shrugged. "I don't have the faintest. But I'd be willing to bet you are the only one who can read it. Your father would have made sure of that." Her face darkened. "And I bet your 'friend' Tak would love to get his hands on it."

Dai's mind went back to her friends. They'd gone to the pavilion; they could be captured or worse. She stood up. They had to get out of there.

"Dai, what are you doing?"

"I'm getting us out of here," Dai said determinedly.

She looked through the ship's interior. She'd never worked on an assault ship before, but all ships had the same basic parts: engines, life support, etcetera. She just needed to understand where everything was. Seeker had locked them in there, but assault ships weren't designed to hold prisoners; she knew she could get them out.

Dai ran her hand along the wall, feeling for seams while also pulling any levers or switches she came across. It wasn't the most scientific way to do it, but time was short. The door would have a manual override somewhere. They were essential for working on the ship when the power was disconnected.

"Stop," her mother instructed. "We'll get this sorted out. But you open that door, who knows what will happen."

Dai turned toward her mother and raised an eyebrow. "Not so confident about their intentions anymore, are you?"

Her mother blushed, a small wave of red creeping into her tan cheeks. "Just don't want you to be in danger."

"Too late for that, Mom. You're the one who put us here."

Dai gave a shout as she found a small access panel behind a cargo bin on the floor. She rummaged through the bin, looking for something she could use to pry open the panel, and found a tool with a handle and flat edge. Dai wedged the tool into the narrow seam between the panel and hull and began to pry them apart.

With a small ping, the panel flapped open, revealing a tight maze of wires. The ship was clearly of a much higher quality than anything Dai had worked on before. She'd have loved to take the time to inspect every bit of the beautiful machine, but time was a luxury she couldn't afford.

Where's the release? Dai frantically pushed the wires to the side, careful not to dislodge any of them; she didn't know what might happen if she did. Finally, she saw a small lever tucked to the side of the door and pulled it. The door sprang open with a hiss of grinding metal, and a gust of wind and sand burst through the opening.

"What the hell?" a Zzyr shouted outside.

Dai heard the occasional burst of gunfire over the howl of the wind. "Safe?" she asked her mother. "Nothing about this seems safe."

"They promised," Tejal said weakly.

Dai cautiously leaned out the door to find a muzzle pointed directly at her. "You set foot outside that door, and I'll drop you," the Zzyr said. Its body was covered in a tight black tactical suit that pushed its feathers out at its hands and feet. The creature looked so silly that Dai would have laughed if she wasn't worried about getting shot.

She leaned out of the door and looked around, counting the Zzyr needing her alive. Despite the storm, she could make out the pointed tops of the tents and hear gunfire and shouts erupting from around the camp. Small piles of equipment were stacked around the ship, and Dai was gratified to see a few of the mercs lying on the ground nursing wounds. The Orbiters of the Triple-Deuce wouldn't just lie down.

She felt a surge of anger and worry as her eyes came across Szan, unconscious with his hands restrained behind his back. At least he was alive.

"We need to talk with Seeker," Dai said to the guard.

"Why?" the Zzyr asked, its weapon still held at the ready.

"If he promises not to hurt my friend, I think I can help find him."

The Zzyr had a brief conversation over his headset and then turned to Dai. "He's coming."

Rather than ask for permission, Dai made her way out of the ship and sat down on the ground near Szan. She glanced down at her friend as her mother hesitantly followed her out of the ship and sat next to her. Other than his pallid skin, the Nashoban seemed to be fine.

"Do you know what you're doing?" Dai's mom asked.

"Hell no," Dai hissed back.

Seeker's sinuous form appeared from the tents in front of them, striding forward like a cat stalking its prey. He stood out, even with the wind and sand swirling around him. "You know where he is?" Seeker demanded, standing above Dai.

"You promise not to hurt him?" Dai asked.

"I'm not here to kill anyone," Seeker said earnestly, the sporadic gunfire coming from the camp behind him. "We need to take him to the authorities. They'll decide what to do with him."

"There's a place just outside the camp where we agreed to meet up if anything happened," Dai said.

"Take me there," Seeker ordered, easily pulling Dai into a standing position.

Tejal started to stand as well.

"You stay here," Seeker commanded. He turned toward a Zzyr merc. "Watch her."

"I should go, too," Tejal said defiantly. "I'm the one who called you here."

"It's for your own protection," Seeker said, not even trying to sound sincere, as he pulled Dai away from the ship. "Now, take me to your friend."

Tak leaned around the edge of the tent to check out the assault ship. A single Zzyr stood in front of the ship's door, its rifle held casually at its side. Dai's mother sat nearby with Szan's unconscious body near her. Several wounded Zzyr mercs lay scattered on the ground. The one thing Tak didn't see was Dai.

Tejal saw Tak and jumped slightly, like she was going to say something, but suddenly stopped and doubled over as if coughing.

The Zzyr merc turned and said something to her. He could see her shake her head, and the guard turned back and leaned back against the assault ship.

Tak waited to see if anyone came out of the ship, but the door remained closed. He figured Dai must be inside. Fortunately, the guard didn't seem too concerned about Tejal and Szan trying to escape; perhaps Tak could use that to his advantage.

He didn't have many options. He'd only survived his first encounter with a Zzyr through pure luck. There wasn't anything around him he could use, and even though they were injured, the other mercs lying on the ground could still shoot at him.

Tak's eyes landed on one of the piles of discarded equipment that lay in the area in front of the ship. A black tactical vest lined with grenades sat on top. He'd seen enough holos to know that the one in white was a disabler. Throw that at a group and it would incapacitate almost anyone—including Dai's mother and Szan.

Now I just have to reach it without dying, Tak thought.

He skirted around the tent, hoping the wind was loud enough to cover the sound of his movement. The wounded Zzyr didn't look up or move a muscle as he reached the edge of the tent closest to the front of the ship.

Tejal seemed to be focused on the ground, but he saw her eyes dart toward him and back down as he peered from around the corner of the tent. The grenade-covered vest was no more than ten meters from him, but it felt like a thousand times that.

He took a deep breath, sprinted into the small circle of mercenaries in front of the ship, and pulled a grenade from the vest. The Zzyr noticed and started to move toward him, but it was injured and had to turn around. As Tak ran to the other side of the circle, he armed the grenade by pressing the buttons on either side, then pulled the tab at the top and dropped it.

Just like the holos, Tak thought in surprise.

As the grenade fell, the Zzyr tackled him around the waist and slammed him into the ground.

"Got you, you stupid—"

The Zzyr's words stopped, and Tak felt the arms around him go limp. The dull pain in his head exploded again and he cried out, but somehow, he remained conscious.

Tak lifted his head and looked around. Everyone near the ship was unconscious. The grenade had worked. He'd expected an explosion, or sparks, or *something*. Instead, there was nothing but a throbbing headache and a bunch of incapacitated Zzyr and Humans. For the second time in less than a standard, Tak was confused. What was going on?

"Szan?" He immediately felt stupid for calling out for his clearly unconscious friend.

Tak pushed himself up and rummaged through the packs on the ground, looking for something to tie up the mercs with. Surely, they would have something. In the first pack, all he could find were medical supplies. He went to the next pack and gave a small cheer as he found one of the compartments filled with seemingly hundreds of quick-action restraints. Tak grabbed a handful and methodically went from merc to merc, binding their hands, feet, wings, and tails—all of which Zzyr used as weapons.

Now to get out of here, Tak thought triumphantly.

He ran to Szan and Tejal and shouted while lightly slapping their faces, but they didn't respond. Tak decided to give them a few more tics to recover and opened the assault ship's door. His heart dropped when he realized the interior was completely empty; Dai wasn't there.

What now?

Tak felt himself being pulled in different directions. There were still patrollers out in the camp; he could still hear some sporadic gunfire from its center. If someone came back, they'd be recaptured at best, killed at worst. But Dai was out there, and he had no idea where she was or if she was in danger.

With a frustrated groan, Tak made up his mind. He dragged Szan's and Tejal's limp bodies into the ship, hoping it would buy them a few secs if someone came across them. At least they'd be protected from the elements. He grabbed every weapon and piece of equipment he could find outside the ship and placed it all next to the two unconscious Humans, then shut the door.

"Any thoughts, Syn?" Tak asked.

There was no response. Tak felt around in his pocket and picked up Syn's insect avatar. It was dead, whether from the grenade or the other explosion, he didn't know. The small insect bot dangled lifelessly in his hand.

Guess I'm on my own.

For a moment, Tak felt like running. He could get away. He could take one of the ships at the edge of the camp and leave. *Screw that.* Szan and Dai had done more for him than anyone else in his life, parents included. And the people of the Triple-Deuce didn't deserve what was happening to them. One way or another, he was going to end it here and now.

Tak grabbed a small weapon that he hoped was a shorter and jumped from tent to tent toward the center of the camp, trying to mimic the smooth movements he'd seen Szan do earlier. Other than tripping once or twice, he felt he didn't do half bad.

The fires in the central pavilion continued to blow in the wind, which had dropped from a howl. Many of the attendees were in restraints and stacked like pipes in neat rows on the rough floor. The rest huddled in a group with several Zzyr watching over them. With a shudder, Tak realized one of the rows of Orbiters wasn't moving. Looking closer, he could see burns and bloodstains covering their clothing. Tak turned away and ducked behind a tent, the image already burned into his memory.

Where would she go?

Tak wracked his mind, thinking about where Dai might be. Why would she be separated from the rest? Unless...

The mercenaries must have taken her aside. He tried not to think of why but quickly realized whatever the reason, it couldn't be good. If she wasn't at the center of the camp, then the next most likely scenario was she was at the edge—where no one would see what they did to her.

Don't think like that!

Tak bounded back toward the camp's perimeter. He wasn't trying to hide anymore; there wasn't time. His mind had gone to the worst-case scenario after seeing the row of bodies in the pavilion. With the wind dying down, he was able to see much further than before. He'd need to rely on luck to not get shot.

Go to the wrong location or jump up at the wrong time and he might find himself at the wrong end of a barrel. Tak reached the perimeter and ran along it, his eyes scanning outward, looking for his friend.

A scream rang out in front of him. Dai. Tak sprinted toward the sound with his shorter ready to fire.

Dai tried to take as much time as possible to reach the perimeter. She shuffled her feet and doubled back, then apologized, saying she was having a hard time remembering where the site was. Seeker followed, rarely speaking or giving any sign of emotion. Without facial features, it was almost impossible to tell what a Gyrdra was thinking. But Dai guessed he either had a very low opinion of Humans' intelligence or suspected something was up.

"Oh man," Dai said. "I think we're at the wrong spot *again*."

"Enough." Anger coated the word.

"We need to go that way." Dai pointed to the other side of the camp.

She barely registered any movement before she felt a burst of pain and saw her extended finger twisted ninety degrees. A moment later, the pain crescendoed and flew up her arm in a wave of fire. Dai doubled over screaming in pain.

"Enough of this," Seeker said. "Let's drop this little game. I know you think you're clever. But actually, you've given me an opportunity." He smiled, his fangs peeking out from beneath his lip. "I'll find your friend and get what I need. But there's no reason you need to be alive when I do."

"You need me." Dai held her broken finger to her side.

"I need to know where your father is." Seeker roughly grabbed her face and painfully brought it next to his own. Close enough she could feel his rancid breath wash over her. Close enough she could see her own terrified expression reflected off of his blank face. "Tell me and then we won't have to do anything to your mother."

Dai immediately thought of her pendant. She had no idea where her father was, but if her mother was right, then the necklace was what the mercenary was looking for. She doubted any of them would live if she gave it up, though. There was only one choice: lie her butt off.

"Fine," Dai said, trying to think through the pain. "I'll tell you what I know." She took a breath as she thought of what to say. "I don't know—"

A sudden wave of nausea swept over her, and she fell to her knees. Seeker spun and streaked from the edge of the clearing and into one of the tents on the perimeter of the camp. As the tent collapsed in on itself, Tak ran out from behind it.

"Run," he screamed. "Run!"

"What'd you do?" Dai shouted back as she stood up and staggered as fast as she could along the line of tents. She held out some hope that maybe they could outrun the Gyrdra despite everything she'd seen him do.

"I have no clue," Tak said. "I thought I'd stun him."

"Well, you failed."

"Thanks," Tak panted, giving a quick thumbs-up.

Dai turned and looked at the small mound of fabric where the tent had been. Seeker was nowhere to be seen. She turned around just in time to see his silvery form appear from seemingly nowhere in front of her and Tak.

He lifted them both up and slammed them on the ground, knocking the breath out of Dai. A raw panic seeped into her as she grabbed her chest. *Breathe!* She curled on her side and saw Tak's wide eyes staring back at her. For a moment, she thought he was dead. Then he let out a large, ragged breath and coughed.

"I'm getting pissed," Seeker spat. "Rishi, you and your fargin' family started this. I guess I'll have to end it." The Gyrdra pulled out a small knife. The metal almost seemed to meld with his skin.

"Dergod sent us here," Tak shouted. "I remember everything. I'm here to help."

Seeker smiled, revealing several rows of teeth. "You were supposed to die along with your parents. You'd played your parts. That worm Dergod has played his as well."

"You need me," Tak said.

"We don't need *you*. Just what's inside your head." He slowly brought the knife toward Tak's temple with his eyeless face turned toward Dai, seeming to relish her fear as he did so.

Dai jumped at the Gyrdra, knocking him off Tak. Seeker landed on his back and continued to roll, pulling Dai with him, and then launched her away with his feet. She felt a moment of disorientation and then a wave of pain as she landed. The sting in her side let her know that the landing had dislodged her scab, and she felt the trickle of blood flowing from her wound again.

"You knew what you signed up for, Rishi." Seeker faced her for a moment and then turned back to Tak, the scalpel still in his hand. "Your family wanted power and money, but you never truly cared for the cause. You were never a real Believer, never really one of us." He sauntered over to Tak and knelt down. Dai struggled to get up, but she was in too much pain to get to her feet. She watched in horror as the small scalpel came closer to Tak's temple. As the knife touched his skin, a high-pitched whine, followed by a loud crack, rang through the air.

Seeker convulsed with a snarl and turned. Tejal stood between two of the tents, her eyes narrow and her mouth drawn into a hard line. She pulled the trigger stud again, and Seeker fell back, the snarl dying on his lips.

"Mom," Dai said, relieved.

"Honey." Tejal ran to her daughter's side.

Chapter
Twenty-Eight

Perridion

T ak took a deep hit off his chempen and stared up at the sky while Tejal knelt by Dai, holding her daughter in her arms, both of them crying. Tak needed a moment to process what had happened, and it seemed that so did they. After a tic, they all stood up and crept back toward the mercenaries' ship.

Tak worried about Dai. A trail of blood snaked its way down the lower half of her shirt, her finger was bent at an unnatural angle, and she was clearly still in pain from Seeker throwing her. Despite all her injuries, she refused his and Tejal's help in walking back to the ship.

The wounded Zzyr were awake, as was Szan, who was pacing near the entrance to the ship, clearly still wobbly on his feet. When he saw the three of them, he cracked a smile and uneasily hobbled over for a welcoming embrace. The restrained mercenaries did not need much encouragement to tell Tejal everything she asked. Dai's mother had turned into a completely different woman than Tak had first met. It was as if a switch had gone off. He'd pegged her as someone who was quiet and standoffish, not this iron-willed fighter.

The mercenaries told them exactly where their comrades were and what their orders were, and they even offered a few helpful suggestions on how to best take them out. They were split into three groups, one guarding the prisoners at the central pavilion and two groups of two sweeping the area for any holdouts.

"Aren't you supposed to *not* answer our questions?" Szan asked suspiciously.

"We're paid to fight," one of the mercs said. "Not keep quiet. Besides"—it eyed Tejal, who had a rifle pointed at its head—"you're the ones with the guns."

They gathered the weapons Tak had piled in the ship and armed themselves with shorters and stun grenades. After a quick discussion, they decided to take out the mercenaries guarding the Orbiters first. From what Tak had seen at the ship, the Zzyr didn't seem like they were committed to the cause—or were Believers, whatever that meant.

They made their way to the center of the camp and took positions along the four sides of the pavilion. The Zzyr were lounging in the center, talking to each other in their language, which sounded like insects buzzing. As stun grenades flew at them from four sides, they screeched and started to run, but they weren't able to make it far before the grenades dropped them to the ground.

Tejal took charge and had the three others restrain the unconscious mercs. As they were finishing, they heard the roar of an engine and turned to see the assault ship lifting off from the planet.

The next few standards were a mix of tears and anger as the Orbiters recovered and tended to their wounded. At the final tally, there were five killed, ten injured, and at least another ten missing. Tak seethed inside, knowing that the Zzyr had stun weapons and stun grenades but had still resorted to killing. Despite their actions, the four captured Zzyr mercenaries were treated humanely, and there was already talk of a local tribunal for them. Although Perridion was in the Central Worlds, the Orbiters of the Triple-Deuce were Fringers and believed in Fringer justice.

It was almost morning by the time things had settled. Tak was surprised to find almost all the refugees from the Triple-Deuce still in the pavilion. They were setting down trays of food and drink, re-hanging the lights that had fallen during the battle, and some were even setting up strands of gleaming copper wire as decoration. When Tak asked, one of them explained they had already planned to hold a party that night for Dai's return and "no group of thugs is gonna get in the way of a good time."

An air of sorrow pervaded the event, but there was still laughing and dancing as well. It was as if all the emotions and things that they'd experienced since the destruction of the Triple-Deuce were wrapped into one enormous party. Tak felt like he was a part of the close family of Orbiters around him. He wasn't sure if it was because of the shared trauma of the attack, him being too distracted to keep his guard up, or a combination of both. But he found himself talking to people and listening to their stories without thinking about himself or judging their experiences. It was something he'd never experienced before, the feeling of being part of a group. Among the rich kids of Hkar'Trush, there was no in or out; it was each person for themselves.

"Enjoying yourself?" Szan asked, sliding over to Tak.

"Honestly, yes." Tak couldn't help but smile.

"Me too. Reminds me of Nashoba." Szan looked at the now star-filled sky. "I wonder what they're doing."

"Missing home?"

"Yeah. But not enough to want to go back."

Tak regarded his friend. "After everything you've been through, you don't want to go back?"

"Still no. There's too much to see."

"Ya know, maybe we're both insane, but I kinda think the same thing." Sure, there'd been things that sucked, but Tak didn't want to go back to the boring life of traveling between isolated mining stations. He definitely didn't want to go back to being evil rich kid Rishi Chao.

"Only question is," Szan said, holding up a finger, "where do we go to next?"

Tak knew that Dai was trying to answer that question right at that moment.

Tejal was a proud woman, as Dai knew she should be. She'd worked her way up through the maintenance ranks in the Triple-Deuce while raising her daughter alone. She'd saved that same daughter from a Gyrdra-led mercenary squad just standards ago. Dai knew it was that same pride that kept her mother from meeting her eyes now.

After the celebration—which wasn't the right word, but Dai didn't know what else to call it—started, they'd walked through the morning sun, back to her mother's tent, and sat down. Dai was exhausted, but she had unanswered questions and knew that she didn't have much time left to stay on Perridion. Her mother knew it as well.

"Mom, you know that I have to go," Dai said.

"You just came back to me." Her mother's mouth quivered for a moment. "But I screwed all that up, didn't I?"

"It was always going to be this way." Dai grabbed her mother's hand. "You did what you thought was right."

"Maybe," Tejal admitted, shaking her head. "But I still feel like it was a damn stupid thing."

"At least you've admitted you were wrong."

Tejal's eyes widened. "I didn't say *that*." She smiled. "Just that it was foolish. Sometimes the foolish thing to do is also the right thing. The two are not mutually exclusive."

"There's a lot of wisdom in there, Mom." Dai leaned over and gently tapped the side of her mother's head.

"Don't I know. At least there was enough in there to raise someone like you. So I must have a lot more going for me than it appears at first glance."

Dai smiled back at her mother. She was the woman who had comforted her when she was young and missing her father. Who had reprimanded her when she refused to do the take-home assignments at crèche. The woman that had risked her own life and fought for Dai when she saw her daughter in danger.

"Mom, what else can you tell me about dad and this necklace?" Dai held the pendant out.

"I told you everything I know already," Tejal said.

"There's got to be something. You were married to the man for eleven cycles for goodness' sake." Dai squeezed her mother's hand. "I'm involved in this. There's no going back. No getting out of it. All I can do is go forward. I just need to know where to go to."

Tejal sighed and then studied her daughter's face, a smile playing at the corners of her mouth. "And to think, I wanted you to become a mechanic. You're like your father, alright. There's that fire that he had. The unstoppable faith in what you're doing."

"Anything, Mom."

"I don't have any idea where he went. He never said where he was going. But I would guess that he wouldn't go back to the Central Worlds; he had such contempt for them—and fear. The night he left, when he gave you that necklace, he talked about a place called Zaru. He said that's where he researched the technology and found the materials to make it. I don't know if it's a planet, or city, or something else. But if you want to find your father and get to the bottom of this, then that's where you need to go next."

"Thanks, Mom," Dai said, trying not to let her disappointment show. All they had was a single name. It could be anywhere.

"I've got one more thing to give you," Tejal said, standing up. She walked to the other side of the tent and opened a small box on top of a dresser. "Your father would have wanted you to have this." She handed Dai a small holocube, the kind that tourists bought. Suspended inside the cube was a broad, smiling face. The eyes seemed to twinkle knowingly above the bushy beard.

"Why didn't you give this to me before?" Dai asked, holding the cube in front of her.

"I was—*am still*—pissed at the man." Tejal's eyes narrowed. "I don't care what his reasons were. He just left. Left you and I alone and disappeared."

"Well, maybe I can find him and bring him back," Dai said hopefully.

Tejal snorted and shook her head. "What makes you think I want him back?"

While at the party, Tak ran into Cookie. The woman smiled at him and even ran over to give him a hug. Seeing her with her son brought a small wave of pride. Giving up his seat on the evac ship was one of the few things he'd done right. Little Hu even ran over and gave Tak's leg a tight hug.

The question of *how* they were going to leave Perridion was something he hadn't discussed with Dai or Szan. They still had Syn's ship, but with the avatar dead, Tak knew this was their one chance to get off the bot's radar—at least for a while. Who knew what Syn wanted with them?

When Tak asked Cookie if there were any ships available, the woman told him to wait and ran off into the crowd. Less than half a standard later, she came back beaming.

"Hey, Brain," she said, grabbing him by the shoulder. "I talked to a few people who owe me some favors and got you a ship. It's a giant piece of crap, but it works." She led him to the edge of the camp where there was a derelict merchant ship that looked like it was as likely to fall apart as fly. The ship's bulbous hull was a patchwork of greens and browns with two stubby wings poking out from either side.

"Doesn't look like much, and it isn't. But it'll get you where you need to go. Ships like this, they got good bones. Needs a splash of paint, a few upgraded systems, potentially some patching of critical hull breaches..." She trailed off. "Her name's the *Odessa* and she's yours."

Tak didn't know what to say. No one had ever given him such a gift before. For the people of the Triple-Deuce, people who generally lived hand to mouth, this was a fortune. He turned and grabbed the woman in an embrace, causing her to yelp in surprise.

Szan suggested they loot Syn's ship for some of the supplies, and Tak was inclined to agree. There were still several of the pulse grenades left from the merc attack. Tak threw several grenades into the cabin and then ran inside with Szan and Dai to retrieve whatever they could find. They were able to pull out the viscreens, medical supplies, and several tools. Combined with what they'd salvaged from the Zzyr mercs, they had a decent cache of supplies.

Dai told Szan and Tak what she'd discovered of her father. It wasn't much, but it was at least a start. Either way, they had no choice but to leave immediately. After that, they'd need to figure out where to go to find Zaru—whatever or wherever it was.

The three of them stood at the base of the ship's cargo lift, and the small platform extended from the underside of the vessel and rested on the ground. Like everything on the *Odessa*, it appeared as if it might break down at any moment.

"You ready?" Szan asked, looking at Tak and Dai.

Dai looked at her mother, who was standing at the edge of the ship's blast radius, then turned back to look at her two friends and nodded.

Together, the three of them stepped onto the lift and ascended into their ship. A few tics later, the *Odessa* lifted from the surface and shot into space.

If you enjoyed this book and want to receive additional stories for free then please consider <u>subscribing to my newsletter</u>. You can find a link at my website <u>www.rile ycollins.info</u>. You *will* get free books and short stories and occasionally be notified of new releases and offers. You *will not* be spammed or have your information shared with anyone else.

Chapter Twenty-Nine

T hank you for reading! I hope you enjoyed it. As always, reviews on Amazon and Goodreads are always appreciated.

I started this book with the intention of writing a series that was more lighthearted than my first (Samsara Fleet). My central concept was of a young girl who's lived her life on a space station until it's attacked one day. As I wrote I found the story morphed into what you read here. For me, that's how my stories always start, with a small central concept that balloons into something bigger.

I look forward to continuing the adventures of Tak, Dai, and Szan. I won't spoil what happens next but I hope that you'll stay around.

Also, if you are looking for a grittier and darker military themed series, please check out my Samsara Fleet series on Amazon.

Thank you,

Riley